SOUTHTOWN

Also by Rick Riordan

BIG RED TEQUILA

THE WIDOWER'S TWO-STEP

THE LAST KING OF TEXAS

THE DEVIL WENT DOWN TO AUSTIN

COLD SPRINGS

SOUTHTOWN

RICK RIORDAN

BANTAM BOOKS

New York Toronto London Sydney Auckland

SOUTHTOWN
A Bantam Book / May 2004

Published by
Bantam Dell
A Division of Random House, Inc.
New York, New York

Book design by Karin Batten

Library of Congress Cataloging-in-Publication Data
Riordan, Rick.
Southtown / Rick Riordan.
p. cm.
ISBN 0-553-80184-8
1. Navarre, Tres (Fictitious character)—Fiction. 2. Private
investigators—Texas—San Antonio—Fiction. 3. Fugitives from
justice—Fiction. 4. San Antonio (Tex.)—Fiction. 5. English
teachers—Fiction. I. Title.

PS3568.I5866S68 2004
813'.54—dc22
2003070892

Manufactured in the United States of America
Published simultaneously in Canada

10 9 8 7 6 5 4 3 2 1
BVG

To John and Mona—
for twenty years of kindness
and for raising a great daughter

ACKNOWLEDGMENTS

Thanks to Officer Colleen Baylor, Omaha Police Department; Alan Tillman, master gunsmith; John Klahn, M.D.; Gina Maccoby and Kate Miciak for their help; and most of all Becky, Haley and Patrick for their continuing love and support.

SOUTHTOWN

—✦—

1

Fourth of July morning, Will Stirman woke up with blood on his hands.

He'd been dreaming about the men who killed his wife. He'd been strangling them, one with each hand. His fingernails had cut half-moons into his palms.

Sunlight filtered through the barred window, refracted by lead glass and chicken wire. In the berth above, his cell mate, Zeke, was humming "Amazing Grace."

"Up yet, boss?" Zeke called, excitement in his voice.

Today was the day.

A few more hours. Then one way or the other, Will would never have to have that dream again.

He wiped his palms on the sheets. He shifted over to his workspace—a metal desk with a toadstool seat welded to the floor. Stuck on the walls with Juicy Fruit gum were eight years' worth of Will's sketches, fluttering in the breeze of a little green plastic fan. Adam and Eve. Abraham and Isaac. Moses and Pharaoh.

He opened his Bible and took out what he'd done last night—a map instead of a Bible scene.

Behind him, Zeke slipped down from the bunk. He started

doing waist twists, his elbows cutting the air above Will's head. "Freedom sound good, boss?"

"Watch what you say, Zeke."

"Hell, just Independence Day." Zeke grinned. "I didn't mean nothing."

Zeke had a gap-toothed smile, vacant green eyes, a wide forehead dotted with acne. He was in Floresville State for raping elderly ladies in a nursing home, which didn't make him the worst sort Will had met. Been abused as a kid, is all. Had some funny ideas about love. Will worried how the boy would do when he got back to the real world.

Will looked over his map of Kingsville, hoping the police would take the bait. He'd labeled most of the major streets, his old warehouse property, the two biggest banks in town, the home of the attorney who'd defended him unsuccessfully in court.

He had a bad feeling about today—a taste like dirty coins in his mouth. He'd had that feeling before, the night he lost Soledad.

Exactly at eight, the cell door buzzed open.

"Come on, boss!" Zeke hustled outside, his shirt still unbuttoned, his shoes in his hands.

Will felt the urge to hurry, too—to respond to the buzzer like a racetrack dog, burst out of his kennel on time. But he forced himself to wait. He looked up to make sure Zeke was really gone. Then he slipped Soledad's picture out from under his mattress.

It wasn't a very good sketch. He'd gotten her long dark hair right, maybe, the intensity of her eyes, the soft curve of her face that made her look so young. But it was hard to get her smile, that look of challenge she'd always given him.

Still, it was all he had.

He kissed the portrait, folded it, and tucked it into his shirt.

Something would go wrong with the plan. He could feel it. He knew if he walked out that door, somebody was going to die.

But he'd made a promise.

He put the Kingsville map in the Bible, and set it on the desk where the guards were sure to find it. Then he went to join Zeke on the walkway.

After chow time, Pablo and his cousin Luis were hanging out on the rec yard, trying to avoid Hermandad Pistoleros Latinos. The HPL didn't like Pablo and Luis getting all religious when they could've been dealing for the homeboys.

Luis tried to joke about it, but he still had bruises across his rib cage from the last time the *carnales* had cornered him. Pablo figured if they didn't get out of Floresville soon, they'd both end up in cardboard coffins.

Out past the guard towers and the double line of razor wire fence, the hills hummed with cicadas. Lightning pulsed in the clouds.

Every morning, Pablo tried to imagine Floresville State Pen was a motel. He came out of Pod C and told himself he could check out anytime, get on the road, drive home to El Paso where his wife would be waiting. She'd hug him tight, tell him she still loved him—she'd read his letters and forgiven the one horrible mistake that had put him in jail.

After twelve long months inside, the dream was getting hard to hold on to.

That would change today.

He and Luis stood at the fence, chatting with their favorite guard, a Latina named Gonzales, who had breasts like mortar shells, gold-rimmed glasses, and a wispy mustache that reminded Pablo of his grandmother.

"You want to see fireworks tonight, miss?" Luis grinned.

Gonzales tapped the fence with her flashlight, reminding him to keep his feet behind the line. "Why—you got plans?"

"Picnic," Luis told her. "Few beers. Patriotic stuff, miss. Come on."

Pablo should have told him to shut up, but it was harmless talk. You looked at Luis—that pudgy face, boyish smile—and you knew he had to be joking.

Back home in El Paso, Luis had always been the favorite at family barbecues. He held the *piñata* for the kids, flirted with the women, got his cheeks pinched by the *abuelitas*. He was *Tío* Luis. The fun one. The nice one. Wouldn't hurt a fly.

That's why Luis had to shoot someone whenever he robbed an appliance store. Otherwise, the clerks didn't take him seriously.

"No picnic for me," Officer Gonzales said. "Got a promotion. Won't see you *vatos* anymore."

"Aw, miss," Luis said. "Where you going?"

"Never mind. My last day, today."

"You gonna miss the fireworks," Luis coaxed. "And the beer—"

A hand came down on the scruff of Luis' neck.

Will Stirman was standing there with his cell mate, Zeke.

Stirman wasn't a big man, but he had a kind of wiry strength that made other cons nervous. One reason he'd gotten his nickname "the Ghost" was because of the way he fought—fast, slippery and vicious. He'd disappear, hit you from an angle you weren't expecting, disappear again before your fists got anywhere close. Pablo knew this firsthand.

Another reason for Stirman's nickname was his skin. No matter how much time Stirman spent in the sun, he stayed pale as a corpse. His shaved hair made a faint black triangle on his scalp, an arrow pointing forward.

"*Compadres,*" Stirman said. "You 'bout ready for chapel?"

Luis' shoulders stiffened under the gringo's touch. "Yeah, Brother Stirman."

Stirman met Pablo's eyes. Pablo felt the air crackle.

They were the two alpha wolves in the gospel ministry. They could never meet without one of them backing down, and Pablo was getting tired of being the loser. He hated that he and Luis had put their trust in this man—this gringo of all gringos.

He felt the weight of the shank—a sharpened cafeteria spoon—taped to his thigh, and he thought how he might change today's plans. *His* plans, until Stirman had joined the ministry and taken over.

He calmed himself with thoughts of seeing his wife again. He looked away, let Stirman think he was still the one in charge.

Stirman tipped an imaginary hat to the guard. "Ma'am."

He walked off toward the basketball court, Zeke in tow.

"What's *he* in for?" Gonzales asked. She tried to sound cool, but Pablo knew Stirman unnerved her.

Pablo's face burned. He didn't like that women were allowed to be guards, and they weren't even told what the inmates were doing time for. Gonzales could be five feet away from a guy like Stirman and not know what he was, how thin a fence separated her from a monster.

"Good luck with your new assignment, miss," Pablo said.

He hoped Gonzales was moving to some office job where she would never again see people like himself or Will Stirman.

He hooked Luis' arm and headed toward the chapel, the rough edge of the shank chafing against his thigh.

"Like to get a piece of that," Zeke said.

It took Will a few steps to realize Zeke was talking about the

Latina guard back at the fence. "You supposed to be saved, son."

Zeke gave him an easy grin. "Hell, I don't mean nothing."

Will gritted his teeth.

Boy doesn't know any better, he reminded himself.

More and more, Zeke's comments reminded him of the men who'd killed Soledad and put him in jail. If Will didn't get out of Floresville soon, he was afraid what he'd do with his anger.

He was relieved to see Pastor Riggs' SUV parked out front of the chapel. The black Ford Explorer had tinted windows and yellow stenciling on the side: *Texas Prison Ministry——Redemption Through Christ.*

The guards only let Riggs park inside the gates when he was hauling stuff—like prison garden produce to the local orphanage, or delivering books to the prison library. The fact the SUV was here today meant Riggs had brought the extra sheet glass Will had asked for.

Maybe things would work out after all.

Inside the old Quonset hut, Elroy and C.C. were hunched over the worktable, arguing about glass color as they cut out pieces of Jesus Christ.

Will let his shadow fall over their handiwork. "Gonna be ready on time?"

Elroy scowled up at him, his glass cutter pressed against an opaque lemony sheet. "You make me mess up this halo."

"Should be white," C.C. complained. "Halo ain't no fucking yellow."

"It's yellow," Elroy insisted.

"Make Jesus look like he's got a piss ring around him," C.C. said. "Fucking toilet seat."

They both looked at Will, because the picture was Will's design, based on one of his sketches.

"C.C.'s right," he said. "Can't have the Savior looking less than pure. Might disappoint those kids today."

Elroy studied him.

He could've snapped Will in half, if he wanted to.

He was a former wildcatter with arms like bridge cables, serving forty years for second degree murder. His foreman had called him a nigger one too many times and Elroy had punched the guy's nose through his brain. The left side of Elroy's face was still webbed with scars from the white policemen in Lubbock who'd convinced him to give a full confession.

"You done shown me the light, Brother Stirman," Elroy said, real sober-like. "Can't disappoint those children."

C.C. tapped the stained glass until it split in a perfect curve along the crack. "You both full of shit. You know that?"

Elroy and Zeke laughed.

C.C. was a nappy-haired little runt with skin like terra-cotta. He could talk trash and get away with it partly because Elroy backed him up, partly because he was so scrawny and ugly his bad-ass routine came off as funny. He also worked in the maintenance shop, which made him indispensable to Will. At least for today.

At ten o'clock, the buzzer sounded, signaling all trustees to their jobs, the rest of the inmates back to their cells. Pablo and Luis arrived a minute late, completing the flock.

Pastor Riggs came out of his vestry. They all joined hands for prayer.

Afterward, the Reverend went back in the vestry to write his sermon. The trustees settled back to their work, getting ready for the juvies' visit at one o'clock.

Will wrote notes for his testimonial. Luis and Pablo got out their guitars and practiced gospel songs in that god-awful Freddy Fender style they had going. Elroy, C.C. and Zeke worked on the stained glass.

The panel would show Jesus in chains before Pontius Pilate. It was supposed to be finished by the time the juvenile hall kids got here from San Antonio, so they could hang it behind the preacher's podium, but the trustees knew it wouldn't be ready. Pastor Riggs had agreed they could work through lunch anyway. He'd seemed pleased by their enthusiasm.

Two civilian supervisors showed up late and plopped folding chairs by the door. One was a retired leatherneck named Grier. The other Will had never seen—a rookie, some laid-off farm-hand from Floresville probably, picking up a few extra dollars.

Grier was a mean son-of-a-bitch. Last week, he'd talked trash to Luis the whole time, describing different ways HPL was planning to kill him. He said the guards had a betting pool going.

Today, Grier decided to pick a new target.

"So, C.C.," Grier called lazily, palming the sweat off his forehead. "How'd you get two Cadillac jobs, anyway? Gospel *and* Maintenance? What'd you do, lube up your nappy ass for the warden?"

C.C. said nothing. Will kept his attention on his testimonial notes and hoped C.C. could keep his cool.

Grier grinned at the younger supervisor.

Reverend Riggs was still in his vestry. The door was open, but Grier wasn't talking loud enough for Riggs to overhear.

"Good Christian boy now, huh?" Grier asked C.C. "Turn the other cheek. Bet you've had a lot of practice turning your cheeks for the boys."

He went on like that for a while, but C.C. kept it together.

Around eleven, the smell of barbecue started wafting in—

brisket, ribs, chicken. Fourth of July picnic for the staff. The supervisors started squirming.

About fifteen minutes to noon, Supervisor Grier growled, "Hey, y'all finish up."

"We talked to the Reverend about working through lunch," Will said, nice and easy. No confrontation. "We got these kids coming this afternoon."

Grier scowled. Continents of sweat were soaking through his shirt.

He lumbered over to the pastor's doorway. "Um, Reverend?"

Riggs looked up, waved his hand in a benediction. "Y'all go on, Mr. Grier. I don't need to leave for half an hour. Get you some brisket and come back. I'll keep an eye on the boys."

"You sure?" But Grier didn't need convincing.

Soon both supervisors were gone, leaving six trustees and the pastor.

Will locked eyes with Pablo and Luis. The Mexicans reached in their guitar cases, took out the extra sets of strings the pastor had bought them. At the worktable, Elroy pulled a sweat-soaked bandana off his neck. C.C. handed him a half-moon of white glass, a feather for an angel's wing. Elroy wrapped the bandana around one end of it. Zeke unplugged his soldering iron.

Will got up, went to the Reverend's door.

For a moment, he admired Pastor Riggs sitting there, pouring his soul into his sermon.

The Reverend was powerfully built for a man in his sixties. His hands were callused and scarred from his early years working in a textile factory. He had sky-blue eyes and hair like carded cotton. He was the only hundred percent good man Will Stirman had ever known.

This was supposed to be a showcase day for Riggs. His prison ministry would turn a dozen juvenile delinquents away from crime and toward Christ. The press would run a favorable story. Riggs would attract some big private donors. He'd shared these dreams with Will, because Will was his proudest achievement—living proof that God's mercy was infinite.

Will summoned up his most honest smile. "Pastor, you come look at the stained glass now? I think we're almost done."

The old preacher went down harder than Pablo had hoped.

Riggs should have understood the point of the glass knife against his jugular. He should've let himself be tied up quietly.

But Riggs acted outraged. He said he couldn't believe everything he'd worked for was a lie—that all of them, for months, had been using him. He tried to reason with them, shame them, and in the end, he fought like a cornered *chupacabra*. Elroy, Pablo and Stirman had to wrestle him down. Zeke got too excited. He smashed the old man's head with the soldering iron until C.C. grabbed his wrists and snarled, "Damn, man! That's his skull showing!"

Pablo took a nasty bite on his finger trying to cover the preacher's mouth. Elroy had blood splattered on his pants. They were all sure Riggs' yelling and screaming had ruined the plan. Any second the guards would come running.

But they got Riggs tied up with guitar string and taped his mouth and shoved him, moaning and half-conscious, into the corner of the vestry. Still nobody came.

Elroy stood behind the worktable so anybody coming in wouldn't see the bloodstains on his pants. C.C. and Zeke huddled around him, staring at the stained glass as if they gave a damn about finishing it. Zeke suppressed a schoolboy giggle.

"Shut up, freak," Luis said.

"*You* shut up, spic."

Luis started to go for him, but Pablo grabbed his shirt collar. "*Both* of you," Stirman said, "cool it."

"We got Riggs' car keys," Elroy murmured. "Don't see why—"

"No," Stirman said. "We do it right. Patience."

Pablo didn't like it, but he got a D-string ready. He curled the ends around his hands, moved to one side of the door. Luis took the other side.

Stirman sat down in his chair, in plain sight of the entrance. He crossed his legs and read through his testimonial notes. The son-of-a-bitch was cool. Pablo had to give him that.

Pablo's finger throbbed where the pastor had bit it. The copper guitar string stung his broken skin.

Finally he heard footsteps on gravel. The rookie supervisor appeared with a heaping plate of ribs.

Stirman smiled apologetically. "Pastor Riggs wants to talk to you. Prison major came by."

"Hell," said the supervisor.

He started toward the vestry and Pablo garroted him, barbecue and baked beans flying everywhere. The supervisor's fingers raked at the elusive string around his neck as Pablo dragged him into the corner.

The rookie had just gone limp when Grier came in.

Luis tried to get him around the neck, but the old marine was too wily. He sidestepped, saw Zeke's soldering iron coming in time to catch the blow on his arm, managed one good yell before Elroy came over the table on top of him, crumpling him to the floor, Grier's head connecting hard with the cement.

Elroy got up. He was holding a broken piece of white glass and a mess of red rags. The rest of the glass was impaled just below Grier's sternum.

Grier's eyes rolled back in his head. His fingers clutched his gut.

C.C. slapped Elroy's arm. "What the hell you do that for?"

"Just happened."

They stood there, frozen, as Grier's muscles relaxed. His mouth opened and stayed that way.

Five minutes later, they had his body and the garroted rookie stripped to their underwear. The rookie was only unconscious, so they tied him up, taped his mouth, crammed him and Grier's corpse into the tiny vestry with the comatose Reverend.

Elroy and Luis got into the supervisors' clothes. Grier's had blood on them, but not that much. Most of Grier's bleeding must've been inside him. Elroy figured he could cover the stains with a clipboard. Luis' clothes had barbecue sauce splattered down the front. Neither uniform fit exactly right, but Pablo thought they might pass. They didn't have to fool anybody very long.

Elroy and Luis put the supervisors' IDs around their necks. They tucked the laminated photos in their shirt pockets like they didn't want them banging against their chests.

C.C., still in prison whites, made a call from Pastor Riggs' desk phone, pretending he was the Maintenance Department foreman. He told the back gate to expect a crew in five minutes to fix their surveillance camera.

He hung up, smiled at Stirman. "They can't wait to see us. Damn camera's been broke for a month. We'll call you from the sally port."

"Don't screw up," Stirman told him.

"Who, me?"

With one last look, Pablo tried to warn Luis to be careful. He couldn't shake the image of his cousin getting shot at the gate, his disguise seen through in a second, but Luis just grinned at him. No better than the stupid gringo Zeke—he was having a grand time. Luis threw Pablo the keys to the Reverend's SUV.

Once they were gone, Stirman picked up the phone.

"What you doing?" Pablo asked.

Stirman placed an outside call—Pablo could tell from the string of numbers. He got an answer. He said, "Go."

Then he hung up.

"What?" Pablo demanded.

Stirman looked at him with those unsettling eyes—close-set, dark as oil, with a softness that might've been mistaken for sorrow or even sympathy, except for the hunger behind them. They were the eyes of a slave ship navigator, or a doctor in a Nazi death camp.

"Safe passage," Stirman told him. "Don't worry about it."

Pablo imagined some Mexican mother hearing those words as the boxcar door closed on her and her family, locking them in the hot unventilated darkness, with a promise that they'd all see *los estados unidos* in the morning.

Pablo needed to kill Stirman.

He should take out his shank and do it. But he couldn't with Zeke there—stupid loyal Zeke with his stupid soldering iron.

Thunder broke, rolling across the tin roof of the chapel.

"Big storm coming," Stirman said. "That's good for us."

"It won't rain," Pablo said in Spanish. He felt like being stubborn, forcing Stirman to use *his* language. "That's dry thunder."

Stirman gave him an indulgent look. "Hundred-year flood, son. Wait and see."

Pablo wanted to argue, but his voice wouldn't work.

Stirman took the car keys out of his hand and went in the other room, jingling the brass cross on the Reverend's chain.

Pablo stared at the phone.

Luis, Elroy and C.C. should've reached the back gate by now. They should've called.

Or else they'd failed, and the guards were coming.

In the corner, wedged between the unconscious supervisor and Grier's body, Pastor Riggs stared at him—dazed blue eyes, his head wound glistening like a volcanic crater in his white hair.

Out in the chapel, Zeke was pacing with his soldering iron. He'd done an imperfect job wiping up Grier's blood, so his footprints made faint red prints back and forth across the cement.

Stirman pretended to work on the stained glass. He had his back to the vestry as if Pablo posed no threat at all.

Pablo could walk out there, drive the shank into Stirman's back before he knew what was happening.

He was considering the possibility when Zeke stopped, looking at something outside. Maybe the lightning.

Whatever it was, his attention was diverted. The timing wouldn't get any better.

Pablo gripped the shank.

He'd gone three steps toward Stirman when the guard came in.

It was Officer Gonzales.

She scanned the room, marking the trustees' positions like land mines. Stirman and Zeke stood perfectly still.

Gonzales' hand strayed toward her belt, but of course she wasn't armed. Guards never were, inside the fence.

"Where are your supervisors?" she asked.

She must've been scared, but she kept an edge of anger in her voice—trying to control the situation, trying to avoid any hint she was vulnerable.

Stirman pointed to the vestry. "Right in there, ma'am."

Gonzales frowned. She took a step toward the vestry. Then her eyes locked on something—Pablo's hand. He had completely forgotten the shank.

She stepped back, too late.

Zeke crushed her windpipe with the soldering iron as she tried to scream. He grabbed the front of her shirt, pulled her down, Gonzales gagging, digging in her heels, clawing at Zeke's wrists.

Stirman got hold of her ankles. They dragged her into the corner where they taped her mouth, bound her hands. Zeke slapped her in the head when she tried to struggle.

Pablo just watched.

He was a statue. He couldn't do a damn thing.

Stirman rose, breathing heavy.

"Bind her feet," he told Zeke.

"In a minute," Zeke murmured.

He tugged at Gonzales' belt. He started pulling off her pants.

"Zeke," Stirman said.

"What?"

"What are you doing?"

"Fucking her."

Gonzales groaned—dazed but still conscious.

Zeke got her pants around her thighs. Her panties were blue.

The phone in the vestry rang.

"Zeke." Stirman's voice tightened.

Officer Gonzales tried to fight, huffing against the tape on her mouth.

Pablo wanted to help her. He imagined himself driving the shank into Stirman's back, coming up behind Zeke, taking him, too.

He imagined the back gates opening, himself at the wheel of the Reverend's SUV, the plains of South Texas unfolding before him, Zeke's and Will Stirman's crumpled bodies far behind in his wake. He just wanted to get back to his wife.

The vestry phone rang again.

"Zeke," Stirman said. "Get off her."

"Only take a minute." He was untying the drawstring of his prison pants. His hands, arms and neck were pale sweaty animal muscle.

Pablo took a step forward.

Stirman's kidneys, he told himself. *Then Zeke's carotid artery.*

Stirman turned. He saw the shank, locked eyes with Pablo.

"Give me that," Stirman ordered.

Pablo looked for his courage. "I was just . . ."

Stirman held out his hand, lifted his eyebrows.

Pablo handed over the shank.

Stirman walked behind Zeke, who was now in his underwear, straddling Gonzales' huge bare thighs.

Stirman grabbed his cell mate by the hair, yanked his chin up, and brought down the shank in one efficient thrust.

It should have ended there, but something inside Stirman seemed to snap. He stabbed again, spitting cuss words, then again, cursing the names of people Pablo didn't know, swearing that he had tried, he had fucking tried to forget.

Afterward, Gonzales lay with her clothes half off, her gold-rimmed glasses freckled with blood. Zeke's body trembled, waiting for a climax that was never going to happen.

"Get the phone," Stirman said.

Pablo started. The vestry phone was still ringing.

He stumbled into the pastor's office, picked up the receiver.

"Damn, man." C.C.'s voice. "Where you been?"

C.C. said the way was clear. They'd taken down two more guards—one at the gate, one in the watchtower. The keys to the armory had yielded five 9mm handguns, a 12-gauge shotgun, and several hundred rounds of ammunition. Elroy and Luis were manning the sally port, waiting for the SUV.

Pablo put down the receiver. His hands were cold and sweaty. Some of Zeke's blood had speckled his sleeves. He took one last look at the bound supervisor, Pastor Riggs, Grier's body slumped at their feet.

No other choice, he told himself.

He went into the chapel.

Stirman was kneeling next to Officer Gonzales, dabbing the

blood from her glasses with a rag. Zeke's dead arm was draped across her waist. Gonzales was shivering as Stirman told her it was okay. Nobody was going to hurt her.

Stirman rose when he saw Pablo. He pointed the shank at Pablo's chin, let it glitter there like Christmas ornament glass. "I *own* you, amigo. You are my new right-hand man. You understand? You are mine."

No, Pablo thought.

As soon as they got through those gates, Pablo and Luis would take off by themselves. They would head west to El Paso, as far from Will Stirman as they could get.

But Stirman's eyes held him. Pablo had blown his chance. He'd frozen. Stirman had acted. Stirman had saved Gonzales. Pablo had done nothing.

Pablo clawed at the fact, looking for leverage. He said, "Who are Barrow and Barrera?"

Stirman's jaw tightened. "What?"

"You were saying those names when you . . ." Pablo gestured to Zeke's corpse.

Stirman looked down at the body, then the terrified face of Officer Gonzales. "Couple of private investigators, amigo, ought to be worried today. Now get the SUV."

Eleven minutes later, right on schedule, Pastor Riggs' black Ford Explorer rolled out the back gate of the Floresville State Penitentiary, straight into a summer storm that was starting to pour down rain.

2

I didn't mind bounty-hunting Dimebox Ortiz.

What I minded were his cousins Lalu and Kiko, who weighed three-fifty apiece, smoked angel dust to improve their IQ, and kept hand grenades in a Fiestaware bowl on their coffee table the way some people kept wax apples.

This explained why Erainya Manos and I were waiting in a van down the block from their house, rather than storming the front door.

Our snitch owed Dimebox four grand in cockfighting bets. He was getting a little nervous about Dimebox's habit of setting his delinquent debtors on fire, and was anxious to see Dimebox in jail. He had promised us Dimebox was staying with his cousins. He'd also promised us Dimebox had a date with a lady tonight, and if we staked out the cousins' house, we could easily tail him and snag him in transit.

Six o'clock, the snitch had told us. Seven o'clock, at the latest.

It was now 10:33.

I needed to pee.

I had an empty Coke bottle, but it isn't tempting to use that trick when your female boss is next to you in the driver's seat and her eight-year-old son is playing PlayStation 2 in the back.

Jem wasn't supposed to be with us. The rain had washed out his plans to see the Woodlawn Lake fireworks with his second-grade friends. That left him nothing to do but a boring old stakeout with his mom.

Erainya, with her usual bizarre logic about what was safe for her child, had weighed the risks of a baby-sitter against Lalu and Kiko's grenades, and decided to go with the stakeout. Of course, given some of the surveillance cases we'd worked involving baby-sitters and day-care workers, I supposed she had a point.

So we had the soothing sounds of Spyro the Dragon in the back seat. We had a dark row of clapboard houses and chinaberry trees to look at. And we had the rain, which had been alternately pouring and drizzling all afternoon, and was now reminding my bladder of flow patterns.

I was about to suggest that we call it quits, that not even the munificent sum Dimebox's bail bondsman was offering was worth this, when Erainya said, "We'll wait, honey. He'll show."

The longer I knew her, the more Erainya answered my questions before I asked them. It had gotten to the point where she could slug me when I was even thinking about being a smart-ass.

"Little late for a date," I said.

She gave me those onyx eyes—the Greek Inquisition. "Your payday is Friday, honey. You want a check?"

That I heard loud and clear.

The past few months, since Erainya's archrival, I-Tech Security, had taken away our last bread-and-butter contract with a downtown legal firm, her finances had been slowly unraveling. We'd given up our office space on Blanco. Erainya's high-speed Internet line had been shut off twice. Our information broker would no longer work on credit. We were taking whatever cases Erainya could get just to keep afloat—divorce, workers comp, bail-jumpers. The dregs of the PI business.

I'd thought about making us cardboard signs, *Will Sleuth for Food*, but Erainya had slugged me before I could suggest it.

I reminded myself she had more at stake in the agency than I did.

She'd inherited the business from her husband, Fred Barrow, when he died. Or more accurately, when she'd shot him to death for abusing her, then been acquitted on murder charges.

This was back before I became a calming influence in her life.

After the murder trial, she'd disappeared to the Mediterranean for a year, reclaimed her maiden name and her Greek heritage, and returned to Texas the adoptive mother of a Bosnian orphan boy. She'd taken up Barrow's PI business with a vengeance and had become arguably the best street investigator in South Texas.

Yet she'd never done more than scrape by, no matter how hard she worked. It was as if Fred Barrow's ghost hung over the agency, jinxing her luck. The old rivalry with I-Tech became more and more one-sided until I-Tech dominated San Antonio, while we survived off bounties on scumbags like Dimebox Ortiz.

Lately, Erainya had been taking longer vacations with her boyfriend. She put off paperwork. She mused through old case files, which she would close and lock in her drawer whenever I approached.

She'd been one of the two great mentors of my career. She'd gotten me licensed and bonded, terrorized me into good investigative habits for the past four years. Whenever I thought of quitting PI work and using my English PhD to find a full-time college teaching position, which was about every other week,

Erainya urged me to stick with it, telling me I was a natural investigator. I had a knack for finding the lost, helping the desperate. I chose to take that as a compliment.

The last thing I wanted to admit was that I was worried about her, that I sensed her spirit going out of the job.

So I tried to act excited about watching the Ortiz house.

Erainya polished a .45-caliber bullet. I nibbled on some of her homemade spanakopita, which she brought by the sackful whenever we went into the field.

I got tired of PlayStation noises and switched on the radio. We listened to an NPR interview with an artist who turned roadkill into paintings for New York galleries. I imagined my mother's voice scolding me: *See, dear, some people have real jobs.*

My mother, one of San Antonio's few card-carrying bohemians, had been out of town for almost three months now, knocking around Central America with her newest boyfriend, a chakra crystal salesman who had ridiculous amounts of money. It was probably just as well she wasn't around to lecture me on my career choices.

In the back of the van, Jem said, "Yess!"

I looked at him. "Good news?"

Delayed reaction: "Frozen Altars level. Twenty-eight eggs."

"Wow. Hard?"

Jem kept playing. The rain battered the windows.

Jem's silky black hair was cut in bangs, same as it had been since kindergarten, but over the past year his face had filled in considerably. He looked like your typical San Antonio kid—a something-percent mix of Latino and Anglo; black Spurs T-shirt, orange shorts, light-up sneakers. You would be hard pressed to believe that as a one-year-old he had been a Bosnian Muslim orphan, his parents' mule-drawn cart blown apart by a land mine, his young eyes burned with God-knew-how-many-other images of war.

"Hard level?" I asked again.

No response.

I wanted to tear the game pad out of his hands and fling it into the night, but hey—I wasn't his dad. What did I expect the kid to do for endless hours in the back of a van? Read?

"Yeah," he said at last. "The evil panda bears—"

"Honey," Erainya said, her voice suddenly urgent. "Turn the sound off."

I looked out the windshield, expecting to see some action at the Ortiz cousins' house.

Instead, Erainya was focused on the radio. A news brief about the prison break that afternoon—five dangerous cons on the loose. The Floresville Five, the media had instantly dubbed them—Will Stirman, C. C. Andrews, Elroy Lacoste, Pablo Zagosa, Luis Juarez.

"Not a good day for the warden," I agreed. "You see the pictures?"

Erainya glared at me. "Pictures?"

"On TV this afternoon. Don't tell me you've missed this."

The news announcer recounted how the cons had been left unsupervised in a religious rehabilitation program. The five had overpowered the chaplain, killed a guard and a fellow inmate, driven straight through the back gate in the preacher's Ford Explorer after stealing several handguns, a shotgun, and an unknown amount of ammunition from the prison armory. They should be considered armed and dangerous.

No shit.

The alarm hadn't gone up for almost fifteen minutes, by which time the cons had ditched the SUV in the Floresville Wal-Mart parking lot and vanished, possibly in another car provided by an outside accomplice. A map of Kingsville had been found in one of the cells, leading authorities to believe that at least some of the fugitives might be heading south toward the Mexican border. Police all along the Rio Grande were on alert. The suspected ringleader of the jailbreak, William "the Ghost" Stirman, had been serving ninety-nine years on multiple convictions of human trafficking and accessory to murder. Prison psychologists described him as a highly dangerous sociopath.

"The Ghost," I said. "He'll be the one wearing the sheet with the eyeholes."

Erainya didn't smile. She turned off the radio, fumbled for her cell phone.

"What?" I asked.

She dialed a number, cursed. With the storm, cell phone reception inside the van, especially here on the rural South Side, was almost nonexistent.

She opened her door. The van's overhead light blinked on.

"Erainya—"

"Got to find a clear signal."

"It's pouring."

She slid outside in her rain jacket, and waded into the glow of the only street lamp, where everybody and God could see her.

Since the day I apprenticed to her, she had harped on me—getting out of the car while on stakeout was an absolute no-no. You jeopardized your position, your ability to move. Otherwise I would've peed a long time ago.

I knew only one person she might break the rules to call—her ENT, Dr. Dreamboat, or whatever the hell his name was, whom she'd met during a romantic prescription for cedar fever last winter and had been dating ever since.

But I couldn't believe she would call him now.

I was pondering whether I'd have to shove a cell phone up Dr.

Dreamboat's sinus cavity when the porch light came on at the Ortiz cousins' house.

A heavyset man in a silky black warm-up suit stepped outside. Dimebox Ortiz.

I tried to kill the overhead illumination, found there was no switch. "Shit."

"Owe me a quarter," Jem told me, his eyes still glued to his game.

"Put it on my account."

My "bad word" account was already enough to buy Jem his first car, but he didn't complain.

I leaned and tapped on Erainya's window.

Halfway down the sidewalk, Dimebox Ortiz froze, staring in our direction. The rain was drenching him.

You don't see us, I thought. *We are invisible.*

Dimebox yelled back toward the house—his cousins' names, some Spanish I couldn't catch. He ran for his Lincoln Town Car, and I gave up on discretion.

"Erainya!" I yelled, pounding on the driver's-side door.

She took the phone away from her ear, just catching the fact that something was wrong as Dimebox's taillights flared to life and Lalu and Kiko came lumbering out their front door, their fists full of things I was pretty sure weren't wax apples.

Erainya climbed in, hit the ignition. "Jem, seatbelt!"

We peeled out, hydroplaning a sheet of water into the faces of the Ortiz cousins, who yelled plentiful contributions to Jem's cuss jar as they jogged after us, brandishing their army surplus door prizes.

Dimebox's Lincoln turned the corner on Keslake as the first explosion rocked the back of our van. I looked in the rearview mirror and saw chunks of wet asphalt spray up from the middle of the street where our tailpipe had been a moment before.

"Fireworks?" Jem asked, excited.

"Sort of," I said. "Get down."

"I want to see!"

"These are the kind you feel, champ. Get down!"

The twins sloshed after us like a couple of rabid hippos.

Up ahead, Dimebox's Lincoln Town Car dipped toward the low-water crossing on Sinclair.

A few hours ago when we'd driven in, Rosillio Creek had been full, but nowhere near the top of the road. Now, glistening in our headlights, an expanse of chocolate water surged over the asphalt. Clumps of grass, branches and garbage piled up on the metal guardrail. It was hard to tell how deep the water was. There was no other road in or out of the neighborhood, even if we could turn around, which we couldn't with *Señor* Dee and *Señor* Dum lobbing munitions right behind us.

In the PI business, we have a technical term for getting yourself into this kind of situation. We call it *fucking up*.

Dimebox's brake lights flashed as he approached the crossing.

"He won't make it," I said, as he revved the Lincoln's engine and plunged hood-first into current.

Ka-BOOM. Behind us, the low-water-crossing sign splintered into kindling.

"He'll make it," Erainya insisted. "So will we."

I started to protest, but she'd already nosed the van into the water.

The sensation was like a log ride—that stomach-lurching moment when the chain catches under the boat. Water churned beneath the floorboards, hammered the doors. The van shuddered and began drifting sideways.

Through the smear of the windshield, I saw Dimebox's Town Car trying to climb the opposite bank, but his headlights dimmed. His rear fender slid back into the torrent, crunched against the guardrail. His headlights went dark, and suddenly the Lincoln was a dam, water swelling around it, lapping angrily at the bottom of the shotgun window.

"Go back," I told Erainya.

She fought the wheel, muttered orders to the van in Greek, eased us forward. We somehow managed to get right behind the Lincoln before our engine died.

Our headlights dimmed, but stayed on. I could see Dimebox Ortiz in front of us, waving one arm frantically out his window. His driver's-side door was smashed against the guardrail. Water was sluicing into his shotgun window.

Behind us, Lalu and Kiko were barely discernible at the edge of the water, watching mutely as our two vehicles were trash-compacted against the guardrail.

The railing moaned. Our van skidded sideways. The Lincoln's back left wheel slipped over the edge, and Dimebox's whole car began to tilt up on the right, threatening to flip over in the force of the water.

I grabbed Erainya's cell phone, dialed 911, but in the roar of the flood I couldn't hear anything. The LCD read, *Searching for Signal*. The water inside the van was up to my ankles.

"Rope," I shouted to Erainya. "You still have rope?"

"We have to stay inside, honey. We can't—"

"I'm getting Ortiz out of that car."

"Honey—"

"He won't make it otherwise. I'll tie off here."

"Honey, he isn't worth it!"

Ortiz was yelling for help. He looked . . . tangled in something. I couldn't tell. Nothing but his head was above water.

I looked back at Jem, who for once wasn't focused on the PlayStation.

"Pass me the rope behind your seat," I told him. "You're the man of the van, okay?"

"I can't swim," he reminded me.

His eyes were calm—that creepy calm I only saw when he tried to remember his life before Erainya, his thoughts thickening into a protective, invisible layer of scar tissue.

I shoved him the cell phone. "It's okay, champ. Keep trying 911."

He passed me the rope—fifty feet of standard white propylene. I didn't know why Erainya stored it in the van. I suppose you never knew when you'd have to tie somebody up. Or maybe Dr. Dreamboat the ENT had strange proclivities. I didn't want to ask.

I made a knot around the steering column, a noose around my waist. Then I rolled down the passenger's-side window and got a face full of rain.

I climbed outside, lowered myself into the current, and got slapped flat against the van.

Up ahead, a few impossible feet, the passenger's side of the Lincoln was bobbing in the current. I could see Dimebox Ortiz in the driver's seat, up to his earlobes in water.

I didn't so much walk as crawl along the side of the van.

My efforts spurred Lalu and Kiko into a new round of yelling. I couldn't make out words. Maybe they were arguing about whether they could blow me up without hurting Dimebox.

I kept the rope taut around my waist, inching out a step at a time, not even kidding myself that I could keep my footing. The side of the van was the only thing that kept me from being swept away.

The worst part was between the cars, where the water shot through like a ravine. When I slipped one foot into the full current, it was like being hooked by a moving train. I was ripped off balance, pulled into the stream. My head went under, and the world was reduced to a cold brown roar.

I held the rope. I got my head above water, found the fender of the Town Car, and clawed my way to the passenger's side.

The Lincoln's shotgun window was open, making a waterfall into the car.

Dimebox's hands were tugging frantically at something underwater. He was craning his ugly head to keep it above the water. His face was like a bank robber's, his features all pantyhose-smeared, only Dimebox didn't wear pantyhose.

"Can you move?" I yelled.

He pushed at the wheel as if it were pinning his legs.

"Lalu!" he shouted. "Kiko! Push!"

Push?

Then I realized he wasn't struggling to get free. He was attempting to start the ignition. He expected his cousins to wade out here and give him a jump start.

"You're underwater, you moron!" I told him. "Give me your hand!"

"Fuck you, Navarre!" he screamed. "Get the fuck away!"

"Me or the river, Dimebox."

"I ain't going to jail!"

I didn't understand his stubbornness. Dimebox was up on some stupid charge like assault. He was constantly going in and out of the slammer, constantly jumping bail, which I guess you can do when your bondsman is your brother-in-law. We'd bounty-hunted him plenty of times. I didn't see why he was making such a fuss about a couple more weeks in the county lockup.

Another metallic groan. The guardrail bent, and the Lincoln shifted a half inch downstream. My side of the car began to levitate. For a moment, a ton of Detroit steel balanced on the fulcrum, my armpits the only thing keeping it from flipping.

"Now!" I told Dimebox. "Over here now!"

"Mother of Shit!" Dimebox lunged in my direction, wrapped his arms around my neck, damn near pulled me into the car with him.

A few more seconds—an eternity when Dimebox is hugging you—and I hauled him out the window. The Lincoln seemed to settle with both of us pressed against it, but I wasn't going to take any chances. We inched our way back toward the van, the rain driving needles into my cheeks, Dimebox reeking a lovely combination of wet sewage and Calvin Klein. On shore, Lalu and Kiko yelled wildly, brandishing their hand grenades.

We'd just reached the van when Dimebox's Town Car rose on its side with a huge groan, flipped the guardrail, and crashed upside down in the creek bed, its body submerged, wheels spinning uselessly in the foam.

The guardrail bent like licorice. Our van would go next.

Erainya yelled at me, "Throw them the rope!"

"What?"

"The cousins!" she yelled. "Throw it to them!"

Only then did I realize that Lalu and Kiko weren't waiting around to kill us. They wanted to help.

Forty minutes later, after Erainya's van, Jem's PlayStation, and a bagful of perfectly good spanakopita had been washed into oblivion down Rosillio Creek, Erainya and Jem and I sat in the Ortiz cousins' living room, wrapped in triple-X terry cloth bathrobes, eating cold venison tamales and waiting for the police, who were coming to pick up Dimebox.

The guest of honor sat on the sofa, stripped to his jockey shorts and T-shirt, his ankles and wrists tied in plastic cuffs. He kept muttering cuss words, and Jem kept telling him he owed us quarters.

"You okay," Kiko told me, smashing the top of my head with his paw. "Save Dimebox's sorry ass. Put him in jail. Kiko not have t'sleep on the couch no more."

"Won't do you any good, Erainya," Dimebox snarled. "Bounty money won't help you worth shit, will it? We're both screwed."

"Shut up, Ortiz." Her voice was harsher than I'd ever heard it. "Don't curse in front of my son."

"Stirman's coming. He's got plenty of friends in the county jail. You lock me up, you're signing my death warrant."

"I *said* shut up."

I looked back and forth between them, wondering what I'd missed, or if my brain was still waterlogged.

Then the name clicked.

"Stirman," I said. "The escaped con on the news."

"I ain't staying in jail," Dimebox said. "You know what's good for you, you'll run, too."

Erainya wouldn't meet my eyes.

I remembered her reaction to the radio news, the intense, almost frantic look she'd given me.

"What?" I asked her. "You helped put this Stirman guy away?"

Dimebox laughed nervously. "That ain't the fucking half of it, Navarre. Not the fucking—"

Lalu whacked his fist against Dimebox's skull, and Dimebox slumped on the couch.

Lalu grunted apologetically. "Lady wanted no cussing."

I said, "Erainya . . . ?"

She got up and stormed into the cousins' bathroom, slamming the door behind her.

I turned to Jem, who was paying a lot of attention to the pattern in the couch fabric. I asked him if he still had his mom's cell phone.

I checked the readout, but the call history didn't help my confusion. I could make a dozen guesses who Erainya might call in an emergency, if she were truly faced with an urgent dilemma.

All my guesses were wrong.

The person she'd been so anxious to talk to when she stepped into the storm wasn't her doctor boyfriend. It wasn't the police, or any of our regular helpers on the street.

She'd called I-Tech Security, the direct line to the company president.

Her archrival.

A man she'd sworn never to cross paths with again, until one of them was dancing on the other's grave.

3

Special Agent Samuel Barrera spent breakfast trying to remember the name of the ax murderer.

The guy had tortured and killed six illegal immigrants on a ranch up around Castroville, left their body parts scattered in the woods like deer corn. What the hell was his name?

Sam had a feeling it would be important in the case he was working on. He'd talk to his trainee Pacabel when he got to the office. Pacabel would remember.

The morning was humid after last night's downpour, just enough drizzle to keep everybody sour-faced, staring at the gray sky, thinking, *Enough already.*

Not even Alamo Street Market's coffee and *migas* were enough to compensate.

Sam pulled on his jacket over his sidearm.

He left a ten on the table, got annoyed when the waiter called, *"Hasta mañana,* Sam."

Like Sam knew the guy. Like they were old friends or something. What the hell was wrong with people these days?

Down South Alamo, yellow sawhorses blocked the side streets. Asphalt had come apart in huge chunks and washed away. The sidewalk was buried in a shroud of mud.

Sam picked his way through the debris.

The last few years, people had started calling this area South-town. Art studios had opened up in the old *barrio* houses, funky little restaurants and curio shops in the crumbling mercantile buildings. The changes didn't bother Sam. He liked seeing life come back to his old neighborhood. But it did make him miss the past.

His family home at the corner of Cedar was falling apart. He'd owned it since his parents died, back in the seventies. He hadn't lived there for years, but he always parked in front of it. Force of habit. The FOR SALE was up. The real estate agent called him every day with glad tidings. They had their choice of offers. For this old dump. Sam never suspected he'd grown up in a Victorian fixer-up dream. To him, it had just been *la casa*. Back then, nobody lived here but the Mexicans, because this was where they could afford to live.

He opened the door of his mustard-yellow BMW.

The car was getting old. Like him. But Sam kept putting off a trade-in, irritated by the thought of unfamiliar controls, a dif-ferent paint job. Too much to keep track of, when you got a new car.

He drove north to the field office on East Houston, still think-ing about that rancher whose name he couldn't remember. He'd kept the six illegal immigrants as slaves, killed them slowly, one at a time. It had something to do with Sam's present case.

When he got to the FBI suite on the second floor, he walked into the reception area and found some rookie fresh out of Quantico blocking his way to the inner offices. "Sir, can I help you?"

Sam scowled. There was a time when he would've chewed out this asshole for standing in his way, but Sam didn't feel up to it today. He felt a little off. Preoccupied. "I *work* here, son."

Something disconnected in the kid's eyes. It wasn't the answer he'd been expecting. "You have identification?"

Sam patted his jacket, where the ID should be.

Hell. Was it in the car, maybe? On the coffee table?

Held up from work by a fucking *detail*.

A couple of agents came out from the interior offices and sized up Sam. One of them was an older guy—must've been nearing mandatory retirement. He had thinning silver hair, a big nose blazed with capillaries. Sam knew him, couldn't quite place his name.

"Must've left it at home," Sam told the rookie. He felt the situation slipping away from him. "Cut me some slack."

The agents exchanged looks. By some silent agreement, the silver-haired one stepped forward. "Hey, Sam."

"Yeah?" Sam said.

"Let's take a walk."

"I don't want a walk."

The old guy put a hand on his shoulder and steered him back toward the entrance.

"You know me?" the old guy asked.

"Sure," Sam said.

"Pacabel," the guy said.

Immediately, the name slipped around him like a comfortable shoe.

"Joe Pacabel," Sam said, confident again. "Sure, Joe. Let me get to work, will you? Tell these jokers."

Pacabel looked at the floor. Beige tiles, which seemed wrong to Sam. It should've been carpet. Green industrial carpet.

The other agents were trying not to stare at him.

"Look, Sam," Pacabel said, the words dragging out of him. "You're a little confused, is all. It happens."

"Joe, my case . . ."

"You've got no case, Sam."

"What the hell are you talking about?"

Pacabel's eyes watered, and Sam realized it was from embarrassment. Embarrassment for him.

"Sam, you retired from the FBI," Pacabel said gently. "You haven't worked here in twenty years."

Halfway across town, Gerry Far was pulling dead people out of a trailer.

He hated this part of his job, but he had to help out personally. Otherwise his employees would panic. He'd learned that from his mentor, Will Stirman.

The driver this time was a fruit trucker from Indianapolis. This was his first run. It was all Gerry could do to keep him from calling the police.

"Help me with this *hombre*," Gerry told the trucker. "Jesus, he's heavy."

The smell in the truck was enough to kill—overripe mangos and excrement and body odor. When they'd opened the trailer, the temperature inside had been about a hundred and ten degrees.

As he hauled the big corpse over to the incinerator, Gerry did the math. Fifty-three illegals. Three hundred dollars a head. Twenty-one had died, but of course they'd paid up front.

The thirty-two who lived would be sold off to Gerry's clients—sweatshops, labor ranches, brothels—to "earn credit" for further transportation to Chicago or Houston or wherever they dreamed of going. In reality, none of them would ever be allowed to leave. They'd bring Gerry a sale price of two to five hundred dollars each, possibly more for young women. That was the beauty of the Stirman system—the illegals paid to get

here, then Gerry got paid again for selling them into slavery.
Welcome to America.

Gerry would have to give the driver his cut, plus a little extra
to calm his nerves. There would be a hefty fee to the guy who
ran the incinerator. Still, Gerry figured he would walk away
with ten grand from this load.

He was dragging out the last body when his spotter, Luke,
ran up, looking paler than the corpses. "You hear the news?"

"What the fuck are you doing here?" Gerry said. "Watch the
goddamn gate."

"Stirman's free. Broke out yesterday afternoon."

Gerry dropped the body he was carrying. "You sure?"

Luke swallowed, held up his cell phone. "I just got the call."

"From who?"

Luke hesitated. If Gerry had been thinking more clearly, he
might've picked up on the fact that something was very wrong
with the way Luke was acting.

"Just a friend," Luke said. "Wanted to be sure you were
warned."

"Shit."

"Where you going?" the trucker called.

But Gerry was already fishing out his car keys, running toward
his TransAm.

He'd always known a life sentence wouldn't stop Will Stirman.
Not after what Gerry had done to him. But damn it—yesterday
afternoon? Why hadn't somebody told him sooner?

Gerry drove toward downtown.

He regretted what he'd done to Stirman. He regretted it every
day, but there was no going back now. He had to go through
with his emergency plan.

He ditched the TransAm near the Rivercenter Marriott and
caught a taxi to the East Side. St. Paul Square. From there, it

was a short walk to one of his properties—a place Stirman didn't know about. Nobody knew about it except a few of Gerry's best guys, like Luke. Gerry could lay low there for a few days, make arrangements, then get out of town for good, or at least until Stirman was recaptured.

The property was an abandoned ice warehouse, a four-story red-brick building that didn't have anything to recommend it— no electricity, no water. Just a whole lot of privacy, a good vantage point from the fourth floor to watch for visitors, and the stash Gerry had squirreled away—a few days' worth of food, clothing, extra cash, a couple of guns. Not much. Gerry should've been more serious. But it was enough to get him started, to make a plan.

He was starting to relax as he climbed the stairs. He needed a vacation anyway. Maybe Cozumel.

At the top of the stairs, two men were waiting for him in the shadows.

A familiar voice said, "Gerry Far. Been praying for you every day, son."

The I-Tech corporate offices looked out over the wreckage of north San Antonio—streets pulsing with police lights, swollen creeks turning neighborhoods into lakes. The gray ribbon of Highway 281 disappeared into water at the Olmos Basin. On the horizon, clouds and hills boiled together in a thick, fuzzy soup.

Sam Barrera said nothing to his secretary, Alicia, about why he was late. He hoped Joe Pacabel wouldn't call to check up on him.

He stared out at the drowned city, the streets he'd known all his life.

He wanted to weep from shame.

The first time he'd passed on his medication. One sorry-ass morning he'd tried to go without the little beige pills and the goddamn diarrhea they caused. And what had happened? A nightmare.

So you got confused, he consoled himself. *It could happen to anybody. You were thinking about . . .*

What?

Something had thrown him. Something on the television.

Sam made fists, wishing he could squeeze the confusion out of his mind.

Today was Monday. His doctor had only given him until Friday to make a decision.

It's got to be next week, Sam. I have to insist. Think about it. Talk to your family.

But Sam had no family. No wife, no kids. His other relatives he'd had a falling-out with years ago, over something Sam couldn't even remember now. He'd taken down all their pictures, stuffed them away in the back of his closet.

He had only his work—his talent for weaving facts into patterns, making the perfect investigation. And now, at the unreasonable age of fifty-eight, that talent was betraying him.

Twenty years since he quit the Bureau . . . Hell, of course it had been.

He'd gone into the PI business, built I-Tech from scratch, made himself a reputation.

He reviewed those facts in his head, tried to hold on to them, but it was like those tests at the neurologist's office—name the presidents in reverse chronological order, count backward by sevens from one hundred.

The last month, work had gotten progressively harder. Case files were now almost impossible for him to understand.

Mornings were better. He tried to finish work early, get home before afternoon when his mind got cloudy.

But he relied on Alicia more and more. She knew something was wrong. She'd stopped teasing him about getting absent-minded in his old age. Now, she just watched him uneasily.

Five days to decide.

He stared at his desk—a disgraceful clutter of unread reports, notes to himself stuck everywhere. The work surface had once been pristinely organized. Now it was deteriorating into chaos.

Across the room, a bank of televisions played security footage from I-Tech's major accounts, along with news from the three local stations.

The news was all disaster coverage—befuddled weathermen predicting the second hundred-year flood in four years.

Sam doubted that's what had unnerved him.

Why should he be surprised if the town hit a century mark every four years? He'd lost twenty years in a single morning. Time was collapsing around him. Chronology meant nothing anymore.

He got out his Post-it notes and a pen, checked his private line for messages.

There was only one—last night, 10:48 P.M. Erainya Manos.

The name snagged on his memory as he wrote it down.

The case he was working on . . . but Joe Pacabel said there was no case.

Erainya Manos said they needed to talk. Absolutely urgent. Sam would know what it was about.

But he didn't know what the woman wanted.

He stared at her phone number until something on the television caught his attention—a reporter breaking in, a convenience store shooting in New Braunfels. Three masked gunmen had fatally shot a clerk, made away with several thousand dollars. Police were investigating for a possible link to yesterday's jailbreak—the Floresville Five. Will "the Ghost" Stirman, four other wanted men.

A mug shot of Will Stirman filled the screen, and the world shifted under Sam's feet.

The convict's face was gaunt and hard, like weathered marble. He had dark, preternaturally calm eyes, and a faint triangle of buzzed black hair. If Sam didn't know better, he would've pegged the man as a white supremacist, or an abortion clinic bomber. His expression suggested the same quiet confidence, the same capacity for fanatic violence.

Sam knew this man. This was who he'd seen on television earlier. This was the news that had shaken him.

He reached into his pants pocket, pulled out a crumpled yellow Post-it note he'd forgotten.

In his own shaky cursive, the note read:

Stirman is free. He'll be coming. I can't *go to the police.*

Sam stared at it, then looked at the newer message from Erainya Manos.

He picked up the receiver, began to dial Erainya Manos' number, then hung up again.

He had a bad feeling about this woman.

He had to think clearly.

Sam felt bitterness rising in his throat. It wasn't fair for life to throw him one more problem. Not now, when he was struggling just to get by.

But it wasn't Sam's nature to surrender. He never played defense. The only way to survive was to plow forward, like he'd always done, right the fuck over anything and anyone who stood in his way.

He would let Erainya Manos do the talking. She would fill in the gaps. He had become an expert at covering his lapses that way, letting others talk into his silence.

He couldn't remember why, but Will Stirman was lethal. If Sam didn't handle this just right, if he didn't stay in control, he would be destroyed.

He picked up a pen and wrote himself a new note: *I'm calling Erainya Manos. Be careful. I'm pretty sure she's my enemy.*

4

Tres Navarre's dating advice: If you're going to meet your girlfriend for dinner, you might as well do it in the middle of a flood, when there are dangerous convicts on the loose.

While you're at it—go to a restaurant where the maître d' wants to kill you. It makes your romantic outing so much more special.

The forty-five-minute drive to San Marcos took me three hours, thanks to a flooded stretch on I-35 and a police roadblock north of New Braunfels. By the time I got to Pig Falls Café, the rain clouds had broken for the first time in twenty-four hours, and an insultingly beautiful sunset was bleeding to purple.

I spotted Maia Lee at a balcony table overlooking the waterfall. Robert Johnson in his carrying case was tucked discreetly under her chair. Since Maia moved to Texas, we'd had to work out a joint custody arrangement. It was now my week to play servant to the Cat Almighty.

Maia was tapping her fingers on a menu, nursing what probably wasn't her first margarita.

I was working up my nerve to walk over, formulating my most sincere apology, when the maître d' put his hand on my arm. "May I help— Whoa, shit."

He was in his mid-twenties, stocky and bald, with freckles the color of nacho-flavored Doritos.

I spun the mental Rolodex, came up with a name. "Quentin Yates."

"If I had a fucking gun . . ."

"Tough break," I agreed. "How's life on the lam?"

He started to make a fist.

"Careful," I said. "Bet your employer doesn't know your history."

His orange brow furrowed . . . kill Navarre or stay out of jail. A decision that has troubled greater criminal minds.

"You gonna snitch me out?" he demanded.

"Of course I'm going to snitch you out. But I want to eat first. Gives you a good head start, doesn't it? See you, Quent."

I strolled out to the balcony and sat across from Maia Lee.

She pretended to study her menu. "Trouble at the low-water crossings?"

"Don't say those words."

Under her seat, Robert Johnson said, "Row."

Maia arched an eyebrow, glanced over my shoulder. "What's your history with Freckles?"

Very little escapes Maia's notice. I had no doubt that if the need arose three weeks from now, she would be able to tell me what I was wearing tonight, how much the meal cost, and what most of the people around us had been talking about.

"That's Quentin Yates," I told her. "He isn't running away in terror yet?"

"No. He just . . ." She muttered what must've been the Chinese word for *ouch*. "He just seated an old lady, gave her the Heimlich maneuver. Now he's glowering at you."

"Quent was a buddy of mine for two weeks, a few years ago, while I was working undercover at his boss's restaurant."

Maia's beautiful face turned grim at the word *undercover*. "Embezzlement?"

"Credit cards. Quentin was the bartender."

"Capturing account information," she guessed.

"Well, hey—you got these perfectly good numbers, why not charge a home entertainment system or two? After I turned him in, he skipped bail, beat up his ex-boss with an aluminum bat, threatened to come after me. Then he disappeared. Apparently Pig Falls doesn't do background checks."

"You want to call the police?"

"Dinner first. I'd recommend we pay in cash."

"Sensible."

Maia, I soon discovered, had already arranged things. At a nod from her, the waitress cranked into high gear, bringing plates of crabmeat flautas, bowls of tortilla soup, Gulf Coast shrimp with fresh avocado slices. Having spent the whole day staring at a computer monitor and sorting through paperwork, I should've been more interested in the food, except that Maia herself was pretty damn distracting.

You'd think, after twelve years, I would no longer stare.

Everything about her still startled me—her glossy black hair, the caramel skin of her throat against the V of her silk blouse, her fingers, her lips, her eyes. She was a perfect mix of war and beauty, like a Zhou Dynasty noblewoman—one of the imperial courtesans Sun Tzu had trained to fight.

"It's been too long," I said.

She gave me a dry smile. "One week."

"Like I said."

"You could solve that problem. A hotshot attorney in Austin has made you a damn good offer."

"Lee and Navarre . . . your stock value would plummet."

"I beg your pardon. No one said anything about your name on the billing."

Maia let her offer float in the air, weightless and persistent, where it had lingered during our last few dinners together. She snuck the cat a crabmeat flauta. Every so often, her eyes would track something behind me, and I knew she was keeping watch on Quentin, the glowering maître d'.

"So, the Erainya Manos Agency," Maia said, trying hard to keep the distaste out of her voice. "Things have been good . . . bounty-hunting and whatnot? Driving into floods?"

The stubborn side of me wanted to rise to Erainya's defense, but Maia knew me too well. She had trained me as an unlicensed investigator before Erainya turned me legitimate. During our years together in San Francisco, Maia had used me as a secret weapon to keep cases from going to court, taught me all the dirty, borderline illegal, ruthlessly effective methods of investigative blackmail that Erainya had tried so hard to erase when she got me licensed. Each woman thought the other unprofessional, mostly because they both kept bad company—like me.

"Erainya's distracted," I admitted. "Increasingly."

"Maybe it's her boyfriend. Men affect one's judgment."

I decided not to take the bait. I watched the swollen San Marcos River tumbling into the grotto thirty feet below us. The sky darkened. The water churned red.

"Something's bothering you," Maia decided.

"Those escaped convicts yesterday afternoon."

"The Floresville Five."

"How much have you heard?"

She shrugged. "Just what's on national news. Fugitive Task Force found a map of Kingsville in a cell, so they figured the convicts were heading south. Then there was the holdup this morning in New Braunfels, so maybe the map was a decoy. The cons seem to be staying together and heading north, which is pretty unusual. The ringleader, William Stirman, sounds like a great human being."

"Erainya's husband put Will Stirman in jail."

Maia set down her margarita glass. "Fred Barrow. The husband she shot."

"Fred and another private investigator. Samuel Barrera, his biggest rival. Eight years ago, they collaborated to put Stirman behind bars. Now Erainya's afraid Stirman will come after them. Barrera, for sure. Maybe her, too."

"She told you this?"

"She won't talk about it. I read some of the agency's old files, some of her husband's case notes."

"Behind her back?"

"I kind of borrowed her file cabinet."

"How do you kind of borrow your boss's file cabinet?"

"We closed the Blanco office. A lot of stuff went into storage. I have the keys."

Maia looked at something across the room. "The news said Stirman was a coyote, smuggled people across the border. He was convicted on six counts of accessory to murder. You find out details?"

I picked at a crabmeat flauta. I was reluctant to recall the images I'd seen in Fred Barrow's files, copies of old police crime scene photos. "Yeah. I found out details."

"Knife," Maia interrupted, suddenly tense. She was looking over my shoulder. Quentin Yates must be coming to say hello.

I held my fingers three inches apart. "Knife?"

She held her hands apart twelve inches. "Knife. In four, three, two—"

I launched a backward elbow strike at groin level.

Quentin Yates grunted, stumbling forward with his meat cleaver off target. He stabbed the table as I grabbed his shirt and used his own momentum to launch him across our crab flautas—Maia calmly lifting her margarita glass out of the way as Quentin went over our table, over the railing, and into space.

A tiny *galosh*, the squawk of a startled duck, and all was quiet again except for the sound of the waterfall. Few patrons had noticed. Those who did quickly went back to their meals. Perhaps, they must've thought, this was like cherries jubilee, or a sizzling pan of fajitas brought straight to the table. Perhaps the high-diving maître d' was a new kind of food delivery panache.

Maia and I were fine, except for a few sprinkles of margarita on her blouse, a knee-print in my guacamole, and the twelve-inch meat cleaver shuddering in the tablecloth.

Robert Johnson said, "Row?"

"Yeah," I agreed.

Our waitress swept over with an oblivious smile and a leather-bound bill. "Well! Anybody save room for dessert?"

The hotel room was too expensive—not even a hotel room, but a ranch-style bungalow with a mauve and crème bed, a canopied frame of rough-hewn oak and a Guatemalan rug on the flagstone floor. The fireplace was filled with dried sage and baby's breath. A nest of birds chirped and echoed somewhere up in the old limestone chimney.

Maia paid cash, signed our names Mr. & Mrs. Smith—her little joke, emulating so many Mr. & Mrs. Smiths we had tailed, photographed, strong-armed into divorce settlements back in the old days.

We stood on the deck, Robert Johnson purring next to us on the railing.

Beneath us, the cedars dropped away into a ravine, the red and silver ribbon of I-35 in the distance, heading north and south to our respective homes. I imagined some poor PI down below us, sweating in his car, pointing his telescopic lens this way, hoping to catch a clear, lurid, unmistakably guilty shot.

I felt the need not to disappoint a hypothetical brother. I pulled Maia close. We kissed.

"So how would it be," she said, "if Erainya married this doctor of hers? Got out of the business. Got time to be a mother. That's a possibility, isn't it?"

"A scary one, I suppose."

Our fingers laced. Down in the woods, a few late fireflies were blinking—something I hadn't seen in San Antonio since I was a kid.

"Then I'd only have the whole city of S.A. to contend with," Maia decided. "Your roots."

She said the word *roots* like she might say *cancer*. If Maia believed in roots, she never would've had the courage to leave Shaoxing as a girl, smuggled aboard a Shanghai freighter by her uncle, who told her she would have to see America for both of them. If she believed in roots, she wouldn't have left San Francisco, her adopted home, to be close to me.

She never rubbed it in, never mentioned the fact that she'd left everything, come two thousand miles, followed me here because I would not stay in the Bay Area. She had resettled in the only palatable Texas port of entry for a Californian—Austin. Couldn't I close the last seventy-five miles?

"Six deaths," I said. "All women, all illegal aliens."

It took her a moment to follow my thoughts. "You mean William Stirman."

"The accessory-to-murder charges. Six women were killed over a twelve-month period at a ranch in the Hill Country. Chopped to pieces with an ax."

"Stirman killed them?"

"No. The murderer was a rancher named McCurdy. He ate a 12-gauge when the police surrounded his house. Stirman supplied the victims. He supplied slave labor to ranches all across

South Texas. He promised immigrants safe passage north. Instead, they were worked to death. This case—the ax murderer—was the only one where Stirman got nailed. He knowingly sold those women to be victims of a killer."

Maia leaned against the railing, staring toward the distant highway. "Barrow and Barrera proved that?"

"They worked from different ends, hired by different clients, but they cooperated. Barrow and Barrera broke the case, tied Stirman to the murderer and the victims, hand-delivered him to the police."

"Stirman won't hang around," Maia said. "He's heading north, probably on his way to Canada."

I turned the idea around in my head, trying to believe it.

"Besides," Maia persisted, "why take revenge on the PIs? There must've been a lot of people involved in the case—police, attorneys."

I didn't bother to answer. We both knew PIs made more satisfying targets—easier to hate, easier to get to. Policemen and lawyers were impersonal parts of the criminal justice machine. Your typical sociopath got little satisfaction from killing one, and then the wrath of the whole system came down on you.

Nobody worked up much righteous indignation when a private investigator got smoked. PIs were everybody's punching bag. In an average week, the Ortiz cousins had lobbed hand grenades at me and Quentin Yates had attacked me with a meat cleaver, all over trivial grudges. In a matter of serious vengeance, I didn't want to think what a sociopath like Will Stirman would do.

"You can't lose sleep over it," Maia said. "Even if Stirman is coming, he wouldn't go after Fred Barrow's widow. And even if he did, what could you do?"

Fireflies blinked in the cedars. The cicadas hummed. In the distance, clouds were choking out the stars. It seemed impossible that it could rain again, but July wasn't playing by the usual rules.

"You'd stick by Erainya," Maia answered herself. "I'll give you this, Tres Navarre. You're loyal. Once someone is in your life, you'd never willingly let them down."

I brushed a lock of hair behind her ear. "A compliment?"

"A reminder."

"It's hard," I said. "A hard time for me to just quit."

She circled my waist, kissed me lightly on the mouth.

"Next week," I promised. "I'll give you an answer by then."

But Maia wasn't hearing me. She was concentrating on the moment—before the rain returned, before the morning separated us for another seven days. She tugged at my fingers, led me inside to the canopied bed, where all night long our slightest movements caused a flutter of birds in the hollow heart of the chimney.

5

Tuesday morning, Luis risked a call to tell Pablo about the amputation.

The Guide had insisted on another heist, so they'd picked a sporting goods store in Oklahoma City—right next to the highway, a Monday evening, hardly a car in the parking lot. They'd been driving all day since the convenience store holdup in New Braunfels that morning, but they were still high on adrenaline.

So there was Luis, leaning against the service counter, bullshitting some college girl cashier. Pablo remembered the drill. Luis would smile real good. He'd be all, *I love these water skis, but oh, damn, I forgot my wallet. Can you wait till my roommate brings me my money? We live right down the street. It's really gotta be tonight, 'cause we're going out of town.*

So they let him stay after closing, and he was chatting up the pretty cashier. All the other clerks went home. The manager was impatient, but trying to be polite, because hey, it was a six-hundred-dollar purchase. Luis was dressed in a nice workout suit, gold chains. He looked like he could afford good things. Why not humor the customer?

The sky turned purple. These huge locusts started dropping from the sky, right on the sidewalk. Hundreds of them crawling over the asphalt, like red cigarettes with legs. Luis figured the whole area used to be farmland, and the bugs were wondering where all the crops went.

He thought of that story Pastor Riggs used to tell—Pablo remembered the one—how the locusts came as a plague to Egypt.

Luis thought: *God must be fucking pissed.* But he kept smiling and bullshitting the cashier, because the plan depended on him being so damn charming they wouldn't kick him out.

The van pulled up, right by the entrance. His make-believe roommate, C.C., got out.

Pablo interrupted the story: *C.C.? They opened the door for C.C.?*

Yeah, Luis said. *He cleaned up pretty good for a scrawny-ass nigger.*

Anyway, C.C. was wearing this flashy Italian suit, like a damn lawyer. He came to the door, looked straight through the glass at Luis, and shook his head like he was irritated. He held up a wallet. *Naughty, naughty.*

The manager turned the key and let him in.

The manager started to say, "Normally I wouldn't—" when C.C. drew a gun and shot him in the face.

The cashier screamed.

The manager knelt, hands going out to break his fall even though he was already dead. He curled into fetal position at C.C.'s feet.

Elroy and the Guide busted inside, both wearing ski masks, carrying shotguns.

They took the flanks, rounded up a couple of stock boys from the back of the store.

Luis told the girl cashier, "We're going into the office now and open the safe."

"He—" The girl pointed toward the thing that used to be her boss. "He's the only one who knows how."

The Guide looked at C.C. "What the fuck you shoot him for?"

"Fuck you," C.C. said, but it was an act. C.C. was getting off on being the bad-ass, and the Guide was happy to let him.

We make a little mess, the Guide had told them their first day heading north. *Every once in a while, we surface and give them a new headline. That's the price for your freedom.*

C.C. loved it. He thought he was goddamn Jesse James. He'd taken to wearing two pistols. He was the one who shot the convenience store clerk in New Braunfels, and a gas station attendant Sunday night in Seguin that the police hadn't tied to them yet. C.C. was the one who delivered the headlines. He'd also be the one who got them a lethal injection, if they were ever caught.

They herded the employees to the manager's office and tied them up. The Guide said to forget about the safe—just get the cash from the registers. They went shopping—grabbed some new clothes, a shitload of ammunition. Elroy picked up a bow-and-arrow set and Luis was like, "What the fuck are you doing?"

The big black man smiled. "Always wanted to be Robin Hood, brother."

The Guide said, "Time to leave."

He went back to the office and gave the employees a spiel—don't yell for help, don't try anything funny or we'll hunt down your families and kill them.

Luis knew what they'd remember—the guy in charge was an Anglo in a ski mask, medium build, West Texas accent. The police would figure it was Will Stirman. They'd figure the five of them were still together, heading north. Four guys did the heist. The fifth stayed in the car, playing lookout.

As it turned out, it would've been better if there *had* been a fifth on lookout.

As soon as they got outside, there was a blaze of headlights. Some guy was shining his brights on them. A red Chevy. The driver wore some kind of uniform. Luis couldn't tell through the glare—an off-duty security officer, maybe. The guy was leaning out his window, training a gun on them. He yelled, "Freeze!"

C.C. and the Guide opened fire. Luis and Elroy took off toward the van, locusts crunching under their boots.

The guard's Chevy revved and careened forward, toward the van, and Luis knew he was going to die. At the last minute the Chevy swerved toward the glass storefront, where C.C. was standing, a pistol in each hand, firing away. C.C. didn't have time to jump before the red Chevy plowed into him, slamming him through the glass.

Luis ran up. The Chevy's engine was grinding. It wasn't going anywhere, steam billowing out the hood, gas leaking from its belly. Behind the blood-spattered web of glass that used to be the windshield, the driver was dead. He wasn't a security guard— he was a cop. Fucker must've been on his way home from his shift, spotted the holdup, had to stop and play hero.

The worst was C.C. He was sprawled on the cement, half under the Chevy, broken glass and locusts all around him. He was screaming, and his leg was pumping like a busted pipe. The Guide yelled, "Get pressure on that!"

Luis stripped off his shirt and tried to bind the wound. But then he saw what had happened. A plate glass shard had gone clean through C.C.'s calf like a guillotine blade. Nothing was holding the leg together but a few shreds of fabric.

Luis managed to wrap the mess with his shirt, tying off the sleeves like a tourniquet, but C.C.'s eyes were rolling back in his head. He was shivering.

Luis looked at Elroy, and they didn't need to say anything. They were both thinking about stained glass, a broken angel feather stabbed in an old supervisor's gut.

The Guide said, "Get him in the van."

"He needs a doctor," Elroy said. "We can leave him here, call 911—"

"No," the Guide said. "Nobody leaves the group."

So they got C.C. in the van and gunned the accelerator, made it to the highway. They drove north into the dark plains of Oklahoma, listening for sirens that never came.

C.C.'s breath smelled like raw meat. The wound oozed.

They'd just passed the city limits sign when C.C. spat up blood, tried to wipe his chin and shuddered for the last time.

They dug C.C. a shallow grave in the red earth of a creek bed. They shoveled dirt on his open eyes. A little sneer traced his mouth, like he was going to tell Satan a thing or two.

The Guide took it in stride. He kept the same calm expression as when faced with police roadblocks, or WANTED signs in grocery stores, or the hotel night manager who had the fugitives' faces on the television as they checked in for the night. The Guide was a Freon-blooded son-of-a-bitch, just like his boss, Will Stirman.

Third day together, now, and Luis still didn't know the Guide's name. Luis didn't trust him any more than when they'd first met in the Floresville Wal-Mart parking lot, when the Guide had given them all fresh clothes and guns, cell phones with clean numbers—Luis and Pablo exchanging looks, silently promising they would keep in touch.

Stirman had said, "Take these folks to Canada. Get 'em set with paperwork and cash. Anything they want."

Luis had never trusted that promise. He tried to believe it would happen, because he had nothing else. He'd never really cared about going home to El Paso. And there was no chance he or Elroy could have made it so far on their own. The Guide had saved their asses a dozen times already.

Luis knew the Canada trip was a diversion. It was a false flare to make the police think Stirman was going north. Luis just hoped he and Elroy wouldn't end up like C.C.

"Least we take some heat off you, cuz," he told Pablo. "Hope you get back to Angelina. Brother Stirman treating you right?"

Pablo stared out the warehouse windows, over miles of San Antonio railways.

Angelina. All he wanted was to see her.

Pablo didn't have the heart to tell Luis what he and Stirman had been doing—how C.C.'s death sounded like a joyride compared to his last two days.

I own you, amigo, Stirman had told him. *You are my new right-hand man.*

Pablo remembered yesterday morning, in this room, holding a video camera for hours as Will Stirman interrogated the former owner of this warehouse, who used to be Stirman's right-hand man.

"I'm cool," Pablo told Luis. "Just be careful. I keep thinking, maybe me and Angelina—"

"Guide's coming, man," Luis whispered. "I got to go."

The line went dead.

Pablo kept his eyes on the rain. He didn't want to turn and see the work that was waiting for him.

He thought about the night four and a half years ago in El Paso when he'd lost everything, drinking straight tequila in a bar on Airway Boulevard while a so-called good neighbor stoked his worst fears into anger. *He was over there again last night while you were at work, ese. I hate to tell you this, but there ain't no doubt. If I was you . . .*

Pablo remembered very little about loading his shotgun, driving home.

He rubbed his eyes to get rid of the memory.

Stirman had promised a chartered plane from Stinson Field. There was a drug runners' airstrip near Calabras, in the mountains south of Juárez, only a few miles from El Paso. Pablo would be able to contact his wife from there. All he had to do was a few more days of service for Stirman.

Pablo mastered his nerves.

He turned. Behind him, waiting patiently in their metal chairs, were two corpses—a pair of fucking nobodies he had to dispose of before Stirman got back. Stirman hadn't even hated these guys. They just happened to have some information he wanted. They'd recently seen some people Stirman was looking for. So after their heartfelt conversation, Stirman had let them die pretty easy, which was why you could still sort of recognize Lalu and Kiko Ortiz's faces through the burn marks.

Will Stirman focused on the boy.

Fred Barrow's widow was in the drop-off line for the school summer camp. There were nine cars in front of her.

The boy had his arm out the passenger's window. He was drumming his fingers against the Audi's door. He had a mop of black hair, a coffee complexion that was nothing like his mother's.

The people Will had questioned didn't know much about the kid. He was adopted, they thought. From somewhere overseas. Not Fred Barrow's blood, anyway. They looked at Stirman through their pain, as if wondering why the hell he cared. What was one more kid to a monster like him?

Will pulled out of line and parked on the side of the traffic circle. He didn't have much time to think. He had misjudged the kind of place Erainya Manos would be going to. He had tailed her right into this wooded campus for the ultra-rich, the parking lot full of Hummers and Cadillac Escalades. His stolen

Honda Civic stuck out like a skinhead in a Juneteenth parade. Soon, the uniformed security guard directing traffic would wonder what Will was doing.

It pissed him off that a place like this could make him feel so nervous.

Maximum security prison was no problem. But a bunch of moms dropping their kids off at soccer camp—that made Will's palms sweat. It pissed him off that Barrow's widow sent her son to this school. No way could she afford it. It rubbed Will's failure in his face, flaunted what Fred Barrow had done to him.

Seven cars before Erainya Manos reached the drop-off point.

Will thought about the first time he'd met Soledad, in the burning fields.

It had been one of Dimebox Ortiz's stupider ideas. He'd decided to let this group of illegals out of the truck just before the Border Patrol checkpoint, let them walk a few miles through the sugarcane fields, then pick them up on the other side. He forgot it was March—burning season.

Next thing, he was calling Will in a panic. Dimebox was at the rendezvous point and the illegals weren't there. He saw smoke—the whole area where the group was supposed to walk was on fire. Farmers were burning their crops as part of the yearly harvest.

Fortunately, Will had been working a deal down in Harlingen, only a couple of miles away. He dropped what he was doing and got there in under ten minutes.

By that time, he could hear the screaming. And if he could hear it, he figured the farmers and the Border Patrol could, too.

He ran into the fields, toward the fire, and a young woman burst through the sugarcane. She was coughing, smoke rising from her clothes. She smelled like burnt syrup.

She crashed right into his arms and said in Spanish, "There are two more! Right in there!"

Will heard a megaphone in the distance. Border Patrol: instructions in Spanish, warning the illegals to get out of the fields.

"*No tiempo,*" Stirman told the woman. "*La Migra.*"

He started to pull her toward the truck, but she fought him. Her strength surprised him.

"You *will* get them!" she ordered.

Will looked at her seriously for the first time. She could have been a special order. She was that beautiful. Maybe seventeen. Mayan complexion, large eyes, long black hair. She wore a man's denim work shirt and tattered jeans. She was barefoot. But Will could imagine her cleaned up, in a nice dress. Getting her north would be enough to turn a profit from this disaster.

"All right," he said. "Wait here."

He plunged into the fields. The Border Patrol megaphone was getting louder. If *La Migra* found Will, or Dimebox Ortiz waiting in his truck up the road, they would start asking questions. Will would be screwed.

He found two older women collapsed in the smoke, and managed to get them to stand. They leaned on him, coughing and stumbling, and together they got away from the fire. The younger woman helped him get them to the truck.

"What about all the others?" the girl asked.

Will looked at her, ready to hit her, but he restrained himself. "They are dead, or taken. If we don't leave now, you will be, too."

He could tell she didn't like it, but she let him put her in the back of the truck. Will got in back, too. He wasn't sure why. He let Ortiz do the driving.

As they were heading north, the two older women collapsed in the corner, the girl asked him, "Are you really going to let us go in San Antonio?"

Will was about to give his standard lie, but her eyes stopped him. He wasn't used to seeing such fight. Usually the young women were placid. They did what they were told. They were too terrified not to.

He said, "What's your name?"

"Soledad."

Loneliness. He liked that name.

She had a single piece of jewelry—a silver Saint Anthony charm hanging on a necklace between her breasts. Will's cargo rarely wore jewelry. They rarely had any left to wear, after they'd paid him. The medallion must have been important to her.

"You're going to have to work in San Antonio," he told her. "Work for men. Do you understand?"

Her eyes bored into him. He started to feel uncomfortable.

"No, I'm not," she said. "You're not going to let me."

"Why is that?"

"Because of the fields," she said. "You owe me a debt."

"Sorry," he said.

She slapped him across the face.

He was too surprised to react.

They sat there in silence, sweating in the heat and the smell of burnt sugar. Soledad ignored him, but Will kept looking at her, and the more he looked, the more he couldn't stop looking.

In San Antonio, he let Dimebox Ortiz take the women to get cleaned up. Dimebox agreed that Soledad would fetch a good price. Will didn't like the way Dimebox looked at her.

After three sleepless nights, Will showed up at the auction and paid Soledad's price himself. He outbid his own clients. Five thousand dollars.

Something in her eyes told him that Soledad wasn't surprised. She knew he would come. She grabbed his hand and started pulling him toward the door, as if he was the one who had been purchased.

When he hesitated, she said, "Well? Are you scared of me?"

Will had paid for a lifetime with her. Soledad had lived just over a year.

For that, someone owed Will a debt.

There were now three cars in front of Erainya Manos.

Will could step outside, calmly walk over to her Audi. He could get in the back seat, press his gun against the kid's spine, tell Erainya Manos to pull out of line and drive. That would work—simple and clean.

Two cars in front of her.

Will hated that Fred Barrow was dead. The fact this woman had shot Barrow didn't make Will fond of her. On the contrary, she had cheated him. She had messed up his revenge.

The other PI, Sam Barrera—Will knew how to handle him. Barrera was a dealmaker. He would've gotten the video by now. He would follow instructions. He'd think he could control the situation without going to the police, and his overconfidence would kill him.

But Fred Barrow's widow—she was a wild card. Will didn't know her well enough. He couldn't kill her until he was sure he would get what he needed.

One car left in the drop-off line.

He had sworn on Soledad's memory that he would not hurt women or children. Never again. He would not become like his enemies.

He imagined Fred Barrow grinning from his little corner of hell, mocking Will's resolve: *Think you're better than me, asshole? Walk away.*

Will watched Erainya's boy get out of the Audi with his soccer gear.

The carpool attendant clapped the boy on the back. The boy went jogging off toward the building. Fred Barrow's widow pulled away and was gone.

A security guard appeared at Will's car window. Will hadn't even seen him coming.

"Can I help you, sir?"

Will wanted to drive a switchblade into the young man's throat.

Instead he said, "Supposed to get my son. I must've got it wrong. When's pickup for soccer?"

"It hasn't even started yet, sir. You probably read the drop-off time."

"I probably did."

"Pickup time is two o'clock."

"Oh, hell. Two. Sure."

Will pulled out, waving his thanks, and took the school exit at a leisurely ten miles an hour.

Two o'clock. Time to oil his gun and make plans about the boy.

No more indecision.

Erainya Manos would cooperate. Hell, yes, she would.

6

I was sure Jem's soccer coach would cause a general uprising by the end of the summer season.

The guy was an unpaid volunteer who knew next to nothing about soccer. He came in late every day of practice, looking like he'd been up all night doing things a role model for little kids shouldn't do.

On the other hand, the school was too cheap to hire a real coach. None of the parents could or would volunteer. So when the kids were close to tears, thinking their summer season might be canceled, this guy had been the only knucklehead dumb enough to commit every Tuesday and Thursday morning, plus Saturday games, for the rest of the summer.

"Tres!" Jem yelled as I walked in the boys' bathroom. Then he corrected himself. "Coach!"

The Garcia twins were hitting each other with their shin guards.

Paul had dumped somebody's clothes in the urinal.

Jack was climbing over the door of the stall while another kid whose name I couldn't remember tried to climb underneath.

The other boys were in various states of lunacy—pulling shirts over their heads, skating on backpacks, calling each other poop-butts.

I did the only thing a coach can do. I blew my whistle.

"Ow!" they all said, pulling on their ears.

I jumped into the half second of focus I'd created. "On the field, five minutes!"

They probably heard the first two words. Getting directions across to a group of eight-year-olds is akin to Luke Skywalker hitting the meter-wide vent on the Death Star.

I ruffled Jem's hair, told him to hurry out of the bathroom, since I was personally responsible for his safety, then went to check on the girls. From their bathroom doorway, I heard shrill sounds like parakeets being tortured. I yelled, "Five minutes, ladies!" crossed myself, and headed outside.

The practice field sat on a ridge overlooking Salado Creek. From any vantage point, the entire city seemed to spread out below one's feet. Given the school's wealthy clientele, I was pretty sure the visual message was intentional.

Unfortunately for frustrated coaches, the edge of the cliff was fenced, so bad children couldn't go rolling off into oblivion. It also wasn't rainy enough to cancel practice, though the sky was heavy gray and the field was spongy.

I set out cones for a relay race, put all the soccer balls in a neat line, then watched my plans disintegrate as the troops came charging over the hill.

Kathleen and Carmen ran screaming straight into the nearest mud puddle and started jumping on top of each other. Paul kicked all the soccer balls as hard as he could. One of them bounced off Maria, who luckily was the size of a totem pole and didn't seem to notice.

Laura hung on my arm. "I'm going to marry *Jack*!"

Jack, the object of her affections, lolled his tongue out of his mouth and barked like a dog.

"I'm very happy for you," I said. "Now everybody on the line!"

No results.

Even Jem, my faithful sidekick, was right there in the mix, tangling himself in the goalie's net while the Garcia twins kicked puddle water at him.

I blew my whistle. "On the line!"

Nothing.

"Last one is a rotten egg!" I yelled.

A few of them ran to the line.

"Oh, look," I announced. "Kathleen's not the rotten egg! She's here!"

"Yay!" Kathleen said, and proceeded to run away, but the others had gotten the idea.

"I'm not rotten!" said Jack the dog.

"Me! I'm here!" Laura told me. "I'm going to marry *Jack*."

Pretty soon I had the whole team of sixteen on the line.

We practiced kicking around the cones, plowing straight through the cones, picking up the cones, putting them on our heads and singing "Happy Birthday."

We did throw-ins, passes and dribbling, stopping approximately every three minutes for a water break. Jack kept barking. Maria kept getting whacked in the head with the ball and not noticing.

Some of the mothers had gathered on the bleachers to watch and gossip. I wondered: If they have off at this time of day, why didn't *they* volunteer?

I answered myself: Because they are intelligent.

One hour into practice, it started sprinkling. I considered calling an early stop, sending the kids to the extended care building for snacks and board games, but Jem said, "Can we scrimmage now, Tres? PLEEEASE?"

"Yeah!" Paul said. Then the Garcia twins started in: "Please, Coach! Please?"

Suddenly I had sixteen little rain-freckled faces crowding around me. Jem and Paul pulled on my arms.

.I thought: *This is how it happens. This is how people can have a second or third kid, even though one is enough to kill you. They're occasionally cute enough to make you suicidal.*

"All right," I said. "Eight on eight."

"Yay!" Jack shouted. "Best coach ever!"

We kicked off and all strategy was forgotten. Kids crowded the ball, moving back and forth down the field in a multi-legged clump. Paul was our best kicker, except he tended to boot it the wrong direction. Maria was a natural halfback, since the ball bounced off her anytime it came her direction whether she meant it to or not.

Jem played keeper. After only five minutes, the other team had scored three goals off him.

All that hand-eye coordination from playing video games didn't seem to translate to sports. He moved slowly, grabbing for the ball right after it went past him. He dove in the wrong direction. I yelled, "Hands!" and he tried to block with his foot. The whole time, he kept a huge grin on his face, as if the other team was cheering for him whenever the ball sailed into the net.

My heart sank. I'd been working with him one-on-one all the previous week, ever since he announced he wanted to play goalie in our first game against Saint Mark's. I didn't want to see the poor kid get blamed for what promised to be an absolute slaughter.

Somebody's dad—a pale Anglo in an Oxford and khakis—joined the mothers at the bleachers. I checked my watch. Only twenty minutes left of practice, and now the rain was really starting to come down. Typical.

Jack the dog boy kicked from the edge of the penalty box—a slow, weak shot. Jem lunged for it, just the way he and I had practiced. He fell on his side, a foot short, and the ball wobbled into the net.

"Yes!" Jack yelled. "Woof!"

Laura clapped for him. His team yelled hooray. Jem got up, grinning happily, his left side caked in mud.

We were still a few minutes early, but I decided it was time to stop.

I told the kids to line up. We would walk together to the extended care building, where they could play until their parents came.

They heard the "extended care" part, cheered for joy, and scattered.

"Pick up the balls!" I yelled after them, but of course it was too late.

Jem and I cleaned up equipment. The rain came down heavier, sizzling against the grass. We gathered the balls and cones, stuffed everything into the supply sack. Jem skipped around in his muddy yellow goalie vest, punching the air.

"Wasn't I great?" he asked. "Goalie rocks!"

"We'll keep working on it, champ."

"Can I play goalie the whole game, Tres? Please?"

"Remember, you have to give the others a turn."

"Aw, please?"

We lugged the gear bag to the storage shed, out by the kindergarten parking lot. Rain drummed against the aluminum roof.

I'd just finished padlocking the door when I noticed the silver BMW idling by the curb. The father in the Oxford and khakis was walking toward us.

"Looking for your child?" I asked.

"No, no," the man said. "Got him in the car."

The BMW's windows were so dark he could've had the whole soccer team inside and I wouldn't have been able to see them.

Technically, he shouldn't have parked in the kindergarten lot. It was off limits for the summer. Everybody was supposed to pick up at the main entrance, where the security booth controlled access. But the back lot was closer to the field, there was easy egress to neighborhood streets, and many parents, like their kids, had trouble believing school rules applied to them.

"I'm Alec's dad," the man said. "Jerry Vespers."

His hand was callused, odd for a BMW driver. His accent West Texas—an oil man, maybe.

"Tres Navarre," I said.

I tried to picture his son. There were still a couple of kids' names I was shaky on, but Alec Vespers?

The father's skin was fish-belly white, his black hair shaved in a severe military cut. His eyes, behind the gold wire rim glasses, were wrong somehow—calm but intense, like he was staring down a rifle scope.

"I don't know Alec," I decided. "He isn't on the team."

"No," Mr. Vespers agreed. "Couldn't get him interested. I told Erainya we'd pick up Jem."

"Pardon?"

"The play date." Mr. Vespers smiled thinly. "I'll have Jem home by supper. Or Erainya can call, if she'd rather come get him. Come on, Jem."

Jem was looking at Mr. Vespers with a curious expression, as if he'd just been offered a dangerous present. He took a tentative step forward, but I put my hand on his shoulder.

"I don't know anything about a play date," I told Mr. Vespers.

"Erainya must've forgotten to tell you," he said. "How about I call the agency? She at the 315 extension?"

He took out a cell phone, started to dial. He seemed keen to prove that he knew Erainya's business number.

"No need," I told him. "Jem's going with me."

Vespers closed his cell phone. He slipped it into his pants pocket. "You the boy's parent, Mr. Navarre?"

"I don't know you. Erainya wouldn't forget to tell me."

He shifted his gaze to Jem. "Alec's in the car, son. How about you come say goodbye to him, at least?"

Jem looked agitated now. He was chewing on his thumbnail.

"Mr. Vespers," I said tightly. "You need to leave."

Vespers lowered on his haunches. His eyes narrowed, rain speckling his glasses. "What's the matter, boy?"

"You're making my stomach feel queasy," Jem murmured.

Vespers' stare was unpleasantly hungry.

"You need to leave," I told him again, trying to keep my voice level. "Before I call the police."

Vespers rose.

"You think I'm a predator?" he asked. "You think I like little kids, is that it?"

I took out Erainya's cell phone. For once, I was grateful she'd made me take it on the trip to San Marcos. "I'm calling campus security."

"This ain't personal between you and me, Mr. Navarre," Vespers said. "Think about that before you insult me. I need to talk to the boy."

"The hell you do."

Vespers' hand drifted toward his side. He had something in his pocket—a lump I should've noticed before, maybe large enough to be a small gun.

Fifteen years of martial arts training told me that if I was going to act, I had to do it now.

But Vespers looked down at Jem again, and the rifle-scope intensity of his eyes dissipated, as if something much too close to target had moved into his field of vision.

"Tell your mother you saw me," Vespers said. "She knows what I want. She'd best give it back."

By the time I got Chuck Phelps, the school security captain, on the phone, the BMW's taillights had disappeared onto Hundred Oaks. I gave Chuck the BMW's model and license plate, told him to call the police.

I could hear Chuck flipping pages in his master directory. "Thing is, Mr. Navarre, that *is* Mr. Vespers' car. He does have a kid, Alec, in Jem's grade. Alec's in summer art class. Mr. Vespers waits on the street over there all the time."

"Call anyway."

Chuck said okay, but I got the feeling my request had just been bumped down to low priority, and I didn't insist it was an emergency.

I'd have plenty of time to kick myself about that later.

It would be almost a week, long after the worst had happened, before the police would find the silver BMW abandoned in a sorghum field in the north part of the county, the body of the real Jerry Vespers curled in the trunk. His death would become a mere sidebar to the story of the Floresville Five, a life cut short merely because it served Will Stirman's purpose to assume another identity for a few minutes.

But that afternoon, driving Jem back to his mother's house, I was slow to process the obvious.

Nothing can prepare you for the moment a child you care about is threatened. Doesn't matter if you're a cop or a social worker or a private eye.

My upper brain functions shut down. My senses went feral. I was a cat under attack, crouching and blinking, smelling my own blood, thinking of nothing beyond my claws.

We were halfway to Erainya's before I realized who I'd been talking to, how close I'd come to dying.

Jem curled up in the cab of the truck, put his head on my lap like he used to in kindergarten.

"That isn't safe, kiddo," I told him. "We're driving."

But he was already asleep, his body trying to absorb a trauma bigger than he was.

I turned on Nacogdoches to avoid the flooding on Loop 410, but that proved a mistake. The low-water crossing by the YMCA field had become a river, black water cresting at the tops of the speed limit signs. A house was floating across the road.

Dozens of people had left their cars. They stood with umbrellas by the waterside, watching the prefab model sail slowly over the bridge. The house had white aluminum siding, a gray-shingled roof, blue curtains and a sign in the window that read, NO MONEY DOWN!!!

I should have backed up, but I sat in my truck, watching the spectacle, my hand on Jem's feverish forehead.

I had failed to recognize Will Stirman, even though his disguise had been nothing more than a pair of glasses and the fact that he had appeared out of any context I would've anticipated.

I had failed to take him down when I had the chance. I told myself I *could* have taken him.

But the truth was: Jem and I were alive for only one reason. Will Stirman had let us go to deliver a message.

Tell your mother you saw me. She knows what I want.

The prefab house snagged on something, made a grinding noise as the current bent its walls. It careened sideways and continued its stately journey.

Will Stirman had tried to take Jem. He had dared to step into a little boy's world.

I promised myself I would get the bastard for that.

I watched the house bob past the line of silent spectators with umbrellas, an American flag fluttering bravely on the doorpost as the building slipped off the bridge and glided downriver.

7

Erainya held the line for ten minutes before Dimebox Ortiz's brother-in-law came on.

"He's a no-show," the brother-in-law said, clearly reluctant to share the information. "Hearing was set for ten o'clock."

Erainya swore. "You fronted bail for him *again*? The judge went for it?"

"Well . . . you know. It's just Dimebox. He's got a good lawyer. Besides, he's not exactly a serious threat . . ."

"Ike, he sets people on fire."

"That's never been proven."

"Jesus Christ." But Erainya couldn't help feeling a little relieved. Ever since she'd turned over Dimebox to the police, two days ago, she kept remembering what he'd said about her signing his death warrant. "Listen, Ike. I've got to talk to him. On the off chance he's stupid enough to call you—"

"Hey, Erainya, don't stress it, right? It's another day's work for you. I'll be happy to pay the regular bounty."

"You're a lunatic, Ike."

"He's my wife's brother, okay? I'll give you a bonus. Probably just staying with Lalu and Kiko again."

"Lalu and Kiko are nowhere," Erainya said. "I've checked. They haven't been seen in at least twenty-four."

A pause. "Should I be worried?"

"Nah," Erainya said, sarcastically. "It's just Will Stirman on the loose. He's not exactly a serious threat."

"Oh, shit—you don't think—"

Erainya hung up the phone. Ike and Dimebox were only related by marriage, but they seemed like blood brothers when it came to stupidity.

She turned back to the television. Constant flood coverage was giving her a headache. She kept waiting for news on Will Stirman—anything that would confirm he had really gone north. All she got were pictures of livestock standing belly-deep in water, people riding a boat down a street in New Braunfels.

Her nerves were frayed. She'd had two hang-up phone calls in the middle of the night, both from blocked numbers. She'd yelled at Jem that morning for something stupid—leaving his cereal bowl where she could trip over it. The memory of his shocked expression made her sick with guilt.

Taking him to soccer practice, she'd almost convinced herself she was being followed. She came very close to not letting Jem go. Then she decided she was being paranoid. Missing practice would crush the poor kid. Besides, Tres would be there the whole time. She couldn't ask for better protection than that.

Now . . . Sam Barrera was ten minutes late. For all his other faults, Sam was never late.

Erainya's mind raced with wild possibilities of what might've happened to him. If he *did* show up, what would she tell him? How far was she willing to go to save herself?

Sooner or later, Will Stirman would contact her. She knew it. She wanted desperately to believe he would just disappear, or if he did go after Barrera, at least leave her alone, but she knew better.

She remembered last spring, when her best friend Helen Malski lay dying of lymphoma. Erainya had been with her in the hospital, holding her hand, as Helen labored to speak. "You can't keep silent forever, Irene. You can't."

Helen had been one of the last people who remembered Erainya as Irene, who dared to call her by the meek, Anglicized, failure-laden name of her marriage.

"I know," Erainya had said. "I'll come clean."

And Helen smiled, the grip of her hand loosening as she drifted off to sleep.

Erainya had lied to her best friend. She had no intention of telling anyone the truth.

She opened her desk drawer, stared at her Colt .45.

It won't come to that, she thought. *Not this time.*

She picked up the photo of her dead husband. It was the only photo of Fred she kept in the house, and she kept it right under the gun—to remind her.

The picture showed a very young Fred Barrow, just after he'd left the Border Patrol to become a PI. His nose was broken from his days as an amateur boxer. His black hair was parted in the middle and feathered in that wretched late-seventies style. His smile had not yet gone sour, nor had he started drinking heavily, so it was possible to think he looked confident rather than bullheaded, strong rather than brutal—the way Erainya had thought of him when they first met.

She'd been a shy, nervous college girl, working part-time in the county records office. Fred's flirtations overwhelmed her whenever he came in to see a land deed or a tax record. He'd complimented her efficiency, her jewelry, her clothes and her eyes. A real private investigator—paying attention to her. The fourth time he visited, he sat at the corner of her desk and picked up her letter opener. As he talked, he kept testing the blade. Years later, Erainya would wonder if he'd been making a subconscious threat, or even trying to warn her.

He said he needed a good helper. His PI business was boom-
ing. He needed somebody who could double as a secretary and
a life partner. The proposal made her dizzy. She found herself
spilling her dreams to him. She wanted children, the kind of
big family she'd been denied, growing up. She told him about
her parents, first-generation immigrants who'd been killed by a
hit-and-run driver when Erainya was seven. She told him about
the cold godparents who'd raised her, renamed her Irene, spent
years trying to erase everything un-American and unladylike
from her character. Fred listened sympathetically. He didn't say
no to a big family. She convinced herself he would make a good
father. They were married two months later.

At first, the partnership had gone well. Erainya had been prepared to take the back seat to a man. Her foster parents had
prepared her for that ever since she was a child.

Then Erainya made two startling discoveries. The first was
that she liked investigations. Informants trusted her. They would
tell her things they'd never tell Fred. She involved herself more
in the cases. She was sure if she showed Fred what she could
do, he would eventually see that it made sense to give her more
responsibility.

The more she did this, the more irritated Fred became. He
began accusing her of butting in, messing up his business. And
the more irritated he became, the more determined she was to
try harder, and prove him wrong.

The second discovery was worse. After three years of trying,
she was still not pregnant. Fred didn't want to talk about it. He
began drinking, and yelling. Finally, the doctor assured Erainya
that the fertility problem was not hers. Erainya's friend Helen
told her she really had to speak to Fred. It took Erainya a
month to get up her nerve, but finally she broached the subject.

That was the first night Fred ever hit her. It wasn't the last.

Erainya was slow, painfully slow, to realize her marriage and her dreams were incompatible.

She slipped Fred's photo carefully back under the .45.

She looked at the clock. Sam Barrera was now twenty-two minutes late.

She cursed herself for putting the old case files into storage, leaving Tres a key. Of course he would go through them. That was his nature. It had been stupid of her to leave him that opening.

There wasn't much he could find, unless he knew what to look for. But he was smart. Damn smart. She had to hope he wouldn't look at the case from the right angle to see what was wrong about it.

The doorbell rang.

Sam at last. Or what if . . .

Erainya reached for her gun.

Fred's picture stared up at her from so many years ago—a reminder of how quickly things could go wrong, how reckless Erainya could get when it came to protecting her secrets.

She left the gun where it was, and closed the drawer.

She went to answer the door, convincing herself she could handle whatever came without violence. As long as she was safe, and Jem was safe, nothing else mattered.

8

"*Dios mío*," Ana DeLeon said when she came on the phone. "Thought the operator was kidding me."

"Long time," I said. "How's it going, Sergeant?"

Ana hesitated, tacitly acknowledging the mention of her new rank. I hadn't seen her in over a year, hadn't called to congratulate her on the promotion, or any of the other news I'd heard.

"Business is brisk," she said. "Flood washed up some interesting corpses. Had one float out of somebody's basement last night."

I pinched the cell phone to my ear, turned my pickup onto Erainya's street. "So who's handling the Floresville Five?"

"Ugh. Not us, thank God. Department of Criminal Justice. Fugitive Task Force. They've got a command post here, though with the Oklahoma City shooting yesterday, the search has gone federal. Most of the manpower has pulled out and headed north. Why do you ask?"

"What happened in Oklahoma City?"

She told me about the sporting goods store manager and the off-duty cop murdered; a positive ID on two of the fugitives; fairly good evidence that Will Stirman led the robbery.

"With a cop down," she said, "you know how it goes. FBI,

U.S. Marshals—everybody wants a piece of this now. What's your interest?"

"Stirman isn't in Oklahoma."

"No," she agreed. "He's heading north. They're setting up roadblocks on every highway in the Midwest. Problem is: The shit-bag specialized in human trafficking. He's got contacts everywhere. Knows how to hide and move."

"Stirman's here in town."

Next to me on the bench seat, Jem sighed. He turned over in his sleep.

I was halfway down the block before DeLeon spoke again.

"Okay," she said warily. "Aside from the fact that San Antonio would be a very stupid place for Stirman to be, seeing how many people know him here—and aside from the fact that every law enforcement agency in the country places him as about halfway to Canada . . . Why are you telling me this?"

I pulled in front of Erainya's house. Two unwelcome surprises were waiting for me in the driveway—her boyfriend's Lexus and an older BMW so god-awful yellow it could only belong to Sam Barrera.

"Tres?" DeLeon asked.

It had taken me a mile of driving to decide to call DeLeon, one of my few friends in law enforcement. I had to tell somebody about Stirman. It couldn't wait until I spoke to Erainya.

I stared at the cars.

When I'd called Erainya from San Marcos that morning, she'd encouraged me to take Jem out to lunch after soccer, let her catch up on some paperwork. She wouldn't be expecting us for another hour at least. She'd said nothing about a meeting with Barrera.

"I'm still here," I told DeLeon. "How much do you know about Stirman's arrest eight years ago?"

There was a long pause. "Since the jailbreak, the old-timers won't stop gabbing about it. Fred Barrow—your boss's dead husband—he was involved. Erainya must've told you the story."

"Pretend she hasn't."

I could almost hear DeLeon's mental gears turning, trying to figure my angle, deciding how much she wanted to tell me.

"All right," she said. "A rancher named McCurdy tortured and murdered six illegal alien women over the course of about a year. The women were supplied as slave labor by Will Stirman. Would-be victim number seven managed to escape. She got the county sheriff to believe her. When the deputies closed in, McCurdy killed himself. National media came in, started looking into allegations that the county knew about McCurdy's slave ranch for months, had previous complaints about mistreatment, even returned one woman to his place when she tried to run away. The county needed a scapegoat before their asses got fried in federal probes and lawsuits, so they decided to find the guy who supplied the slaves. Sam Barrera and Fred Barrow both worked the case—Barrera for the county, Barrow for some of the victims' families. Folks were laying bets the two would strangle each other before they found anything, but they ended up working together. They lined up three solid material witnesses who tied Stirman to the rancher—the illegal who survived and two members of Stirman's smuggling ring who agreed to turn on their boss. The PIs delivered statements to the police, gave the district attorney more than enough for an indictment."

"You sound like you don't approve."

Another pause, like she was censoring herself. "There are rumors Barrera and Barrow got their results by doing what the cops couldn't. They bent rules, used bribery, threats, whatever it took."

"But the case stood up in court."

"Stirman was scum. The jury would've handed him a death sentence if that was an option."

"What about the arrest itself?" I asked. "Fred Barrow's notes on the case—he makes it sound like he apprehended Stirman personally."

"He did. Would've been late April '95. Will Stirman got tipped off things were going against him. He made plans to flee the country. Barrow and Barrera got word of this, like, the night he was planning to leave. Instead of telling the police, the two of them decide to play cowboy and show up at Stirman's apartment with guns blazing. Just the kind of cool, methodical detective work you'd appreciate. A woman was killed in the crossfire—one of Stirman's prostitutes. Stirman was critically wounded. He just about bled to death before the police and paramedics arrived. There were some other . . . irregularities about that night."

"Irregularities."

"That's all you get for free," she told me. "How do you know Stirman is in town?"

I didn't answer.

"Look, Tres—I get the revenge angle. The Task Force has considered it. I know SAPD called Erainya and Sam Barrera, along with the attorneys who prosecuted the Stirman case. They were all offered protection."

"They were?"

"And they declined. The point is—Stirman isn't stupid. He wouldn't hang around here. Unless you have evidence that would change my mind . . ."

I stared at Sam Barrera's yellow BMW. "Can I come by tonight?"

"I'll be at the office until six. Or you can come by the house."

"I can make the office by six."

An uneasy pause, the wipers going back and forth across my windshield. Ana said, "Ralph would love to see you, Tres."

"Same," I said. "It's just . . . I don't want to barge in, with the baby and all."

"You wouldn't be barging in."

I said nothing.

"Okay then," she said. "So . . ."

"By six," I told her. "Count on it."

I folded up the phone.

I waited for a break in the rain before gathering Jem in my arms and carrying him to the front door.

Inside, the television was going. Live footage of drizzle, as if there wasn't enough of it right outside. The weatherman warned that three area dams were already over capacity.

A leather briefcase sat next to Erainya's living room couch. Spread out on the coffee table was a picnic lunch—a checkered cloth, bouquet of wildflowers, bottle of wine, cheese, baguette, kalamata olives.

Erainya's boyfriend was a few steps down the hallway, his ear pressed to the door of Erainya's study.

"Hear anything good?" I asked.

He straightened, faced me with as much dignity as a caught snoop could.

He was a gray-haired Latino, trim, chocolate eyes, a pencil mustache and impeccable taste in clothes. Early sixties, but he could've passed for ten years younger. He would've been the heartthrob of any retirement community.

He held a finger to his lips, pointed to the heavy sleeping bundle in my arms.

I carried Jem past him, down the hallway to the bedroom.

Jem mumbled something about goalie position as I laid him on his bed and tugged off his soccer cleats. On his TV, a video game character was suspended mid-jump over an exploding barrel, probably paused since Jem had left that morning. The video system was a duplicate of the one Jem lost in the flooded van. A gift, Jem had told me earlier, from the nice doctor.

I turned off the monitor.

On the way back down the hall, I heard voices coming from behind the study door, where Dr. Dreamboat had been eavesdropping.

Erainya yelled, "Goddamn it, Barrera!"

Sam Barrera said something I couldn't quite make out.

I was tempted to eavesdrop myself, but the doctor was watching me, so I joined him in the living room.

He poured a glass of merlot from the tabletop picnic. "Tres, may I offer you some?"

I shook my head. "How long has she been in there?"

"About twenty minutes. I was hoping to surprise her with lunch, as you can see."

"Inconvenient."

He set down the wine bottle. "You know this man Barrera?"

I nodded. "An old rival."

"They were shouting. I was concerned. That's why I was at the door."

"You don't have to explain yourself, Doctor."

He studied me as if I were a patient, as if he were scanning for allergies lurking behind my eyes. "Would it hurt to call me J.P.?"

"Yeah. Probably would."

He managed a smile. "From Jem, I expected resentment. But from you? Give me a chance, Tres."

The problem was: He was right. Erainya was crazy about this guy. Jem thought he was right up there with fruit rollups. And I resented him why—because he was too old for Erainya?

Because he lavished Jem with presents? Maybe I feared he was after the tens of dollars in Erainya's bank account.

"Sanchez," I said. "That's your last name, right? Dr. Sanchez?"

He raised his eyebrows. "So you think you might try to remember it, after all?"

"I don't know," I said. "But I suppose a glass of wine wouldn't hurt."

He was about to pour when we heard the gunshot from the study.

9

Even before the crazy woman picked up the gun, Sam Barrera wasn't having a good day.

He'd spent the last twenty-four hours making careful notes from his case files, trying to understand what he'd gotten himself into eight years ago. Unfortunately, the information he needed most wasn't in the files. He wouldn't have committed incriminating evidence to writing.

After breakfast, his real estate agent called. She had a quarter-million-dollar offer for the Southtown house, but she needed an answer by Friday. He told her he'd have to think about it.

A few minutes later, his doctor called—the goddamn neurologist who'd adopted him.

"Sam, did you visit?" he wanted to know.

"Yeah, I visited."

"And?"

What was Sam supposed to say? The place had scared him to death.

"It's your best chance," the doctor assured him. "It really is. But openings don't happen often. We have to jump on this right away. I need an answer soon."

Again, Sam said he had to think about it.

He hung up and drew a picture of the neurologist with devil horns. By the time he'd finished drawing it, he'd forgotten who it was supposed to be.

Then, as if all that wasn't enough, a courier delivered the videotape.

Sam had watched the video four times, even though it was one of the most horrible things he'd ever seen. He hoped the images would keep his memory from fading, keep his sense of urgency alive.

When he'd called Erainya Manos, he asked for a morning meeting. But she had insisted he come at noon, when her house would be empty.

Words were slippery for Barrera at noon. So far, he had let her do the talking. Mostly, that consisted of ranting.

She spoke with her hands. She was short and wiry and seemed to blame Sam and her late husband for everything, including Will Stirman, her business problems and the state of her housekeeping.

While she paced around, yelling at him, Sam focused on the room. He remembered being in this den before. The old Sony Trinitron with rabbit-ear antennae. The leather reclining chair that smelled of pipe tobacco. The limestone fireplace with the moldy twelve-point buck's head above the mantel. The watercolor fishing scenes.

This was Fred Barrow's den. It pleased Sam to come up with the name without looking at his notes. Maybe it was because the woman kept yelling that name.

Fred Barrow and Sam had sat here, in this room. They had made a temporary truce, a plan to catch the man they both hated—Will Stirman.

Sam wondered why the woman hadn't changed the decor, if she hated her deceased husband so much. Two reasons occurred to him—she didn't use this room; or changing it would've deprived her of something to complain about. The way she slapped the air when she spoke—this woman liked targets. Probably, she kept the den intact for the same reason people keep their boss's face on a dartboard.

He felt satisfied with his analysis, then found himself staring at the striped pattern of the woman's dress and he forgot where he was. Goddamn it. He checked his notepad.

"How can you sit there so calm?" the woman demanded. "What—you're taking notes on me? Jesus, Barrera. What did Stirman say?"

Sam had the videotape in his lap. For lack of a better idea, he said, "Maybe you should watch this."

The woman grabbed the cassette and stuck it in the VCR.

The dusty old television flickered green, then showed a badly beaten man tied to a chair. Sam had written the man's name in his notepad—Gerry Far. He'd underlined it once for each time he watched the tape. Sam still didn't recognize the man's face. That could have been because there wasn't much left to recognize.

"Barrera?" An off-screen voice—male, West Texas accent. "You remember Gerry Far? He's going to give a statement now—little different story than the one he told at my trial. I thought you'd like a preview before I send it to the media in forty-eight hours. You ready, Gerry?"

The camera centered on what was left of Gerry Far's face.

The woman in the striped dress paced in front of the television, cursing in a language Sam didn't recognize.

Gerry Far got about ten sentences out of his ruined mouth before the woman snarled, "I won't listen to this."

She punched the TV's *off* button. "Goddamn it, Barrera!"

"Turn it back on," he said calmly. "You need to see it."

She made a fist in the air. Then she hit the *on* button.

Gerry Far told his story in slow painful gulps.

Sam had always been best at reading places, reading people. The way the image shook, the jerky zoom motions, meant a handheld camera rather than a tripod. Stirman's midsection could be seen moving behind Gerry, his hand occasionally patting Gerry's shoulder. Stirman had an accomplice doing the filming.

The room had brick walls, large rectangular windows. Two of the windows were boarded up, but one was not. The bad quality of the video bleached the view outside, but Sam could just make out one cabled support column of the Alamodome. Clouds obscured the angle of the light, but Sam guessed the film had been shot in the late afternoon. If he read the orientation correctly, the building was somewhere just northeast of downtown. A brick warehouse near St. Paul Square. A leap of deduction, maybe, but he was hardly ever wrong.

"Did I do anything to you, Gerry?" Stirman was saying. *"Did I deserve this?"*

"I'm sorry, Will," Gerry Far whimpered. *"I'm sorry."*

"Was I innocent?"

"You were innocent. It was their idea. Their idea."

"You hear that, Sam?" Stirman asked. *"You tell Fred's widow— she's not off the hook either. Forty-eight hours."*

That's when the woman opened the desk drawer and took out the gun.

Barrera didn't think she would shoot him. Then he flashed on a memory—she *had* shot someone, hadn't she? In this very room. Her husband.

How had he known that?

"Gerry," Stirman said. *"Tell them I'm serious."*

"You're serious, sir," Gerry said. *"You are fucking serious."*

"I think they need proof." Stirman pressed the muzzle of a gun to the man's temple.

Gerry Far blinked furiously, his lips trembling.

Just as Sam was about to watch him die for the fifth time, the woman raised her own pistol and blew out the television screen. Glass cracked. Electronic innards sparked.

The woman ripped the video from the machine and started tearing out long silky loops of ribbon.

Two men burst into the den.

"Erainya?" The older of the two men stared at the gun, then at Barrera, accusingly, as if Sam had done something wrong. "What the hell's going on?"

He was a gray-haired Latino in an expensive blue suit. Soft hands, gold school ring, silver pen in his lapel pocket. Sam pegged him for a doctor. His accent was buried deep under years of affluence, but Sam recognized it—Southtown Spanish. A local boy, a self-made *vato*, like Barrera himself.

The woman said, "Everything's fine, J.P. Just go. Tres, you, too."

The younger guy was in his mid-thirties, Anglo, dark-complexioned, jeans and a white American flag T-shirt that said YMCA COACH.

Barrera had seen this guy before.

He was a PI. He worked for Erainya. She'd just said his name, but Sam hadn't been prepared to catch it.

"Put the gun down, Erainya," the coach said. "Jem's taking a nap."

She threw the pistol on the desk, which gave her two free hands to better destroy the videotape. She cracked it across the edge of the TV, wrapped it in a section of newspaper, tossed it into the fireplace. She took a box of matches off the mantel.

From a professional point of view, Sam was thinking this was a highly inefficient way of destroying evidence. Acid would be better. Or a wood chipper.

The doctor was still glowering at him. Must be her boyfriend, Sam figured. Meanwhile, the young coach was zeroing in on the important stuff—the battered courier's envelope, the video in the fireplace, Barrera's notepad.

He tried to read Barrera's expression.

Good luck, Sam thought.

Sam calmly picked up his pen and wrote, *YMCA Coach. Erainya's PI.*

He underlined it. He'd had a run-in with this guy in the past. He was sure of that.

The woman crouched by the fireplace, striking matches. She lit the corners of the newspaper.

The coach scooped up the woman's gun, unloaded it. "Video-tape won't burn that way."

She said, "I know what I'm doing."

"Erainya, we need to talk. Jem's all right. He's fine. But we had a visitor at school."

Her eyes blazed. Sam was suddenly glad the coach had taken her gun.

"J.P.," she said, her voice tight, "would you check on Jem, please?"

The doctor started to come toward her. "Erainya . . ."

"Please, J.P. Go see about Jem. I'll only be a minute."

Sam could tell the doctor wasn't used to feeling unwanted. He swallowed, nodded reluctantly, then closed the door on his way out.

"All right, what happened?" the woman demanded.

The coach told them about Will Stirman visiting the school soccer field, trying to take Jem.

Sam took notes—put a question mark after the name *Jem*. The woman's son?

"Stop that," the woman snapped.

Sam looked up, realized she was talking to him.

"Put away the damn notebook," she said. "You should have killed Stirman when you had the chance. You and Fred couldn't even do that right."

"We weren't out to kill anybody," Sam said. He felt pretty confident it was the truth.

The woman rose. "We are now. We have to find Stirman."

The flue of the chimney must've been closed. The smell of burning paper and melted tape filled the room. A rag of ash sailed past the woman's head.

The coach said, "You seriously think the two of you can track him down alone? You think you could pull the trigger?"

Judging from the woman's expression, Sam thought he could answer the second question.

"You're not thinking straight," the coach said. "Call the police."

The woman slapped the air. "I *can't*."

"No police," Sam agreed.

The coach picked up the courier envelope. There was nothing inside. No sender's address. Sam Barrera's office address had been typed.

"You refused police protection," the coach said. "You knew Stirman was coming. Now he's threatening Jem. And you won't call the police. Why?"

"They won't catch him," the woman said. "Even if we told them he was here, even if they believed us, Stirman would vanish. He'd be back next month, next year, five years from now. I won't live like that, knowing he's out there. I won't risk my son."

The coach could probably sense there was more, just as Sam could. The woman, Sam remembered, had never been a good liar. It was one of her professional liabilities.

"What's on the video?" the coach asked.

"Gerry Far's execution," Sam put in. "Stirman's old lieutenant."

"One of the men who testified against him," the coach said.

Sam nodded. The young man was making him uncomfortable. He was a little too intelligent, a little too curious. He was the kind of detective who would dig for the sake of digging, who wouldn't abide loose ends even when he was told to. If he'd worked for I-Tech, Sam decided, he would've been fired long ago—insubordination, breach of policy, something. Sam decided he would never let himself be alone with the coach. The coach would dig into him. He would sense the cracks.

"There were two other witnesses," the coach said. "What about them?"

"Dimebox Ortiz," the woman said weakly. "He skipped bail again yesterday. He'll be long gone."

"And the illegal alien woman?"

"Long gone as well," Erainya said.

"Gloria Paz," Sam said. "That was her name."

It bothered Sam that he suddenly remembered that, the same way he'd remembered Erainya Manos had shot somebody in her den. His mind seemed to spit out only the most dangerous facts, like rocks from a lawn mower.

"Ana DeLeon can help us," the coach said. "I told her I'd come by."

"You've already talked to her?" the woman demanded.

"I haven't told her anything yet, but she can be trusted."

"No." The woman was adamant. "I'll take care of this myself. With Sam, if he's got any guts. But you can't go to the police, honey. You can't do that to me."

Her tone made the coach hesitate.

The coach put his hand inside the courier envelope. "If Stirman just wanted to kill you, you'd be dead. He's pressuring you. What does he want?"

"I don't know," she murmured.

The coach wasn't buying it.

Sam wished he could lie for her. He wished like hell he could remember what they were trying to hide. Most of all, he wished the woman had fired this young man a long time ago. No wonder she did so badly in the business. Never hire operatives who are better than you are.

"I'll wait on talking to DeLeon," the coach decided. "And *you* two won't do anything stupid. That's the trade-off."

The woman wiped her nose. "I have to take care of Jem."

"Austin."

She winced.

"There's no one better suited to protect him," the coach said. "You know that. And Jem likes her."

He offered Erainya the phone.

Reluctantly, she placed a call.

"Maia," she said into the receiver. "It's Erainya Manos. Yeah, I bet you didn't. Listen, I . . . Tres and I . . . we have a favor to ask."

Another minute making arrangements, and the woman hung up.

"I'll take him up in the morning," she said. "Jem and I can spend tonight at J.P.'s."

The coach nodded.

He looked at Sam. "One more condition. You tell me what you're holding back. Now."

He hadn't asked Erainya Manos. He had picked out Sam as the weak link, just as Sam would've done in his place.

Sam tried to keep the panic off his face. He stared at his notes, but he knew they wouldn't help him.

Places. He did best with places. This den, for instance. The past had come back to him when he sat here.

He thought about the ax murderer, McCurdy. The ranch near Castroville. He remembered something about Gloria Paz, the woman who'd gotten away.

Don't be alone with the coach, he warned himself. *He'll try to manipulate you.*

But Sam needed a delay. Time to remember. He needed a place.

"The third witness," he said. "You can hear it straight from her."

That threw the coach off balance. "I thought she was long gone."

Sam felt the initiative shifting back to him, the way he liked it.

For once, he wasn't afraid of *not* remembering.

He was afraid that once he got to the McCurdy spread—once he breathed the evil air of that ranch house again, the stone walls would tell him more than he wanted to remember, and some of it might be about him.

"I'll pick you up in the morning," he told the coach. "I'll show you why if you were going to kill anybody, Will Stirman would be a damn good candidate."

10

"Have to walk a piece," the deputy told us. He swung open the gate. "Road's out 'cause of the floods."

I gave him credit for understatement. The strip of yellow mud that led into the McCurdy Ranch looked like it had been used for heavy artillery practice. About a half mile back in the soaked hills, I could just make out the glint of a metal roof.

"Gloria Paz?" Barrera asked.

"Still there." The deputy spat a stream of brown tobacco between the bars of the cattle guard. "Last owner set this place up as a trust. She gets to live here free the rest of her life. Damned if I know why. Then the bank gets it."

"You know about Will Stirman?" I asked.

He gave me traffic cop eyes—like he could either shoot me or wish me a nice day. It was all the same to him. "We got worse problems. Evacuating this whole area. One more day of rain, that dam upriver is going to break. This whole valley's gonna be under ten feet of water."

"You warn Ms. Paz?"

"She ain't going nowhere."

"How do you figure?"

He made a dry, rasping sound that might've been a laugh. "You'll see."

He touched the brim of his hat and ambled back toward his cruiser.

Barrera looked wistfully at his mustard BMW, sitting useless on the side of the two-lane. We hiked into the ranch.

After a few yards, my boots were caked in limestone frosting. I was dripping with sweat. The mosquitoes were having a picnic on the back of my neck.

Barrera looked perfectly cool. His shirt and tie betrayed no speck of mud, not a single wrinkle. Something they taught at Quantico, I guessed. Staying Starched Under Stress, Course 2101.

"You've been out here since the trial?" I asked.

Barrera looked at me blankly. He returned his attention to the muddy slope. "No."

He was never what you might call a sparkling conversationalist, but during the hour trip to Castroville, he'd been even less effervescent than usual.

That could've been because he had a lot on his mind, which was a guess. Or because he didn't like me, which wasn't.

"Who was the last owner of this place?" I tried.

"Businessman from San Antonio. Died a while back. Don't remember his name."

"He let Gloria Paz live here for free?"

No response.

Okay. Thanks, Sam. That clears it up.

I wished I was in Austin with Erainya—getting Jem settled, seeing Maia Lee, keeping the peace between the two heavily armed women in my life.

But Barrera was the key to understanding Stirman. I was sure of that.

He'd brought me out here to tell me something he didn't want to say in front of Erainya. If I could get through the morning without killing him, I might find out what.

I tried to keep my mind off the mud and insects. I appraised the McCurdy spread from a business point of view. It struck me as more scenic and a lot less useful than my own family ranch in Sabinal.

The terrain was rocky and uneven—hills and limestone cliffs hugging the Medina River Valley, poorly suited for crops or cattle. Tourism might've worked. Summer cabins for tubers. Or goat ranching. Exotic game. But the McCurdy land didn't appear to have been managed for any purpose in a long time. Cattle feeders stood rusted and empty. The barn was falling apart. A single emaciated heifer stood under a mesquite tree. Three vultures waited patiently on the branch above.

We were almost on top of the ranch house before I realized it was abandoned—a limestone shell in a thicket of live oaks. The windows were square holes of crumbling mortar. The doorway was an empty frame. The roof had been partially stripped, leaving a patchwork of metal and cedar beam.

Barrera hesitated in the doorway.

He didn't need to explain why. The place radiated a quiet malevolence.

Inside were three empty rooms, a fireplace, a doorway in back that probably led to the kitchen. A mildewed watercolor of a fly fisherman hung crooked over the mantel. Most of the living room floor had been stripped to beams, revealing a cellar below. That was unusual in a Texas house. In most parts of the state, the winters were too mild, the soil too close to bedrock to make a cellar practical.

Barrera stepped carefully across rotten floorboards toward a set of descending stairs. I'd never been a fan of underground, but I followed him down.

The back half of the cellar was stacked with building materials—slabs of Sheetrock and plywood, buckets of paint and caulking, all covered in plastic tarp, tied off with bungee cords. The stuff looked like it had been there for a while. The tarp was tattered, pools of rainwater crusting in the folds. Rats, or maybe cockroaches, had been chewing the labels off the paint cans.

Two black iron hooks protruded from the wall.

The limestone bore stains like rust or moss, but the streaks suggested spray patterns. I'd seen walls like that before—in a Hill Country abattoir that had served generations of deer hunters.

"The table was here," Barrera said.

He stood in the center of the room, holding his palms out as if warming them over a fire. "McCurdy thought the room was soundproof. But up in the cells, they could hear the screaming."

A raindrop hit my face. I looked up through the open squares in the roof. I reminded myself I was just ten easy steps to the surface. The floor beams above me were not prison bars.

I thought about the businessman who had bought this place after McCurdy's suicide. I imagined his optimism as he started tearing up the house—thinking he'd gotten an incredible deal. This load of building materials would fix up the place, make it new and clean again.

I understood now why he'd never finished the job, why the materials were still sitting here unused and the ranch would eventually revert to the bank.

"Stirman knew what would happen to these women?" I asked.

Barrera picked up a small piece of metal, a broken link from a chain. "Stirman wouldn't have cared."

"That doesn't answer my question."

Barrera slipped the link of chain into his pocket. "Come on. Gloria will be waiting."

He led me back outside, down toward the river. Under the cypress trees stood half a dozen cinder block sheds and a small cabin. The smaller structures might have been kennels. Each had a metal gate. In the center of each cement floor was an iron ring, where you might attach an animal's chain.

Then I noticed the lidless steel toilets.

Barrera didn't say anything. I didn't ask.

After almost a decade, a cold acrid smell still hung in the air. Human misery, like old bloodstains, is hard to wash away.

The little cabin at the end was so different from the cells that it took a moment for me to realize it was part of the same row of buildings. Two cinder block cells had been built together, expanded, treated with stucco and painted dark gold. Rust-colored curtains trimmed the windows. Statues of saints lined the roof. River rocks marked off a little garden filled with oregano and mint. It could have been any dwelling on San Antonio's West Side—poor but cozy, proud of its eccentricity.

Barrera knocked. The plywood door rattled in its frame.

The woman who opened it was probably no more than fifty-five, but her frayed white hair made her look decades older. Her face was deeply etched, her eyes milky. Her determined expression, and the shotgun held loosely across her waist, made her look as if she'd just charged the throne of God and been blasted by divine light. She was obviously blind.

She said, "*Señor* Barrera."

How she knew without seeing him, I wasn't sure. Perhaps Barrera's cologne was the not-too-subtle giveaway. She turned toward me, angling the shotgun in the general direction of my chest.

"*¿Quién es el gringo?*"

I hadn't moved or spoken, but she knew I was there. She knew I was male, and Anglo.

"We came to check on you," Barrera said in Spanish. "This is a friend of Fred Barrow's."

I wasn't sure why he introduced me that way, but the woman took her finger off the trigger, lowered the barrel.

"They want me to leave because of some rain," she said. "I had to fire a warning shot at the deputy. Come in. I'll make coffee."

Inside, the tiny living room was painted cornflower blue, hung with dried garlic and chili *ristras*. On the stereo turntable, Lydia Mendoza sang "Dos Corazones," her heartache cutting straight through the scratch and hiss of the old vinyl.

There was no air-conditioning. The windows let in a breeze from the river. The curtains were dappled with raindrops. With the shade of the cypresses, the room felt just warm enough for a nap.

Barrera kept speaking to Gloria in Spanish, simple questions— was she getting enough to eat? Did the locals bother her?

Gloria heated water in a pan on a gas stove. She knew exactly where to find her extra cups, her tin of instant coffee, her spoons.

"Does your friend speak Spanish, *Señor* Barrera?" she asked.

I said, "*Sí, señora.*"

She turned to face me—a moment of adjustment as she let me into her linguistic world.

"*Ya lo veo,*" she said. "Then please tell Mr. Barrow I pray for him."

I looked at Sam, who seemed to see nothing unusual in the request.

"*Señora* Paz," I said, "Will Stirman escaped from jail. One of the men who testified against him has been murdered."

She poured boiling water into each cup. "You came all this way to tell me? I am sorry to have troubled you."

"But, *señora* . . ."

An electronic riff of Mozart collided with Lydia Mendoza's song. The new music was coming from Sam Barrera's pocket.

Barrera frowned, fished out his phone. I was surprised he could even get a signal out here.

He said, "Yes?"

A moment of listening. He paled. "Alicia, I'm in Castroville . . . Of course I told you."

He took the phone away from his ear, looked at us with embarrassment. "Excuse me."

He took his call outside, leaving me alone with Gloria Paz.

"Would you like milk?" she asked. "It is goat's milk."

I glanced at the tin of Folgers Crystals on the stovetop. Plain, or with goat's milk. The kind of rock-and-a-hard-place decision tough PIs must face. "Why not?"

She brought over a tray, sat next to me on the sofa. She passed me the blue metal cup. Her hands were rough and warm.

"*Señora* Paz," I said, "you realize you're in danger?"

"No, *señor*. I am done with fear."

This blind, prematurely aged woman, alone on a ranch, with the dam upriver about to burst and a killer on the loose, was telling me she had nothing to fear. The hell of it was, I believed her.

Her tone was confident, oddly familiar, though I was sure we'd never met.

"A warning shot won't be enough," I told her. "Not against Stirman."

Her milky eyes seemed to stare past my shoulder, as if keeping tabs on an unruly spirit. "*Con permiso.*"

She reached out and touched my cheek. Her fingertips traced my jaw, my nose, my lips. "An honest face. Like Mr. Barrow's."

Erainya had used many adjectives to describe her late husband. *Honest* was not one of them.

"I'm not his friend, *señora*," I said. "Just a friend of the family."

"Tell him not to worry. We did the right thing. It was not a lie."

"*Señora?*"

"Stirman lured many others to a similar fate. It is the same, whether he served *this* devil or some other."

It had been a long time since I'd felt unsure of my Spanish, but I wasn't certain I'd understood her correctly. I set down my coffee.

"*Señora,* how did you come to this ranch?"

"The Green Highway."

"*¿Mande?*"

"The power lines."

I knew what she meant. The power line poles that ran through the South Texas plains were kept clear of brush and cactus, making a perfect path for illegal immigrants who wanted to stay off the roads without getting lost. The Green Highway. A determined illegal could walk for hundreds of miles along those grassy corridors, straight into Uvalde or San Antonio.

"So . . . you never met Will Stirman?"

She shook her head, her expression apologetic. "McCurdy would not trust someone else to pick his women. He knew what he wanted—the kind who made him angry. He would pretend to be a border agent and search the Green Highway himself. He separated me from two friends, promised to let them go if I co-operated. I thought I knew what he wanted. I was wrong. He brought me here. He went slowly with me. My blindness ex-cited him, I think. But it also made him careless. He did not re-member the lock, the third night."

She related the story without faltering, without showing any emotion other than grim satisfaction. I imagined her alone in the dark, tired and beaten and bloody, escaping and stumbling down to the river, following it as she'd followed the power lines, trusting her sense of direction to lead her out of McCurdy's property. Somehow, she had found help. She had made the sheriff believe her.

"After all that," I said, "you chose to come back. You made a home . . . here."

"You cannot move away from the dead, *señor*. When I spoke against Stirman, I spoke for all of the women like me. I live here now for all of them."

I could translate the words, but her meaning seemed alien to me. I could not imagine doing what she had done.

"Stirman will come after you," I said. "He will not be kind."

She turned her face to receive a wet breeze from the window. I realized she knew more about pain and fear than I could ever imagine. I could say nothing that would scare her.

"This is my home," she said. *"Velo tú."*

I looked at the garlic *ristras,* the sunlight on the cornflower walls, the pot of steaming water on the stovetop. I did see.

Gloria Paz had exorcised fear from this place—from this small part of McCurdy's ranch. I wondered if that was why the new owner had allowed her to live here. Gloria had succeeded where he had failed.

"Tell Mr. Barrow to come visit," Gloria Paz said. "It has been too many years. He can bring me more shotgun ammunition. Tell him not to despair."

Only then did I realize who she reminded me of—her small frame, her stubborn expression, the tense set of her shoulders, as if she were ready to lead a charge. She reminded me of Erainya.

I managed to say, "I'll tell him."

Sam Barrera came back inside. He muttered an apology. He slipped the cell phone into his pocket, looked around the room as if he'd misplaced something.

"Are we done?" he asked me.

It seemed a strange thing to say, since he hadn't participated in any of the conversation. Perhaps he could see from my expression that I'd learned what I needed to know. Or perhaps he saw the goat's milk and Folgers on the stovetop and decided not to risk it.

"Yeah," I told him. "I guess we're done."

On the drive back through Castroville, we passed our friend the deputy. He was leaning against the hood of his unit, supervising a group of men placing sandbags across the entrance of Haby's Bavarian Bakery. He tipped his hat to us. I imagined he was congratulating himself on being right—the city folk were beating a hasty retreat after a hopeless visit with the crazy woman.

The hills retreated behind us. I waited for Barrera to speak.

When he didn't, I said, "You framed Will Stirman. Gloria Paz lied for you."

Just when I thought he wasn't going to acknowledge my statement, he said, "So now you know."

"At the risk of sounding rude—were you fucking insane?"

"Did you miss the chains?" Sam asked. "The bloodstains on the wall?"

"That was McCurdy. Will Stirman had nothing to do with those women."

"Not *those* women, maybe. But a thousand others. He sent them to sweatshops, brothels, slave ranches. Fred and I knew. We had both crossed paths with Stirman before. He was a monster. This was our chance."

"You used the public outrage about the McCurdy case. Your clients wanted a scapegoat and you knew Stirman was an easy sell."

"We started the investigation thinking it was him. Fred and I both. When we found out . . . Gloria admitted there was no supplier. McCurdy handpicked the women he wanted. Fred and I were too far along at that point. We'd gotten in Stirman's face. We'd already convinced a couple of his men to turn on him and provide evidence. How did we know they were lying? That they just wanted an excuse to divide up the boss's business? After we realized the truth, we decided . . . what the hell? Gloria was willing to cooperate. We would bring Stirman down."

"You. Sam Barrera. Mr. By-the-Book."

"Circumstances were different, eight years ago." His voice was tinged with bitterness.

"Erainya knew about the frame-up?" I asked.

"Fred wouldn't have told her."

"Then why is she reluctant to call the police?"

He hesitated. "We have too much to lose."

"*Your* reputation. She did nothing wrong."

He gave me a wary look.

There was more to it. He wasn't worried about looking bad, having his frame-up exposed eight years later. Who would believe the truth anyway, or care? No prosecutor would be anxious to file charges against Barrera and an old Mexican lady for taking a demon like Will Stirman off the streets.

We were back in the city now. Barrera turned south on I-10—not the way to my place.

He exited on Commerce and headed through downtown.

I didn't want to talk to him, but finally I said, "Where the hell are you going?"

He drove to South Alamo and turned right, into Southtown.

Under different circumstances, this would've been fine with me. Invariably, Southtown was where I ended up whenever I had free time. I loved the dilapidated houses, the palm trees and crumbling sidewalks, old cantinas next to new art studios, tattoo shops, folk magic *botánicas, pan dulce* bakeries.

Back when I was still speaking with my best friend Ralph, we would kick around down here, occasionally kicking heads when business called for it. Two Northsiders, we would joke that this was the neighborhood we should have been born in. Southtown was where San Antonians came to remember why we lived in San Antonio.

Barrera parked on Cedar, in front of a big blue Victorian with a FOR SALE sign out front.

"What?" I asked.

He looked at me like the answer was obvious. "Home."

I didn't know what the hell he was talking about. Sam lived in an upper-middle-class two-bedroom in Hollywood Park. His street was sleepy and safe and white-bread and about as far from Southtown as you could get.

"Look, Sam, as much as I love shopping for houses with you—"

"Real estate agent called. She's got an offer of a quarter million. A quarter goddamn million."

I hesitated. "This is your family place?"

He kept his eyes on the house. "I was walking home as a kid—right on the corner there. Couple of *cholos* drove by and shot at me. The bullet ripped a hole in my jacket, embedded in our front porch. You can still see the groove in the floorboards."

"Wow," I said. He was starting to scare me.

"Mom was too afraid to call SAPD," he continued. "They wouldn't have done shit anyway. Next day at school, those *cholos* asked me how I liked the drive-by. They laughed, like it was a big joke. I beat the shit out of them. Otherwise, they would've tried it again. That's the day I decided to become a cop. Not the local assholes. Somebody bigger. FBI."

"Sam?"

No response.

I touched his shoulder. "Sam."

He started, as if I'd appeared from nowhere.

"Just remembering," he said.

His face had gone pale. He looked sick with worry.

"Let's call the police," I said. "You're not in any shape to be running down Will Stirman."

"I'm fine. I'm just tired."

He started the car, pulled away from the curb. In a few minutes, we were back on 281, heading toward the North Side.

"What did you take from Stirman?" I asked Sam. "What is it he wants back?"

Sam kept driving, checking his rearview mirror as if looking for a tail. "I got a full slate of meetings today. Missed a lot, carting you around. Unlike Erainya, I've got accounts to handle."

"You're not sure," I said. "Are you?"

He shifted the strap of his shoulder holster. Sweat stains had appeared in the armpits of his shirt. "I know where to find Stirman. I don't need anyone's help bringing him down. Not from you. Not from that goddamn Manos woman."

It was something he might've said at any time during the years I'd known him, as his company rose to power at the expense of that goddamn Manos woman.

Same old Barrera. Irritating, arrogant, dependable.

But as he drove me home, I felt an uneasy pull in the pit of my stomach.

Barrera's hands stayed steady on the wheel, his left turn signal still blinking from the entrance ramp on Commerce, blinking all the way across town with a reassuring, meaningless rhythm.

11

"That your old place?" Pablo asked.

Will didn't answer. He closed the car door, brushed the rain off his shoulders.

They had parked outside the abandoned plumbing supply shop on Avenue B—a big white building with a razor wire fence and stacks of corroding pipe in the yard.

Will had walked the perimeter first. He'd noticed how much thicker the honeysuckle was on the fence, how the roof was falling apart. The windows on the second story, where he once lived, were now painted over. There was still a bullet hole visible in one pane of turquoise glass.

Finally, he'd built up the courage to go inside.

Upstairs, ratty sleeping bags, old needles, piles of clothes indicated junkies had been using the place to shoot up. Nobody there at the moment, which was fortunate for them.

Will found what he was looking for under a loose floorboard, right where he'd left it, as if it were too small, too insignificant to have been disturbed. He took what he needed to take, then left his sketch of Soledad in exchange. It seemed the right thing, to leave her image here in this building—the place she'd been happy.

Or perhaps that wasn't his only reason.

Crouching in the silence of the ruined apartment, Will thought about his encounter with Tres Navarre and Jem Manos. Revenge would be much harder, much more complicated than he'd imagined.

Perhaps he was leaving Soledad's picture here because he was no longer sure he could do what she would've wanted.

It was a long time before he trusted himself to get up, walk outside again, and join Pablo in the car.

"We shouldn't be here, man," Pablo said.

Will knew he was right.

Dimebox Ortiz had found this place for him, years ago. He had said, *Nobody will ever think to look for you here, man. It's one of those places that you just drive by. It's invisible.*

They had searched all morning for Dimebox Ortiz. Will wanted to make him eat those words.

"Any news?" Will asked.

Pablo shook his head. He'd been manning the phone. They had hired a guy to tail Erainya Manos, just to make sure she didn't do anything stupid.

Pablo had made the calls, dropped off the payment, just like he'd done the face-to-face work asking after Dimebox Ortiz. Nobody knew Pablo in San Antonio. That's why Will kept him alive.

Across the street, the San Antonio River was flooding its banks. Soledad used to walk along the edge of the water there. She used to talk to the man who sold hubcaps from his front porch. She'd make jokes with the boys who fished off the oil drums in the shade of the sycamore trees.

The tail on Erainya was costing them two hundred bucks. The video camera they'd gotten for a hundred bucks at one of the Arguello pawn shops.

Even with the stash Gerry Far had provided, they were getting low on money and food. Will hated banks. He hated anything that left a paper trail. But he should risk a trip to the ATM, dip into the emergency fund his friend had set up for him. He didn't have time to be knocking around the old neighborhood.

Will put the car in drive.

He eased across the Grand Avenue Bridge, through a half foot of water. He parked in front of the San Antonio Art Museum.

"Hey, man . . ." Pablo again, nervous.

The museum was a big limestone castle with two turreted towers, a glass skywalk connecting them. It used to be the Lone Star Beer Brewery, and in Will's opinion that had been a better use for the building. He'd only been here once before, with Soledad, and for her sake, he hated the place.

It had been two weeks after the McCurdy Ranch story broke. Will had been pissed about the media coverage. It would mean trouble for him, for everybody in his line of work. Then came the call—the invitation for a meeting he never should've attended.

He got out of bed at midnight, as quietly as he could. A full moon was coming in the window.

Soledad sighed in her sleep. Her silver Saint Anthony medal glinted at her throat.

Four months she'd been sharing his bed. He kept waiting to get tired of her, for the feeling of wanting her to pass. But the feeling didn't pass. He was no longer worried about her running away. He didn't have her watched, or lock the doors when he left.

She said she loved San Antonio. This was where she was meant to live. And the way she treated him in bed—maybe it was a lie, but she acted as if she wanted to be with him. If it was a lie, he didn't want to know.

She had put on some weight since he'd bought her, but he didn't mind. She had been too thin, anyway. Now she looked healthy. Her skin and hair had a glow that hadn't been there before.

She stirred as he was getting dressed, and opened her eyes. "Where are you going?"

"The museum."

The answer, he realized, was absurd. She laughed, and it was impossible not to laugh with her.

"It's closed, *loco* boy!"

"Not for me," he said. "I've got to meet somebody there."

"I like the museum."

"You've been there?"

"Got to do something while you're gone all day. Take me with you."

Her smile made him want to take off his clothes again, join her under the covers. A lot more pleasant than what he had to do.

"I can't," he said. "These aren't good men I have to see."

Her eyes widened. "Are they worse than you?"

"No."

"Then I got nothing to worry about, do I?"

He couldn't tell her no. She dressed quickly. Together they walked down Jones Street in the dark, holding hands under the full moon.

The museum was all lit up.

They walked straight up to the doors. The security guard wore an I-Tech patch on his uniform.

He didn't look happy about it, but he let them in. "Fourth-floor skywalk."

They walked upstairs, Soledad pointing out paintings. She made faces at the abstract stuff. She thought the nude models looked sad.

"You draw better," she told him. "Why couldn't your stuff be in here?"

She was one of the few people who'd ever seen his sketches—the drawings he did late at night, when he woke up haunted by some illegal immigrant's face, one of the hundreds he'd imported that week. He didn't know why some faces stuck with him and others didn't. He didn't know why sketching them made him feel better. But it allowed him to sleep. It got their faces onto the paper and out of his dreams.

Soledad stopped in front of an eighteenth-century seascape. "I wanted to live on the beach, when I was little."

Another security guard passed by, pointedly ignoring them.

"Why San Antonio then?" Will asked her. "No beaches here."

Soledad pinched her medallion. "My father's. He gave it to me before I left. San Antonio was his patron saint. Said the city would be lucky for me."

San Antonio. Saint Anthony. Will had lived here since he was eight, when his parents moved from West Texas hoping to escape the oil fields, but he'd never thought about what the city's name meant. "Why lucky?"

Soledad raised an eyebrow. "You don't know about Saint Anthony?"

Will shook his head. At the time, he knew almost nothing about religion.

"I'll tell you sometime," Soledad promised.

On the fourth floor, she squeezed his hand. She let him go forward without her.

Two men were waiting for him on the skywalk.

"Hey, Stirman," Fred Barrow said. "I see you brought your daughter."

Will said nothing. It had been a mistake to bring Soledad. If Barrow said another word about her, Will would break his neck. He could fix a lot of things with the police. He spread money around in a lot of places. But he wasn't sure he could fix murdering Fred Barrow, not with a witness, with armed security guards.

Barrow took the unlit cigar from his mouth. He had a nose that had been broken at least twice, a knife scar on his jaw. He wore a suit that fit his broad shoulders poorly. His eyes were not very different from the eyes of Will's clients—the ones who appraised women for purchase.

"We want a confession," Barrow told him.

Will looked at the other man, Sam Barrera. It was common knowledge the two PIs hated each other, which was why Will had agreed to this meeting. Despite the risks, despite Will's dislike for them both, he was curious. He wanted to hear what they were calling an "urgent business proposition." What could possibly bring these two men together?

"You give us a statement," Sam Barrera said, "we can talk to the D.A. this morning. He's willing to go with human trafficking only, drop the accessory-to-murder charges. You've just got to admit to supplying the women. You'll be out in five to ten."

Will shook his head. "What are you talking about?"

The two private eyes exchanged looks.

Immediately Will remembered why he hated them. They thought they were so goddamn superior. Will had crossed paths with both of them before, on separate missing persons cases. Families in Mexico had hired them to find kin who had crossed illegally and disappeared. Unlike most gumshoes, Barrow and Barrera wouldn't take Will's money. They wouldn't go away. They just kept digging as if Will was beneath them, as if it would be insulting to cooperate with him. So Will had taught

them a lesson. He had made sure the people they were looking
for disappeared permanently, all traces of their existence wiped
out. He'd made sure the PIs knew it, too. Their investigations
went nowhere. They couldn't touch Will.

"You went too far this time, Stirman," Fred Barrow said. "Six
women were murdered."

Will made the connection. "You're talking about the
McCurdy Ranch. Those women weren't mine."

Fred Barrow laughed. "Every slave laborer in South Texas
has your handprints all over them."

His eyes drifted over to Soledad.

"You look at her again," Will said, "I'll kill you."

"That wouldn't be wise," Sam Barrera said.

A security guard drifted into view at the far end of the skywalk.

Will had been stupid to come here. Barrera controlled the
guards. They could set Will up, find some pretext to kill him.

"I'm not confessing," he said. "I didn't do anything."

"We'll get you anyway," Sam Barrera warned. "This is huge,
Stirman. People want blood on the McCurdy case. We're going
to give it to them."

"Not my blood."

Barrera said, "We've got witnesses who can tie you to
McCurdy."

Will knew he was bluffing. He had to be. There'd been nothing for anybody to witness.

"Thanks for the private tour, Barrera," he said. Then to Fred
Barrow: "Stay the fuck away from me. You understand?"

Barrow bit off the tip of his cigar, spat it at Will's feet. "Stick
around and enjoy the artwork, Stirman. We'll meet again soon.
And, um, give your Mexican daughter a kiss for me, okay?"

The two men walked back across the skywalk.

Will found Soledad running her fingers over the head of a Greek statue—a half-naked woman lying forlornly on a sofa. The card said, *Ariadne waits for Dionysus. DO NOT TOUCH.*

"Don't let them anger you," Soledad told him. "They aren't worth it."

"You heard?"

She turned, wrapped her arms around his waist, kissed his chin.

She made him feel worse than Barrow and Barrera ever could.

He was a smuggler. A murderer. He had disposed of human bodies like they were animal carcasses. He had put Soledad up for sale, and a thousand women like her.

"You can leave, if you want," he told her.

She looked up at him, mystified. "I told you, *loco* boy. San Antonio is my lucky town."

"Wherever you want to go," he said. "The seashore. Wherever. I'll give you money. You're free to leave me."

She grabbed his wrist, moved his hand to her belly, warm and slightly swollen under the cotton dress. She said, "That wouldn't be a good idea, *mi amor.*"

Somewhere in the middle of a long kiss, he finally understood what she was saying, and the knowledge terrified him.

It was months before Barrow and Barrera found him again. Long enough for Will to lower his guard, and believe that they had forgotten about him. Long enough for him to come to terms with his fear, and believe that Soledad might be his salvation.

Eight years later, the museum hadn't changed. The towers were still there, the skywalk and the glass entrance.

An idea started to form in Will's mind. An idea that had some justice to it.

He got out of the car, ignoring Pablo's protests.

He walked to the entrance. It was the middle of the day, but the sign said CLOSED.

Inside, he saw shattered windows in the back of the entrance hall, tables covered in plastic. He tried the doors. They were locked.

Will knocked on the glass, knowing he was taking an absurd chance. But no one expected him here. No one would think to look for Will Stirman at an art museum.

Finally a guard came up and frowned at him.

The patch on the guard's uniform said *I-Tech*. Sam Barrera's company still held the security contract. Good.

The guard unlocked the door, cracked it open. He kept one hand on his holster. "We're closed, sir."

Stirman said, "Why?"

"Flood damage."

The guard said it like it should be obvious. The broken windows. Plastic covering the patio tables. Pools of water on the tile floor.

Perfect.

What had Sam Barrera told him, when he called to set up the meeting, eight years ago? *It'll be a private place to talk. Secure. Hell, I own the security.*

Will smiled apologetically at the guard. "Okay. Sorry."

The guard locked the door. He stood at the glass, his hand still on his holster as Will walked back to his car.

Pablo waited on the hood of the car, trying to ignore the rain.

He wanted to throw the phone across the museum parking lot. He'd just heard from their man watching Erainya Manos, and the last thing he wanted was to share the news with Stirman.

It had been bad enough, dealing with a private investigator. It brought back too many memories of his big mistake—the stranger he'd found in Angelina's bedroom, four and a half years ago.

So far, Pablo had resisted the urge to call his wife. He needed to be on the plane first, on his way to Mexico. He just hoped Angelina had read his letters from jail, and understood his veiled directions about what she should do if he ever got free.

But what if she'd burned the letters? He kept thinking about the look on her face the night he came home with the shotgun.

In the month or so leading up to that night, she'd acted cagey, nervous. Money had vanished from their checking account without explanation, and they never had any extra money to spend. She would go out and tell him she was visiting a sick friend, or seeing a doctor—little excuses that didn't add up.

At first Pablo was too bewildered to be angry. He was used to Angelina depending on him for everything. She'd come to the country illegally years before, gotten separated from the rest of her family in transit, when they'd run into some vigilante ranchers in the high desert. She had only Pablo, who'd given her citizenship through marriage, a good home, all the love she could want. She would never betray him.

Then his next-door neighbor told him about the man who was visiting her while Pablo was at work—twice he'd come to see her, over the last week.

And when Pablo had walked in that last night, and found the man talking with her on their bed—on *his* bed . . .

Angelina had looked up, and screamed at Pablo to stop.

He would give anything to take back those few seconds, as the man rose to face him, and Pablo's finger found the trigger.

"Yo, amigo. Wake up."

Stirman's presence jarred Pablo out of his thoughts.

"What's wrong?" Stirman demanded.

"Bad news," Pablo managed to say.

He told Stirman about their private eye, who had followed Erainya Manos out of town that morning. She'd taken I-35 north—her and her boy, Jem.

"Running?" Stirman asked.

"No. She came back."

"Where did she go in Austin, then?"

Pablo shifted uncomfortably. "Our guy lost her when she turned off on Ben White. He missed the exit, never found her again. He drove back to San Antonio and sat on her house, in case she came back. She did—a few minutes ago. Without the boy."

Pablo saw the rage building in Stirman's face.

They both knew what the PI's news meant. Erainya Manos had hidden her son. She was trying to protect him, insulate him from danger, which meant she probably wasn't going to cooperate. She would try to double-cross them.

"The woman is a problem," Stirman decided.

"She's still got twenty-four hours," Pablo said halfheartedly. The last thing he wanted was another death, especially a woman's. "Maybe she'll come through. We just got to stay low and wait."

"No," Stirman insisted. He took a deep breath, and Pablo knew he was filling himself with that cold, homicidal sense of purpose Pablo had seen too many times over the last few days. "Change of plans, amigo. We've got work to do."

12

Robert Johnson was a great help going through the agency's old files.

He would crouch at the far end of the living room, get a running start, and dive straight through them like a snowplow. Then he would look at me, wild-eyed, a manila folder tented over his head.

"Yes, thanks," I said. "That's much better."

In terms of finding important information, however, neither of us was having much luck.

The only things that belonged to Erainya in the locked file cabinet were mementos of her transitional year, from Barrow's wife to self-made PI. There were stacks of clippings about her defense trial in Fred's murder. Her change-of-name paperwork, officially declaring her to be Erainya Manos. Her U.S. passport, stamped for Greece. Jem's adoption paperwork from a Texas-based agency called Children First International. His birth date, which Erainya had told me was a guess—April 28, 1995. His birth parents' names: Abdul and Mariah Suleimaniyah. The usual signatures and medical work. A letter from some government official in Bosnia-Herzegovina, authorizing Jem's release to Erainya's custody.

An early picture of Erainya and Jem. Jem looked about one year old. His dark eyes were wide with amazement as the woman with the frizzy black hair held him up to the camera and kissed his cheek.

I went through some of Erainya's correspondence. Several notes of support from women's advocacy groups. Fan letters from women who admired her for shooting her husband.

I put those down. They made me nervous.

The rest of the stuff was from Fred Barrow's time.

I'd always thought of Fred as an old man, but the only photograph I found showed him looking not much older than me. It must've been from the early eighties. Fred's greasy black hair was parted in the middle, too long at the collar. He had a square face, battered from years as an amateur boxer. His eyes were sly and shallow, his smile insincere. He looked like a wife-beater, in the middle of saying, *Look, officer, you know how these women are.*

I didn't want to find anything that would make me like him, but he did seem to have a soft spot for illegal immigrants. His first job out of college was ten years with the Border Patrol, and the experience must've affected him. After opening the PI agency, he'd taken on a number of cases, either pro bono or at reduced fees, to help families in Mexico find missing kin in the north, or to help prosecute coyotes like Will Stirman.

He liked fishing and hunting.

He relished divorce cases. Even his enemies admitted he was a tenacious investigator.

He almost lost his PI license once when he'd assaulted a federal agent who'd questioned his integrity in a high-profile drug trafficking case. Fred Barrow had been working for the defense. The federal agent made a comment about Barrow's testimony being "the best fabrication money could buy." Later, at a bar near the courthouse, Barrow decked the agent with a left hook. A judge friendly to both parties managed to smooth things over, at least legally. The federal agent's name was Samuel Barrera.

There was nothing to indicate the two men had framed Will Stirman. Just meticulous notes on their interviews with Gerry Far and Dimebox Ortiz, outlining Stirman's operation, and confirming that McCurdy had been a regular client. In exchange for their testimony, Far and Ortiz had escaped prosecution. Far had taken over Stirman's operation. And Dimebox Ortiz . . . what had he gotten out of the deal?

I wrote on my otherwise blank notepad: *Dimebox Ortiz?*

I set that question aside for the moment. If Dimebox had any brains, he was several hundred miles away by now.

Robert Johnson dive-bombed the stack I'd just gone through and sent papers flying.

"Thanks," I said.

As I was picking them up, I noticed something I hadn't seen before. It was a piece of stationery that must've been stuck between envelopes in Erainya's correspondence. The note was from a woman. I could tell that from the handwriting. She wrote:

Irene, You'll be acquitted and back with us before you know it. Don't worry. And the package from Fred—relax. It's safely hidden.

Love, H.

The package from Fred?

I read the note again. It still said the same thing.

Will Stirman wanted something from Barrera and Barrow, something Erainya felt guilty about.

I looked at the cat. "You're a genius."

He looked at me wild-eyed. He probably couldn't believe it had taken me so long to catch on.

I needed to strong-arm somebody for more information.

Somebody who wasn't Sam or Erainya; they would only lie to me more. Somebody who knew Will Stirman, and wasn't dead yet.

I looked at my notes. I'd written two words: *Dimebox Ortiz?*

At this point, under normal circumstances, I would've called my friend Ralph Arguello, Ana DeLeon's husband. He specialized in finding lowlife scumbags. He delighted in strong-arming them. But I hadn't talked to Ralph in almost a year. The longer the silence got, the more stubborn I felt about not breaking it. Besides, I had an unreturned message from his wife on my answering machine, asking why I hadn't shown up at the police station last night like I'd promised.

I'd have to go this one alone.

Was it worth searching for Dimebox?

I looked at the cat. "If he has any brains, he'll be far, far away."

The cat's expression told me I'd just answered my own question.

"You're right," I said. "He'll be in town."

I told Robert Johnson to sort the rest of the files for me. Then I grabbed my car keys.

The normal axiom is *Follow the money*. In the case of Dimebox Ortiz, it's *Follow the poultry.*

Dimebox might've been a bail jumper hiding from a crazed killer, but he still had to place his cockfighting bets. Sooner or later, I knew he would show up at the pits, or with a bookie. I asked around, said I had a couple of grand to spend on the right bird, and within an hour I had a list of places to try.

I found Dimebox back in Southtown at Rosario's restaurant, about to enjoy a skillet of sizzling fajitas with a particularly oily cockfighting bookie named Travis the Spur. There were various rumors about how Travis had gotten the nickname, none of which involved the local basketball team.

I came up behind Dimebox, pulled his arm behind his back, and slammed his head onto his flour tortilla, making sure his face was close enough to the heated skillet so he would catch the pops from the grease.

I told Travis the Spur to cluck off. He was only too delighted to oblige.

Dimebox struggled.

I applied a little more pressure to his arm. "Nothing like a good fajita."

"Navarre?" He was blinking from the grease, drooling on the tortilla. "Jesus, thank God it's you."

"Saved you again, have I?"

"Stirman's looking for me. He got to Kiko and Lalu—I think . . . shit, he might've killed them, man. I was just leaving town—"

"You seem to have trouble finding the city limits."

"Just gonna make a couple more grand for the road. You know. How the hell did you find me?"

"Talk to me about the night Stirman was arrested."

"What?" He tried to shrug, which was not easy to do in his position. "What's there to say?"

"Your face needs garnishing, Dimebox. How about some of these?"

I made a lightning grab for the jalapeño bowl, poured them on Dimebox's face, then reapplied pressure to keep his head against the plate.

"Agghh!" he said. "Jesus!"

The juice started running into his eyes.

I let him struggle.

There wasn't much of a crowd in the restaurant, this time of afternoon—a few guys drinking margaritas at the bar; a couple of businessmen having a late lunch. They'd been admiring the wraparound view of the corner of Alamo and Presa, but they all stopped watching that and started watching me.

A waiter came over nervously and asked if there was a problem. Did he have to call the police?

"Everything's fine!" Dimebox groaned, blinking pepper juice out of his face. "No police! Everything's cool!"

"Cable company," I informed the waiter. "He's three months behind on premium service."

"Oh." I could see the waiter's mind working, trying to remember if he'd paid his cable bill. He left quickly.

"You testified against Stirman at his trial," I said to Dimebox.

"Yeah. Yeah, okay. Jesus, Navarre. Lemme up."

"Gerry Far took over the operation. What was in it for you?"

"Stirman was a maniac. You guys would get along. You think I liked working for a maniac?"

"Not good enough. What does Stirman want from Erainya and Sam? What did they take from him?"

"I don't know."

I picked up some *pico de gallo* and splashed it in his face.

He struggled a little more, spit the tomato chunks out of his mouth. "Jesus, Navarre!"

"You're looking pretty appetizing, Dimebox," I said. "I think we're about ready to pour on this sizzling meat here."

"No! Look— His wife. Stirman's wife."

"What wife?"

"Soledad. She died in the gunfire. One of the PIs shot her. I don't know which."

"I heard the woman who died was a prostitute."

"Yeah, well—she was more to Stirman. She was . . . you know . . . pretty fine. They killed his woman."

Something in his tone . . .

"That's what you wanted," I decided. "You wanted her."

"No. Hell, no."

"You figured with Stirman out of the way, you would get his woman. You set him up because you wanted to get laid."

"No!"

Which meant yes. I cranked up on Dimebox's arm. He yelped.

A businessman in one of the booths got out his phone. He dialed a short number—three digits. I was pretty sure he wasn't calling directory assistance.

"What else?" I told Dimebox. "Quick."

"Nothing. Honest."

"They took something from Stirman. Something he wants back. What is it?"

"Money, maybe. I don't know."

"How much money?"

"Hell, I don't know. The guy used cash for everything. He was leaving the country. I told them that. I said, 'You get him arrested now, tonight, or he'll be gone.' But look, I never thought they'd . . . well, they went overboard. Okay?"

I glanced down South Presa. Some beat cops were strolling along, coming our direction. The businessman with the cell phone had hung up. I had maybe four seconds.

I let Dimebox up, pushed his chair around so he was looking at me, *pico de gallo* chunks dripping off his face. The jalapeños had made burn rings on his cheek.

"You're holding back on me, Ortiz."

"Honest to God."

"Why would Stirman go after Erainya? She wasn't even part of it."

Dimebox stared at me, incredulous. "Are you kidding? When I called the night Stirman was going to escape . . . shit, don't you know . . . ?"

"Speak, Dimebox. Don't I know what?"

He wiped the salsa off his chin. "Erainya was the go-between for me and Barrow. She's the one I called. When they took down Stirman without waiting for the police—hell, yes, she was part of that. It was her goddamn idea."

13

The phone rang for the third time as Erainya was loading her gun.

Tres' voice on the answering machine: "Okay, now I'm sure you're home. Pick up."

She pushed .45 cartridges into the magazine. It was strange looking in the drawer and not seeing Fred's photo, but it had felt damn good to rip the bastard up and throw him away after so many years.

"I'm coming over," Tres said. "See you in ten minutes."

The line went dead.

In ten minutes, she would be gone. Now that Jem was safe in Austin, she knew exactly what she would do. She would start on the South Side, with a heroin supplier whose little girl Erainya had once rescued. He had excellent contacts at the Floresville State Pen. If anyone could find out who Stirman's friends were, where he might be hiding, this guy could.

She slapped the magazine in place, felt the heft of the gun. She would have to use both hands. After firing a clip, her forearms would be sore.

But she could still place a cluster in a man's chest at fifty feet. She was confident of that. She'd let a lot of things slip, over the years, but not her Saturday mornings at the range.

She aimed at the blasted television, kept her sights steady.

Eight years ago, in this room, she had not been so prepared. It almost cost her life. She'd vowed never to let that happen again.

She remembered her right eye stinging with blood. Her mouth had been salty with the taste of her own busted lip.

Fred had never hit her so hard before.

Then again, she'd never threatened him like that before.

You will not do this to me, he told her.

What am I supposed to do? she screamed. *You* destroyed *that family.*

You *destroyed them, Irene. That's what you wanted all along, isn't it? And now you want to blame it on me? I'll kill you both.*

He meant it, too. His face was distorted with rage, his limbs heavy with bourbon.

He knocked her backward into the desk, and she heard one of her own ribs crack.

She clawed open the drawer, found his gun.

In that moment, Irene died—docile Anglicized Irene, who'd married Fred because he needed a good helper, who'd cleaned his house, filed his papers, answered his phone. Irene told herself Fred didn't hit her *that* much. He wasn't really as bad as the spouses they were hired to investigate.

Her fingers closed around the butt of the Colt, and Erainya came back—her childhood self, half remembered like her mother's Aegean lullabies, a little girl who had known how to fight.

She turned on Fred and fired. Once in his shoulder, but he kept coming. So again, into his hip.

He got his hands around her neck, started to squeeze the life out of her as her third shot blew through the side of his chest.

He collapsed on top of her, wet and warm, crushing her, as if he wanted to prove his ownership.

She pushed him off, sat trembling on the desk.

Finally, she called her best friend, Helen Malski.

She heard herself saying, "Listen, honey, I need your help." She realized she'd already formulated a plan. She'd known what she was going to do even before she pulled the trigger.

Self-defense. An easy sell to the jury. Erainya had walked free eight months later.

She raised the matched grip of the Colt, shoved her palm against the butt, imagining a fast reload.

Now, it would not be so easy. The stakes were higher. The man she was fighting was more deadly, but she felt a strange sense of calm.

She would kill Will Stirman.

He would never threaten her or her son again.

The doorbell startled her.

Even Tres couldn't drive that fast. Besides, that damn truck of his always rattled the windows when he pulled in the driveway.

Couldn't be J.P., either. As much as she wanted to see him, she'd begged off his dinner invitation. She'd made it clear she needed the night alone.

She curled her finger around the trigger of the Colt.

She was halfway down the hallway when her visitor knocked—shave-and-a-haircut, slow and heavy. Too familiar for a solicitor or a deliveryman.

She slipped out the back door, moved barefoot through the soaked grass, and sneaked around the side of the house.

No car was parked on the street. That meant her caller had either walked or pulled into the driveway.

She cursed the ranch house design that Fred had always loved. The front bedroom jutted out in a useless fin of bricks so she couldn't see the driveway or front door. If Stirman had someone with him, a helper parked and waiting, she would be stepping into crossfire.

She would only have a millisecond for decisions. If he was alone, she would call his name, watch him turn so she wouldn't have to shoot him in the back. She would put a bullet in the center of his chest.

She crept to the edge of the bedroom wall.

Her front door creaked. The bastard was opening it.

One. She exhaled. *Two* . . .

She swung around the corner, crouching into firing position as her visitor called into the house, "Erainya?"

His voice saved his life.

J.P.'s back was to her. Her Colt was leveled at the stretch of white broadcloth between his shoulder blades.

She caught her breath.

He sensed her, turned in time to see the gun drop to her knee.

He held up his hands, one of which held a bouquet of snapdragons. "May I request a last meal with a beautiful woman?"

She was trembling.

She had almost killed the only man she would never consider killing.

She was furious with him. What the hell was he doing here?

She wanted to drive him off, tell him to go the hell away. Right now she was as dangerous as a downed power line. Murder danced in her nervous system.

J.P. smiled.

How could he look at her like that?

Here she was with her bare wet feet, her grungy work clothes, her bloodshot eyes and her runny nose, ambushing him with a goddamn .45—and he was looking at her like she was the best thing he'd ever seen.

"I could've killed you," she said.

"I was thinking Italian."

She rose, took a shaky breath, and let the gun fall uselessly to her side. "If the last meal is *that* good, honey, I suppose I've got to share it."

According to the radio, half the West Side was underwater. Woodlawn Lake had overflowed, manhole covers burst open, storm drains exploded into geysers. Hundreds of residents were stranded on rooftops. Four teenagers had disappeared, sucked into the current while trying to body-surf a drainage ditch.

Even the affluent North Side had not been spared. Right down the street from J.P.'s chosen restaurant, at the corner of Basse, an elderly couple's Cadillac had turned into an underwater coffin. Erainya could see the police lights flickering through the treetops.

But you could tell none of that from the crowd at Paesano's. The parking lot gleamed with eighty-thousand-dollar cars. Inside, the elite of San Antonio packed the dining room, laughing and talking without concern, the air infused with oregano and expensive cologne.

J.P. made everyone's face light up as he walked through the room.

"Dr. Sanchez!"

Surgeons, trial lawyers, politicians rose from their tables to shake his hand. J.P. introduced Erainya, though it was clear none of them cared about her. J.P.'s arm around her waist, his complete deference toward her, seemed to irritate his acquaintances.

J.P. politely cut short each conversation, declining their offers for a drink.

"You must excuse me," he told them. "When I am with Miss Manos, my time becomes very valuable."

Erainya loved him. She loved the way his friends' mouths hung open, the way their wives stared after her as they wrung their diamond bracelets.

J.P. had managed to reserve the restaurant's best table—a corner spot with windows overlooking the golf course and, across Basse, the man-made canyon that had once been the Alamo Cement Quarry. She could just make out J.P.'s house, there on the far rim of the canyon, its windows bright with buttery light.

Erainya wondered if this was a subtle invitation, eating dinner within sight of his bedroom. But no—she would think that way. J.P. wouldn't.

Last night he had comforted her so patiently, asked no questions, expected nothing in return. He had completely understood when she wanted to sleep next to Jem, so they ended up camping out in his living room, all three of them—down sleeping bags on his plush carpet, bowls of popcorn, flashlights, *Yu-Gi-Oh!* DVDs instead of ghost stories. All night, Erainya lay awake, listening to the easy breathing of her child and her lover, and pondering how she would kill Will Stirman.

J.P. ordered dinner—shrimp Paesano, Parmesan salad, fettuccine Alfredo. He waved aside the wine list and ordered a magnum of '97 Brunello di Montalcino, not making a big deal out of it, but Erainya knew the vintage would cost more than she earned in a week. She'd made a point of learning about wine since she'd started dating J.P.

The bottle arrived. He declined a taste test, sent away the waiter, and poured Erainya a generous glass as if it were Kool-Aid or Strawberry Ripple. "So did you get Jem settled?"

"I suppose. He loves this lady . . . Maia Lee."

"Tres' girlfriend."

"Yeah."

J.P. placed his hand on hers. "If I had to pick *one* eight-year-old to watch my back in a fight, I'd pick Jem. He'll be fine."

She managed a smile. A small knot of worry was twisting in her throat. Jem had never spent the night away from her—at least not since he was very small, before she'd taken permanent custody of him. Baby-sitters, sleepovers . . . she couldn't deal with them. She'd never been able to shake the fear that he would disappear somehow, leave her life as suddenly as he'd entered it.

J.P. seemed to understand how she felt. He knew what a serious emergency it would take for her to send Jem out of town. But still he had asked no questions. He just made himself available, in case she needed him.

She realized that was why he'd shown up on her doorstep tonight, despite her refusal. He knew she shouldn't be alone.

"Hey," he said gently. "I thought you liked shrimp."

She looked down. Appetizers had appeared and she hadn't even noticed.

"I haven't been fair to you," she said. "I've haven't explained anything."

"We agreed not to talk about our jobs. I'm sure you don't want to hear about the sinuses I cleared today."

"Sinuses won't kill you."

"I don't know. There was this big nasty one—"

"I'm serious, J.P."

"You don't have to explain anything," he said. "I trust you. If you don't tell me, you have a good reason."

She wanted to cry. She knew so much about him. Once she'd realized she might actually love this man, she'd run a complete background check. She knew all about his school days, his career, his wife, who had died in childbirth twenty years ago and whose name he had never so much as mentioned. J.P. had never remarried. He'd devoted his life to raising his daughter, who had just recently graduated from college. Except for the one horrendous tragedy of his wife's death, the man had no secrets, no enemies, no skeletons in the closet.

Erainya's closet, on the other hand, was loaded. There was so much she couldn't tell him.

It was easier to concentrate on the wine and the shrimp Paesano.

The sky darkened. Traffic on Basse subsided to an occasional streak of headlights, the rattlesnake sizzle of tires on wet asphalt.

J.P. twirled his fork in the fettuccine. "Have you told Tres our plans?"

Their plans.

"I haven't said anything," she admitted. "Not yet."

He kept his attention carefully focused on achieving the perfect bite-sized forkful of pasta.

"I'll tell him soon," she said.

"Only if it's still what you want."

He tried to sound casual, but she heard the fragility in his voice. He had opened himself up for emotional hurt, for the first time since his wife's death. The fact that Erainya had so much power over him scared her.

They had agreed to get married in the fall. She would quit working, close the agency. He would provide for her and Jem. He had more money than they would ever need.

Did she really want this?

She only had to look at J.P. to know the answer was yes. No one had ever loved her so much. And the sex . . . well, she'd almost consigned herself to a life of celibacy until J.P. came along. The sex was fantastic.

At first, she had resisted the idea of quitting work. She told herself she needed the job. It was part of her identity. But she believed that less and less.

For a few years after taking over the agency, she'd felt good about the work. She'd been exorcising Fred's spirit, becoming a PI in her own right to prove that she could. But business soon began to go sour, deteriorating into a petty grudge match between her and Barrera.

Despite her way with people, her contacts, her face-to-face talents, she wasn't much of a businesswoman. She hated the Internet, computers, information brokers. She liked the human part of the PI business, and that part was disappearing. She was rapidly becoming a dinosaur.

She'd been contemplating quitting, in fact, the day a young man named Tres Navarre had walked into her office, looking for work. Something about him had reinvigorated her—made her want to teach him the trade. He had made the work interesting again, fresh, good. But now . . . she wanted an escape. She wanted to believe she could slip out from under Fred Barrow's legacy, with Jem safely in her arms, and start a new life at age fifty-one.

Almost as soon as she made that wish, Will Stirman had reappeared in her life.

J.P. pushed his plate aside, took a long drink of wine. "All right. I lied."

Erainya realized she'd been silent too long. "What?"

"I *do* want to know. Let me help. Tell me what's going on."

She wanted to. Her anger at Stirman had faded to a dull ache. Her confidence was starting to slip. The enormous Colt in her purse seemed ridiculous in this elegant restaurant, with the affluent people and the candlelight, the shrimp and fettuccine and wine.

"Not here," she said.

"Will you come back to the house?"

The house. As if there were only one—with the bright yellow lights across the canyon, shining through the rain.

Ten years ago, this quarry had been the poorest neighborhood in San Antonio. Workers' shacks lined dusty roads and dump trucks rumbled back and forth, hauling limestone to the rail depot. Now the quarry was a golf course, a clubhouse, a string of fashionable mansions around the canyon rim. Even the old factory with its smokestacks had been transformed into an upscale shopping center.

The very location of J.P.'s house seemed to suggest that anything was possible.

She decided she would tell him everything. She would postpone her hunt, at least until the morning. And if the worst happened, if Stirman got to her first, she would trust this man—a man she had known for such a short time—to do what was necessary to protect Jem.

"Back to our house," she said. "That would be wonderful."

His smile was the best reward, the only reward, she'd had for days.

A battered white Chevrolet was blocking the alley behind the restaurant. It idled at a crazy angle, headlights illuminating the dumpsters, fender almost kissing J.P.'s Lexus.

The man sitting on the hood was a Latino in his late twenties—lean and muscular, military haircut, beige shorts and a green camp shirt.

Nice legs, Erainya thought absently.

Two glasses of '97 Brunello had taken the edge off her apprehension. It was hard to think about danger when J.P.'s arm was around her.

The young man looked at them sheepishly. It didn't take Erainya long to see why. There was a deep gash in J.P.'s car door. The sideview mirror had been sheared off.

Erainya had warned J.P. not to park back here. The lane was too narrow, squeezed between the restaurant and the golf course fence, and it was completely shielded from sight, perfect for car thieves. But the front lot had been full, the alley was convenient, and J.P. cared as little about parking conventions as he did wine prices.

"I'm sorry, sir," the young man said. "I was trying to get around the dumpster."

He turned up his palms, revealing a crucifix tattoo on his inner arm.

The guy obviously wasn't a Paesano's customer. Probably an off-duty waiter, worried he'd get fired for bashing the Lexus.

J.P. looked pained. He knelt down to examine the damage. "Well, it's fixable, anyway."

"Really sorry," the man said again. "Hope we can solve this without insurance."

"I doubt you want to do that," J.P. said. "Probably looking at a few thousand dollars."

Erainya decided the young man wasn't a waiter. Something about his tattoo was wrong, and the way he held himself—not really sheepish, after all. He was coiled like a spring, as if he were used to watching his back. He was staring at her, almost like he was trying to warn her of something.

"You'll have to talk to my boss," the young man said.

He slid off the hood of the Chevrolet and stepped aside.

Erainya realized, too late, what was wrong about him. He moved like a convict.

The Chevrolet's back door opened.

The man who stepped out was tall, with a triangle of black

hair, dark glasses, an expensive leather jacket and pale, pale skin.

He said, "Change of plans, Mrs. Barrow."

The name froze her.

She should have reached for her Colt, but her hand wouldn't obey. She watched the glint of the man's pistol as it emerged from his leather jacket.

J.P. said, "No."

Erainya tried to warn him, to stop him, but he stepped in front of her, shielding her. The gun fired.

The bullet ripped through the white broadcloth above his belt. Erainya wanted to scream. She wanted to move. But the Colt in her purse might as well have been at home.

J.P. crumpled to his knees.

And Will Stirman turned, pointing his gun at the center of her chest.

14

The last person I wanted to find in the Brooke Army Medical Center waiting area was a homicide detective.

Ana DeLeon was leaning against the reception desk, talking to a couple of uniforms and another plainclothes detective.

She might've been mistaken for a young professional—a hospital administrator being hit on by the three male cops—unless you noticed the sergeant's badge clipped to her belt, or the shoulder holster under her blue silk blazer. Or unless you knew, like every guy in SAPD, that the last cop who tried to hit on Ana DeLeon pulled desk duty for a month and still had trouble sitting down without pain.

She saw me approaching, told her colleagues something on the order of: *Here comes Navarre. Get lost or I'll make you talk to him.*

They got lost.

"I stayed at the office until seven last night," she told me. "I keep wondering—if you'd showed, would we be here now?"

"What's the word?"

"No change in condition. And no leads on the shooter, unless you're bringing me something."

I used to have a martial arts instructor who could press his hand very softly on the center of my chest, and no amount of effort could dislodge him. I'd swear he was barely making contact, but after thirty seconds, his touch left a bruise. DeLeon's eyes were like that.

"I'm going upstairs," I told her.

"No visiting hours for ICU."

"The hell with visiting hours."

She studied my face. "I suppose I'll chaperone, in case you need arresting."

After a few conversations with nurses and some badge-waving from DeLeon, we were admitted to the gunshot ward.

J. P. Sanchez lay cocooned in linen and bandages, hooked up to so many tubes and monitors the machines seemed to be feeding off him rather than keeping him alive. His eyes were bruised, his skin as gray as his hair.

"They're trying to stabilize him," DeLeon told me. "They'll do another round of surgery if he makes it through the night."

"Did he talk at all?"

"Tres, he flat-lined in the ambulance. He wasn't in a talkative mood."

I touched the guardrail of his bed. Even through the hospital odors, I could smell his cologne.

I imagined his wry smile. *Give me a chance, Tres.*

"Come on." DeLeon's hand gripped my shoulder. "Buy me coffee."

She steered me toward the elevator.

In the hospital food court, I was vaguely aware of the other plainclothes detective—an Anglo guy built like a linebacker—falling in behind us. He kept his distance, out of earshot.

I bought two tall coffees. DeLeon and I took a corner booth. I drank while DeLeon emptied sugar packets into her cup, three at a time.

"That'll kill you," I told her.

"I've been promised faster deaths." She stirred, sipped without even making a face. "So where is Stirman?"

"Ask your Fugitive Task Force."

"Yesterday, you said he was in town."

I stared into my coffee.

My day had begun with Folgers and goat's milk, prepared by a blind woman on a ranch. Here it was evening, and I felt like I was still drinking from the same cup, no wiser than I had been before.

Erainya was missing. An innocent man was upstairs dying. Sam Barrera was cracking under stress. And I'd been asked to tell the police nothing.

"Around five this evening," DeLeon said, "patrol got a call. One of Erainya's neighbors reported seeing her in her front yard with a gun. She was pointing it at Dr. Sanchez. Then Sanchez calmed her down. They left together before patrol could get there. Two hours later, we found Sanchez bleeding to death behind Paesano's. Erainya was missing. One possibility: She shot her boyfriend and fled."

"That's absurd."

"It's also Major Cooper's working theory." She nodded toward the linebacker, who sat two tables away, feigning interest in the bluebonnet paintings.

"Major," I said. "That's a Department of Criminal Justice rank."

"Fugitive Task Force," she said. "I asked him to come with me. Just in case you had something to say. For the record, Major Cooper does not believe Stirman would stay in San Antonio."

"He wants a few more people to die?"

"He needs convincing."

I tried to look her in the eyes, but it was damn uncomfortable.

In the year since I'd seen her last, her face had filled out. Her skin had taken on that healthy glow you see in new mothers, her hair cut short to keep little baby hands from grabbing fistfuls.

She seemed more confident, balanced. Maybe that came from the marriage, or the baby, or the promotion. I didn't know. The fact that I didn't know made me sad.

I told her about my encounter with Stirman at the soccer field, the videotape he'd sent to Barrera, the McCurdy Ranch, Barrera's admission that Stirman had been framed.

DeLeon listened, and drank her coffee. I knew she was mentally recording every statement.

"Gerry Far," she said, "the informant who sold out Stirman eight years ago. We found him this morning—or what was left of him—floating in the San Antonio River. I called the FBI. They weren't impressed. A guy like Far makes lots of enemies, they told me. Even if Stirman *did* kill him, he did it days ago, on his way north. Their most recent reliable sighting places Stirman last night in Kansas. They get a hundred leads a day, all of them north. Since the Oklahoma City shooting, every crime from Colorado to Missouri, some jittery witness decides he saw the Floresville Five. I'm just another paranoid local cop, in the city where Stirman's least likely to be."

"Stirman's here. I didn't imagine him."

"You want me to call Major Cooper over?"

"So he can dismiss me as paranoid, too?"

"Cooper's good. Best they've got on the state task force. He's skeptical Stirman would be so stupid as to stay here, but he's willing to listen."

"If the manhunt moves here in force, the media will find out. They'll broadcast it. Stirman will feel the net closing. He'll disappear."

"Not if we do it quickly and quietly."

We locked eyes. I wondered if she believed her own words. With a media circus like the Floresville Five, there was no way to handle it quickly or quietly. Every law enforcement officer in the state would want a piece. Catching Will Stirman would be like chasing a speedboat with an aircraft carrier.

"Stirman won't bother with a hostage if he's forced to run," I said. "Erainya will die."

"If she's not already dead. I'm sorry, Tres."

I shook my head. "If he wanted Erainya dead, he would've left her in that alley along with Sanchez. He took her alive. She's got something he wants."

DeLeon stared at the elevator doors.

"You told me there were rumors," I said. "About the night Stirman was arrested."

"Maybe I didn't give you the worst version."

"How much worse can it be?"

"After Stirman was shot, he was ranting in the hospital, okay? A couple of cops who were guarding him heard the whole story. For one thing, Stirman claimed the PIs had stolen his money. He was this low-tech guy, you understand. Didn't trust bank accounts or computers. He said he was about to leave on a chartered jet with two duffel bags full of cash. The PIs supposedly took the money."

"Assuming it existed, how much would we be talking about?"

"Don't know. How much could you fit in two large black duffel bags?"

"Jesus."

I remembered Stirman at the soccer field, his barely restrained rage as he looked down at Jem. *Tell your mother— She knows what I want. She'd best give it back.*

"There's more," DeLeon said.

"The woman who died was his wife."

DeLeon looked momentarily impressed. "Yes, but not just that. Stirman claimed the PIs didn't only shoot her. They shot their baby."

I stared at her.

DeLeon curled her fingers over the stack of torn sugar packets on the table. "There was no baby at the scene. No sign there had ever been one. But according to Stirman, the mother and child were both killed. Maybe accidentally. Barrow and Barrera let Stirman almost bleed to death while they destroyed the evidence and toted away the cash. There was no cash at the scene when the police arrived."

"Did anybody believe Stirman's story?"

"Why should they? Cons say shit about their captors all the time. Of course, Stirman also claimed he was innocent of supplying the women to McCurdy's ranch. Nobody believed that, either."

"Killing a child doesn't sound like Sam Barrera's style."

"Neither does framing somebody."

I glanced over at Major Cooper, who was still admiring the bluebonnet pictures. "Why hide a child's death and not the mother's?"

"Killing an illegal immigrant woman is one thing," DeLeon said. "Killing an infant—that's something else. Even the shittiest public defender could make use of that in Stirman's trial. Let's say Barrow or Barrera panicked. One stray bullet. You've just murdered a child. You're going to live with that on your conscience forever. As soon as the media find out, you'll be publicly crucified. You can guess what happens. We get a dozen cases like this every year. The child's body conveniently disappears. A lot easier to conceal that kind of murder than the death of an adult."

I wanted to say it wasn't possible.

Then I remembered Barrera's haunted look as he toured the McCurdy Ranch, as if he needed to remind himself there'd been justification for what he and Barrow had done.

Erainya had killed Fred Barrow only a few weeks after Stirman's arrest. Fred had been treating her like dirt for years. Maybe something besides the abuse had made her snap—some new proof Fred Barrow was a monster.

"No cop wants to believe a guy like Stirman," DeLeon said. "None of them spread these rumors outside the department. By the time Stirman got to trial, he'd gone tight-lipped. He never mentioned the dead child or the money again. Like he'd already started planning his own revenge. But if you're wondering why Barrera and your boss weren't anxious to bring in the police . . ."

"Give me a few hours," I said. "Let me talk to Barrera."

"Major Cooper is willing to listen now. He might not believe you, but if he gets the idea later that you held back information—"

"I could deal with Stirman more effectively my way."

"You mean Ralph's way."

I didn't say anything. I didn't need to tell her about her husband's track record for finding his enemies, or what he did with them afterward. I knew she wouldn't want Ralph to have any part of this.

She sipped her coffee, no doubt trying to contain her anger. "Tres . . . if somebody killed my baby . . . I wouldn't care how much money they stole from me or where they hid it. Do you understand? I wouldn't trust myself to keep them alive long enough to find out. And this is me talking, the law-abiding one. When I think about how somebody like my husband might react . . ."

She didn't finish the thought. She didn't need to.

"Just a couple of hours," I said. "I'll call you tonight."

She looked at Major Cooper, two tables away. She shook her head.

"You didn't see what Gerry Far looked like when we pulled him out of the river, Tres." She slid out from the booth, pulled on her raincoat. "For Erainya's sake, don't wait too long."

When I got home to 90 Queen Anne, the two-story crafts-man was dark except for my little in-law apartment on the side. Rainwater streamed down the driveway, carrying away petals from my landlord's purple sages and blue plumbagos.

Sam Barrera waited on my stoop in the glow of the porch light. He was catching moths and shaking them like dice.

"We need to talk," he said.

"It'll cost you."

Sam studied me.

I tried to remember if I'd ever seen him with a five-o'clock shadow before, or with his tie loosened.

He said, "Cost me?"

"Yes, sir, yes, sir. Two bags full."

He released his moth, watched it flutter up the side of the screen door. "So you know."

In my younger days, I would've hauled off and decked him, but I'd mellowed over the years. Now I was perfectly willing to breathe deep, thinking rationally, and invest the few extra minutes it would take to invite him inside, find a gun, load it, and shoot him.

"*Mi casa es tu casa,*" I told him.

I unlocked the front door, just missed stepping on the dead mouse Robert Johnson had left for me on the carpet.

The offending feline sat smugly on the kitchen counter. He had one paw in the middle of his empty food dish. A subtle hint.

"Nice to see you, too," I said.

I cleaned up the present and filled Robert Johnson's dish with tortilla chips and flaked tuna.

Sam Barrera made the grand tour of my apartment. That takes about thirty seconds. Once you've seen the futon and the built-in ironing board and the tai chi sword rack above the toilet, you've pretty much seen it all.

"Talk," I told Barrera. "If I have to ask, the bathroom sword is coming unsheathed."

Barrera sat down on the futon. He opened that annoying notepad of his.

"Sam, it's not a lecture," I said. "Put away the notes."

"Fourteen million dollars," he said, quietly.

I set down the tuna can. "Fourteen million."

"How much we stole. Yeah."

My fingers felt numb. I wanted to say that was a hell of a lot of money. Large change. A truckload of kitty nachos. Two big goddamn duffel bags. All I could say was "Damn."

"Stirman called an hour ago," Barrera said. "He wants an exchange for Erainya. Tomorrow night. Any police involvement, she dies."

"Great," I said. "That's fucking great, Sam. So we just hop over to Stop-N-Go with our ATM cards, and we've got it covered."

"I don't have any money. I used my half to build up I-Tech a long time ago. I don't know what Erainya did with Fred's share. She sure as hell didn't put it into the agency."

"Erainya's been scraping for money ever since I've known her. She's got no hidden cash."

"She had to know."

I thought about the note to Erainya from H., telling her the package from Fred was safe.

"She would've turned it in," I said, trying to believe it. *"You should've turned it in."*

"We had to take it," Sam said. "Stirman would've paid for the best defense. That kind of cash . . . we didn't even trust the cops. Stirman had friends in the department, in the state attorney's office. We didn't want any chance he'd get off the hook. There was no choice."

"Doing your civic duty," I said. "A real self-sacrifice. What about Stirman's baby, Sam? Was there no choice on that, too?"

His eyes took on the kind of deadness I was used to seeing in victims of violence, or collared criminals.

"We didn't mean to," he said.

Rain rattled at the window screens.

Robert Johnson pushed his food dish around.

I tried to think of something to say—some condemnation strong enough.

The phone rang. I pulled the ironing board away from the wall.

Sam said, "You've got a phone behind your ironing board."

"You must be a detective." I reached into the alcove, which had been constructed by some day-tripping carpenter in the sixties, and picked up the receiver. "Tres Navarre."

Silence.

Then Will Stirman's voice said: "Shitty little apartment, Navarre. Can't she afford to pay you better?"

I snapped my fingers to get Barrera's attention, but I'd lost him. He was still staring at the ironing board, trying to come to terms with the phone's unorthodox location.

"Put Erainya on, Stirman," I said. "Let me hear she's okay."

He ignored my request. "Instructions: I'll call Barrera's mobile number tomorrow evening, around midnight. I'll tell you where to bring the money. You, Sam and Erainya's boy. Nobody else."

"You think I'm going to bring Jem anywhere near you, you've been locked up in the wrong kind of institution."

There was a pause I didn't like at all. "We'll all be better behaved with the kid around. A lot less anxious for the guns to come out."

There was something about his tone I couldn't quite nail down. What the hell did he want with Jem?

"Nothing that happened to you was Erainya's fault," I said. "It damn sure wasn't her son's."

I looked out the dark windows. Stirman could be on the street right now. Or in the alley. He could've cased my place days ago.

"Mr. Navarre," he said, "eight years ago there was another mother and child. They hadn't done anything, either. I won't hurt the Manoses, as long as you and Mr. Barrow don't disappoint me."

"What makes you think the money is still around, or that I can get it?"

"You're a resourceful young man. And Mr. Navarre, be smart. If I get indications you have talked to the police, it will go very hard on you and everyone you care about. And don't think Austin is far enough away."

He hung up.

Robert Johnson leapt onto the ironing board. He pushed his back against my hand. I wanted to think he was consoling me. More likely, he was reminding me that he liked dessert after tuna nachos.

"Well?" Sam asked.

I told him the details. "How much cash could you raise?"

"If I liquidated everything? Took everything out of savings? I don't know. Nowhere near three million."

"Seven," I said.

"What?"

"Your half was seven million."

He kept his hand on his notepad, as if it were a railing.

"Right," he said. "That's what I meant."

"Where would Fred Barrow stash his loot?"

"Doesn't matter," Sam said. "The money won't save us. Stirman will kill her. We have to find him before tomorrow night. We have to get to him first."

For once, I agreed with him.

"I have to call Maia," I said. "I need to tell her . . ."

What?

Sorry, honeybun—the psychopath knows where you live. Don't forget your AK-47 when you take Jem to the playground.

"We'll figure something out," Barrera told me. "We'll talk on the way."

"The way to where?"

"Castroville."

I stared at him. "What?"

"The McCurdy Ranch. I'm supposed to take you there."

The air thickened around me.

"Sam," I said, "we already went to Castroville . . . this morning."

He hesitated a couple of heartbeats. "I just meant . . . That's what I said. This morning."

I stepped around the ironing board, sat down across from him. "Sam, let me see your notebook."

He didn't move.

I took the notebook out of his hands.

Inside, meticulous notes—where Barrera worked, directions to his house, who he had called that day. Addresses. Phone numbers. Names—his secretary Alicia, Erainya Manos, Will Stirman. Descriptions of each person. My name, with a small notation: *Erainya's PI. Be careful about him.*

"Sam," I said, "do you know who I am?"

His eyes were watery with frustration. "Of course I do."

"What's my name?"

He glanced at his empty lap. "I never forget a name. The whole damn case is in the details."

"When were you diagnosed, Sam?"

Barrera stared at the wall, his jaw tightening. "I'm fine. They gave me some pills."

"Do you remember what happened, the night you took down Will Stirman?"

A long silence. "There was something . . . something important . . ."

He gazed across the room, helpless.

"We're going to get through this, Sam." My voice didn't sound like my own. "I'm going to help you, okay?"

"I don't need any help."

"Are you better in the mornings?"

"Yeah. I'm fine in the mornings."

"I'm going to drive you home then, and keep your car for the night. I want you to sleep. We'll talk tomorrow."

"Damn it," Barrera said. "Goddamn it."

He pushed away my hand, and got up by himself.

We took our second ride together in his mustard-colored BMW.

As the windshield wipers slashed back and forth, I realized I was going to need other help finding Stirman fast.

I was going to have to call on an old friend. A friend I'd rarely called for help without somebody ending up dead.

15

Just before the news hit the networks, the Guide called Will from Omaha to warn him.

Luis and Elroy had fucked up.

The Guide had told them to steal a new set of wheels. He didn't give a shit what kind. Anything from the Target parking lot across the road. A van would be good. Tinted windows, for sure.

It wasn't a fucking calculus problem.

The Guide told them to fill up with gas and meet him back at the motel. They only had to go, like, two blocks. Shouldn't have taken them more than fifteen, twenty minutes.

Luis and Elroy ended up boosting a Toyota Sienna—two child seats in the back, the whole floor littered with Cheerios and juice boxes and trading cards. It was parked on the side of the store, nice and secluded. Doors weren't locked. Might as well put a STEAL ME sign in the window.

But did they notice the FOP sticker? Did they know that stood for Fraternal Order of Police? Fuck no.

Apparently what happened, the police officer's wife came out with her kids, saw her van driving away without her, and cell-phoned her husband. Must have happened that fast, because in a matter of minutes the whole fucking Omaha Police Department knew some stupid shits had stolen an officer's car, and every unit in the area was closing in.

If Luis and Elroy had gotten straight on Highway 64, they might've had a chance, but no—they were supposed to fill up the van with gas, so they parked a block away at the pumps of a gas station—the most obvious fucking target in the world.

Back at the motel, the Guide heard the first dry crack of gunfire.

How it happened: Luis went into the Exxon store for a six-pack of cherry Coke and some candy. He was thinking jelly beans, maybe red licorice.

"You're a fucking kid," Elroy told him. "How about some beer?"

Luis grinned. "You want them carding this baby face?"

He went inside to get his sweets while Elroy worked the pump.

It was a big goddamn gas tank, so Elroy had time to watch the clouds scraping by overhead. There were hills in Omaha. Tall pine trees. Parks with lakes. Elroy never would've figured that in Nebraska.

He watched a big military plane lumbering toward the horizon, and he thought about C.C.

He missed the scrawny bastard's smart remarks. He missed his tough-guy act, his stupid Italian suit and matching pistols. C.C. had been a time bomb, sure, but he'd kept things upbeat. He'd believed they would make it to freedom. Another week, C.C. had told them, and they'd all be partying in Alberta, screwing some Canadian chicks. Now, C.C. was six hundred miles south, under a foot of red earth, food for Oklahoma worms.

Night before last, in a Kansas trailer park, Luis and Elroy had held a kind of memorial.

While the Guide retired inside the rented Winnebago, they had lit a barbecue fire and got drunker than hell, cooking up brisket and talking about C.C.

Elroy took Luis down to the creek, where they shot the bow-and-arrow set Elroy stole in Oklahoma City.

Then they realized they'd have to find the arrows, so they tromped around in the dark and collected a few until they heard a rattlesnake and ran like shit back to the picnic table. They laughed about it afterward, their hearts pounding, and Elroy felt good for the first time since C.C. died.

But they couldn't keep up their spirits. The Guide was always close by, always giving orders. He looked at them like they were heavy, worthless packages he didn't really want to deliver—the same way he'd looked at C.C., bleeding to death in front of that sporting goods store.

Nobody leaves the group.

Walking to Target, Luis had told Elroy, "We can make it the rest of the way, *ese.*"

"You mean without *him*?"

"Fuck him," Luis said. "We steal a car, head north our own damn selves. What do you say?"

Elroy understood why Luis hated the Guide. The Guide was a flesh smuggler, same as Stirman. Probably killed more Mexicans in his life than he'd killed flies. Be like asking Elroy to trust a Klansman.

But Elroy was doubtful. He wanted a new identity, money to start a life, all those things the Guide had promised. He didn't trust the Guide or Stirman worth a shit, but Elroy *had* to get to Canada—for C.C.'s sake, as well as his own.

Here at the Exxon station, this was the moment to decide. As soon as the tank was full, as soon as Luis came out of the store, they could either go up the block to the motel, or they could get on the highway.

Elroy wanted to find a good woman to marry. He wanted to buy a decent house, join an old-fashioned gospel church.

Not that he believed his soul could be saved. He knew better than that. Since the day he drove his fist through that racist foreman's nose out in the oil fields of West Texas, Elroy had accepted the fact his temper would damn him to hell.

But he wanted to get a job, have some kids. Maybe if he raised a couple of children right, that would count for something. He could have his own van with Cheerios and juice boxes in the back. He could take his kids into woods, somewhere up north where the wilderness went on forever, and teach them to shoot a bow. They'd buy an endless supply of arrows, so they'd never have to go looking for them, just shoot them into the sky and watch them disappear.

Elroy didn't hear the police car pulling up behind him until the doors opened.

A cop's voice on the bullhorn: "Driver of the Sienna van. Put both hands slowly on top of your head. Do it now."

Elroy turned.

The policeman yelled, "Do not turn around. Put your hands on your head. Do it now!"

There were two of them, shielded by their car doors, guns drawn and pointed at him. No way could Elroy reach the gun tucked in his jeans, under his shirt.

He started to raise his hands, but he kept hold of the pump nozzle, still squeezing so it came out of the tank gushing. Gasoline sprayed up the side of the van, toward the cops.

That bought him a half second. They weren't expecting it.

Elroy dropped the nozzle and ducked around the front of the van. He hoped the cops knew better than to shoot at high-octane fuel. One of them fired anyway. The shot sparked off the fuel door. Elroy crouched against the front bumper, breathing heavy. He pulled his gun.

He weighed the odds of running, and didn't like them much. He saw Luis come out of the convenience store, a plastic grocery bag under one arm and a gun in the other.

Before Elroy could say anything, Luis let loose a full clip at the police car.

Then Luis jerked back. The glass behind him spiderwebbed. A hole ripped through his grocery bag, then another—cherry Coke and jelly beans dribbling down his shirt.

Elroy thought about his imaginary children, shooting arrows into the sky. He thought about Floresville State, the death sentence that was waiting for him.

Maybe Luis had nailed at least one of the cops. Maybe there would only be one left.

He raised his gun and charged around the side of the van, straight into crossfire from the second and third police cars, which had just pulled up.

Elroy didn't have time to marvel at his bad luck.

He smelled gasoline turning to flame, and the world erupted like a full blast of Texas summer sun.

The Guide pulled out of the motel in a stolen Honda Accord. He could see the black smoke boiling, a couple of blocks away.

The dragnet was already going up, but he eased past the scene at the gas station long enough to get the idea what had happened. The cops stopped him. His Nebraska driver's license was valid. They didn't bother checking his registration. He didn't look like anyone they wanted.

He got on the highway and headed in no particular direction—just away.

Eventually, the police would check motel records. They would get an ID on Elroy and Luis and wonder about the third

man who'd checked in with them—who didn't quite match
Will Stirman's description. They would start wondering where
Stirman had gone.

"We're even," the Guide told Will over the phone. "I'm gonna
disappear for a while."

"You promised me a week," Will reminded him. "I need a full
week."

Nothing on the line but the hum of the highway.

Will felt his old friend's disapproval. Will should have left the
country already. He'd had plenty of time. It shouldn't take him a
week to tie up his loose ends.

"You sure you're thinking straight, Will?" the Guide asked.

Will had trained this bastard. He had saved his life once on
the border.

"You sent them out on purpose, didn't you?" Will asked. "You
knew they couldn't handle anything alone. You knew something like this would happen."

"We're even," the Guide repeated. "And Will? That emergency account I set up? Don't try to withdraw any cash, you
hear? I emptied it."

The line went dead, and Will shattered the phone against the
warehouse's brick wall.

He threw the iron bolt on the storage room door. Inside,
Erainya Manos was sitting cross-legged on an old mattress, her
hands no longer tied behind her back. She was eating chicken
soup out of a can.

Pablo sat by the window, thumbing a *Sports Illustrated,* his
gun and portable radio on the table next to him. The news was
just coming on: *"Breaking story in Omaha, a possible connection
to the Floresville Five—"*

Will turned it off.

"Hey," Pablo complained.

"You heard enough news about yourself."

"What's your problem?"

"What's my problem?" Will repeated. "Who told you to untie her hands?"

"She's got to eat."

"Then spoon-feed her."

"Fuck that."

Will went over to Erainya Manos and slapped the soup can out of her hands.

She didn't even blink. She gave him a look of pure black hate. She held up her spoon, like she was inviting him to slap that away, too.

"Your memory any better today?" he asked.

"I don't have your goddamn money. You're wasting your time."

If she'd shown any weakness, Will couldn't have held back from hitting her. Her anger saved her. That, and the doubt that had started to creep into his gut, the feeling that maybe he'd read things wrong. Perhaps very wrong.

"Put down the fucking magazine," he told Pablo. "Pick up your gun and keep it on her."

Will yanked the woman's wrists behind her back and tied them.

He looked at Pablo. "She stays that way, understand? I'll be back in a couple of hours."

"When do I get to eat? That soup was it."

"When I get some money, you get to eat." And then, sensing rebellion, Will forced himself to add: "A few more days, Pablo. You'll be loving on your wife again. Patience."

Will could tell Pablo wanted to believe him. That was all that mattered. Even a slim hope would keep him in line a little longer. As soon as the money came through from Barrera and Navarre . . . Stirman would figure out the rest.

He walked out, conscious of their eyes on his back. The concrete floor felt spongy under his feet.

Maybe it was the lack of food. How long had it been since he ate? Fourteen million dollars coming, and he didn't have ten bucks for a meal.

From the milk crate by the loading dock entrance, he took a 9mm and a clip of ammunition.

He didn't know where he was going. He didn't have a plan.

For the first time since the Fourth of July, Will thought about his Floresville cell, his Bible sketches blowing in the fan breeze.

You were better off in that cage, he thought. *You're falling apart.*

No. He could keep himself together. He had to, or eight years of praying for vengeance went for nothing. Just a brief errand, now. Something to clear his head.

He tucked the 9mm under his shirt and went out to find cash and food.

Erainya pretended to sleep for almost an hour. She waited for Pablo to nod off, but it was too much to hope for, even though he'd been guarding her all night and half the morning.

After a while, Pablo turned back on Texas Public Radio. Under different circumstances, this would've struck Erainya as funny. A con who liked the Diane Rehm show.

Pablo listened dutifully as Diane refereed a debate between a Catholic priest and a Buddhist monk on the sanctity of marriage. Still Pablo didn't snooze. The guy was made of iron.

A newsbreak came on: two fugitives shot dead in Omaha. Identification was pending, but the men were believed to be

part of the Floresville Five. Police were confident more appre-
hensions in the case were imminent.

Erainya opened her eyes just enough to watch Pablo's
face.

He stared at the wall.

He got up, paced, and turned toward Erainya.

She closed her eyes, willing herself to breathe deeply.

She heard the big iron door creak open. Pablo walked into
the next room.

She wouldn't get a better chance.

Stirman had been angry when he retied her, which made for
sloppy knots. Her fingers had spent the last hour carefully ex-
ploring them. She worked herself the rest of the way free with
little problem.

She'd tried to keep her legs from going to sleep, but they
were sore and stiff when she tried to stand. She wasn't going to
be running anytime soon.

She could hide. She'd been staring at the loose ventilation
grate in the corner. It looked big enough to crawl inside, if she
could just move it. But there wasn't time, it wouldn't be quiet,
and she didn't know if the shaft led anywhere.

Only one other option, even riskier.

What kept her going was the memory of J.P. getting shot. Her
anger braided around her spine like an iron coil.

Pablo's gun was sitting on the table. She heard him in the
next room, rummaging around.

Move, she told herself.

She grabbed the gun and walked to the door.

Pablo was kneeling over a milk crate. He was holding a
phone, cursing as he tried to dial a number.

Shoot him, she told herself.

She aimed.

This one, Pablo, she didn't hate enough.

He hadn't pulled the trigger on J.P. She could see in his eyes he hated Stirman as much as she did. He'd fed her soup.

So fucking what? Shoot!

Then he turned and saw her. His eyes got small.

"Put it down," he told her. "I don't want to hurt you."

"I've got the gun, Pablo."

He took a step toward her. "No bullets in it."

She aimed at the center of his chest.

He took another step and she squeezed the trigger.

Nothing happened.

He grabbed her wrist. She managed to punch him in the nose—a weak effort, but enough to loosen his grip. She made it a few steps toward the stairs before he tackled her and dragged her back into her cell.

She screamed, but there was no one to hear.

He flung her onto the mattress, stood over her, breathing heavy, dabbing his bloody nose. On the radio, Diane Rehm was talking about trusting your spouse.

Erainya felt like crying, but she held on to her anger.

She sat up, touched the back of her head where it had struck the wall.

After a long time, she asked Pablo, "Those were your friends who died in Omaha?"

For a moment, he became that young man in the alley behind Paesano's again—a contrite, harmless kid. "One of them . . . my cousin . . . if he's really dead."

"You've been keeping in touch," she guessed. "You just tried to call him."

Pablo didn't answer.

"Stirman wouldn't approve," she persisted. "Little harder to trace mobile calls, but they can do it. They find your cousin's

phone, honey, they find out he's been making calls to San
Antonio—"

"Shut up."

"Time's running out."

"Just give Stirman his money, and nobody's going to hurt
you. Do that, we're gone."

"I don't have the money."

"Cooperate, lady. You could go home. So could I."

"You believe that, Pablo? Is that what Stirman promised
your friends in Omaha?"

Blood trickled from his nostril. Pablo didn't seem to notice.

If Erainya could just get him on her side . . .

"Honey," she said, more gently, "what were you in prison
for?"

Pablo studied her warily, as if he were afraid she'd make fun
of him. "I killed a man."

"You're not a natural killer. What did this man do?"

"He was . . . I came home, and he was with my wife."

Aha, she thought. *Keep him talking. Be his friend.*

"You still want her back?" she asked. "Will she still be waiting?"

Erainya realized she'd made a mistake when she saw the
anger in his eyes.

"She didn't do anything," he said tightly. "They were talking
on the bed, but . . . it wasn't what I thought."

"Okay, honey," Erainya said, trying to placate him. "So what
happened?"

Pablo looked at his gun. "Couple of weeks, Angelina had
been spending money, going out at weird times. Then a neighbor saw this guy come over to the house twice while I was at
work. I came home with a shotgun one night . . . but it wasn't
what I thought. She'd hired a private eye. Somebody like you.
Angelina had lost her family coming across the Rio Grande

years ago, see. She hired this guy to find them. Didn't think I'd approve of her spending the money. That's why she didn't tell me."

"You shot the PI."

"No, see . . . the PI had some luck." He closed his eyes. When he spoke again, his voice was heavier, chained with guilt. "Angelina had just started meeting this guy he'd located. They were in the bedroom looking at Angelina's photos. They were talking about old times, trying to figure out what happened to their mother. The man I shot was Angelina's brother."

Diane Rehm's grandmotherly voice filled the room. Sunlight pulsed through the cracks in the boarded-up windows, heating the air like steamed cotton.

Despite the fact that Pablo was holding a gun, Erainya felt so bad for the young man that she had a sudden urge to put a handkerchief to his bleeding nose, the way she would do for Jem.

"Honey," she said, "does your wife want you back?"

He blinked. "She'll meet me in Mexico. I wrote her what to do. If she read the letters . . ."

Erainya looked away.

She knew his plans for a happy ending were nothing but smoke. He would never see his wife again. He would be gunned down, or die on Death Row.

"You'll see her," she lied. "But don't wait for Stirman. Even if he gets his money, he won't let either of us go home. This is the only chance we're going to get, Pablo. Your wife wants you back."

She thought she had him, until he pulled a clip of ammo from his pocket and slid it into the gun.

"Shut up," he told her again, softly. "Just shut up."

This time, his eyes told her she'd better do it.

She saw the capacity for rage that had put him in jail. She saw he was capable of murder.

The news came back on—unconfirmed reports from a source close to the investigation: The Floresville Five may not have stayed together as previously thought.

Pablo leaned forward to listen. His newly loaded gun cast a long shadow across the cement.

16

After dropping off Sam Barrera, I spent hours rifling through Erainya's house, looking for seven million dollars.

I opened every locked drawer in Fred Barrow's office. I wiggled every stone in the fireplace. I poked random holes in the walls and dug around behind the Sheetrock. I was rewarded with a 1963 phone book and a Jax beer bottle.

In desperation, I even went through Erainya's bedroom closet.

For a guy, even a private eye, there is nothing more disconcerting than looking through the bedroom closet of a woman you respect. You just never know what you'll find that might ruin her image.

I found nothing incriminating. Not even the dominatrix suit I'd long suspected Erainya might own.

On second thought, perhaps that did ruin my image of her a bit.

I ended the evening with a tequila bottle, doing my thinking and drinking on top of the Olmos Dam—something I hadn't done in a very long time. The last time I'd been there, the water level hadn't been nipping the soles of my shoes.

I tried to concentrate on Erainya, but my mind kept coming back to Sam Barrera, the perplexed look he'd given me from his living room window as I'd driven off in his BMW.

The old curmudgeon probably had family somewhere who could look after him. The fact that he lived alone, that he had absolutely no photographs of relatives in his house . . . Forget it. I had other problems.

I chunked a rock into the flooded basin. It made a deep *sploosh*.

My father, Bexar County Sheriff Jackson Navarre, had been a contemporary of Barrera and Barrow. He hadn't lived as long. One summer when I was home from college, my dad had been gunned down in front of my eyes by a drive-by shooter, an assassin hired by one of his enemies. At the time, I'd gotten a lot of support and sympathy from my friends. Nobody could imagine going through anything so terrible.

But in the last few years, something funny had happened. My older friends' parents had started aging. Now, many of them were dealing with their parents' cancer, dementia, Parkinson's, assisted living nightmares. When my friends talked to me about these problems, I could swear they were giving me wistful looks, suppressing a guilty kind of resentment.

I would never have to go through what they were going through. I wouldn't have that lingering hell to deal with. My dad had died quickly, still in his prime. My mom—well, she was much younger. She never seemed to age. She had told me many times that she intended to go off a cliff in a red sports car as soon as she began doubting her own faculties, and I had no doubt she was telling the truth.

My friends didn't have quite so much sympathy for Tres Navarre these days. I'd had it pretty easy when it came to parents. Death in a drive-by? Piece of cake. In fact my last argument with Ralph Arguello—almost two years ago, after the death of his mother—had been along those lines. But the more I saw of what my friends with aging parents went through, the more I tended to agree—I'd had it easy.

Which didn't explain why I felt so damn empty, or why Sam Barrera's unraveling bothered me so much.

I took another swig of Herradura Añejo.

I stayed on the dam, watching emergency lights flash all across the city, until a National Guard patrol came by and chased me off.

I probably would've slept through the rest of July had the phone not woken me up the next morning.

I opened my eyes. There was a cat on my head. Sunlight was baking my mouth.

Much to Robert Johnson's displeasure, I crawled off the futon, made it to the ironing board, and yanked down the receiver. "Yeah."

"Oh . . ." A female voice, on the edge of panic. "Coach Navarre, I didn't expect you to be home . . ."

Several things went through my head.

First: Where the hell else would I be at—Jesus, did the clock really say ten?

Second: Why was this woman calling me *coach*?

Behind the caller, children were screaming. Then it hit me. I realized why she was close to panic. It was Thursday morning. Jem's summer school volunteer soccer coach was late to practice again.

"Crap," I said. "I mean darn. Um . . . Mrs. . . ."

"Toca," she said. "Carmen's mother? If you can't make it today, I suppose I can watch the children . . ." A pregnant pause—letting me imagine torture with soccer cones, mass destruction in the goalie's box. "But the first game is Saturday. I didn't know if you had the uniforms . . ."

Uniforms. Damn.

Game. Damn.

In my mind, my commitment to soccer had ceased as soon as

Jem wasn't able to make practice anymore. Apparently, I'd forgotten to share that assessment with the other fifteen players and their families.

I should have taken up Mrs. Toca's offer to watch the kids. I could make up an emergency excuse. Like I didn't have an emergency excuse.

Ma'am, there's an escaped fugitive I have to kill. Just tell the kids to work on their passing.

But I heard the team yelling behind her, and the primal fear closing up her throat as she pleaded, "Coach . . . ?"

"I'll be there in five minutes."

"Oh, okay," her voice quavered. "Thank God. I mean, we'll see you in five minutes."

She either hung up or a child broke the phone.

Seventeen minutes later I was on the field—which again had dried out just enough to avoid canceling practice. It was as if God had declared divine protection over this small patch of ground, and scheduled His Flood around practice times, just so I could get my twice-weekly punishment.

Except for Jem, the whole team was there—fifteen miniature tornadoes who'd been cooped up indoors since the last time I'd seen them, two days ago, and were desperate to unwind every ounce of energy at my expense.

A few mothers waited impatiently on the field. No doubt I'd made them late for their manicures at Patricia's.

I circumvented their disapproving looks by brandishing the soccer shirts.

"Sorry," I mumbled. "Trouble getting these."

In fact, the plastic bag full of neon-orange clothes had been sitting in my truck for a week, but the distraction worked.

The kids yelled, "Uniforms!" and mobbed the bag like Somali refugees. The mothers had to retreat or get trampled.

"First game Saturday against Saint Mark's!" I called to the mothers as they left.

My grumpy inner voice: *And I hope you have fun without me.*

The kids were running down the field holding bright orange tube socks from their ears like streamers. The Garcia twins were tackling each other. Laura and Jack were playing leap-frog.

I blew my whistle. "On the line!"

Nobody got on the line, but the chaos moved into a tighter orbit around me. I was making progress.

"I've been practicing my kicks, Coach!" Paul told me. "My dad said you were teaching us wrong!"

"That's great, Paul."

Kathleen pointed at me and giggled. "You look like a cat's been sleeping on your head!"

"Scrimmage!" the Garcia twins screamed.

"We've got to do some drills first, guys," I said.

"Scrimmage!"

Pretty soon the whole tribe had taken up the call.

I relented.

We went eight on seven. Jack took Jem's place as keeper.

Two scrimmages and twenty-seven water breaks later, the rain started coming down—just in time for the end of practice.

I blew my whistle. "Circle up!"

To my surprise, the whole team responded. They sat in a circle around me on the wet grass.

"The game is at ten on Saturday," I said. "What time is it, Laura?"

"Ten on Saturday!"

"Who are we playing, Paul?"

"Saint Mark's!"

Two right answers in a row temporarily stunned me.

One of the Garcia twins tugged at my sock. "Where's Jem? Is he sick?"

"He's . . . out of town."

"He'll be here, right? He's our best goalie!"

I blinked, and wondered if they'd been practicing in some alternate universe last time.

"I don't know," I said. I didn't add that I probably wouldn't be there, either. "Listen, just play your best. Practice your kicks. Saint Mark's is supposed to be a good team, so don't be discouraged . . ."

"We're gonna win!" Paul yelled, and bounced the ball off Maria's head. She didn't notice.

"Yeah!" said Kathleen. "Best coach ever!"

Jack gave me his best loyal dog bark.

"Okay," I said. "Well . . . your parents will be here soon. So . . . let's clean up the equipment."

The team spirit was too good to last. They gave a cheer and went screaming en masse toward the playground.

I watched them go. Then I stared down at the extra uniform in my plastic bag. I'd saved Jem his favorite number: 13. I'd saved him the yellow goalie vest.

Somewhere during the night, I'd decided not to call Maia's. Despite the time crunch, I had to go in person. I had to talk to Jem, face-to-face, find a way to tell him what was going on. He deserved to know.

It would be better not to bring the uniform. The kid wouldn't be playing in Saturday's game. Even best-case scenario—no way.

I shouldn't waste another minute on soccer. I'd lost half the morning and done nothing to help Erainya. I needed to get Ralph Arguello working on my problem. Now. Immediately. Then I needed to get to Austin.

But I took the time to walk the rainy field. I collected the balls the kids had kicked to the far corners of creation. I locked up the supply shed. And I stayed at the playground until my last player got put safely in her parent's car.

"Vato."

Ralph Arguello held out his arms. His gold-ringed fingers and white guayabera shirt and fan of black hair across his shoulders made him look like the Brownsville version of Jesus.

He pulled me into a bear hug, which disconcerted me. I wasn't sure I'd ever touched Ralph before, except maybe for the time I'd pulled him back from killing our high school football coach.

"We were about to eat lunch," he told me, leading me down the hallway. "You like Gerber's tapioca?"

"Tempting, but I'm okay."

Ralph grinned. His thick round glasses made his eyes float like dangerous little fish. "Change your mind, I can fix you up."

"Ralphas, I need help."

A few more steps into their home—past the tintype of Ralph's great-grandfather who rode with Pancho Villa; the tiny altar to Ralph's deceased mother; Ana DeLeon's framed Police Academy graduation picture.

"Ana told me," he said, his voice even. "Come on. Meet my main *chica."*

His den windows overlooked Rosedale Park, so close to the bandstand that in the spring the whole house must have vibrated with *conjunto* music from the annual festival. Marmalade walls were hung with Frida Kahlo prints. Patchouli incense coiled up the blades of a potted yucca. eBay flickered on the computer screen. The bookshelves were crammed with Spanish poetry, homicide manuals and children's stories.

In the center of the carpet, a baby sat suspended in a plastic saucer seat, her tray sprinkled with Apple Jacks.

She had a drool stalactite on her chin, tufts of black hair, and little wrinkled fists. I could tell she was a girl because her ears were pierced and fitted with gold studs. Then again, so were her dad's.

She looked up at Ralph and grinned in a way I'm sure must've been very cute—though her expression struck me as not too different from an *I'm-pooping-now* look.

"There she is—*mi bambina!*" Ralph stuck his face down toward the baby, who squealed happily.

She kicked her feet. The saucer went *whumpity-whump*.

I decided I needed to sit down.

I pulled a teething ring out of the crack in Ralph's brown leather recliner and settled in, outside what I hoped was drool-flinging range.

"So—Erainya." Ralph turned toward me, trying to suppress his parental euphoria long enough to focus on my problem. "Tell me about it."

I filled him in on what his wife the police sergeant didn't know—the fourteen million dollars, Stirman's ransom dead-line, my feeling that Stirman would kill Erainya whether I found the money or not.

Ralph picked up a jar of processed yellow goop. He stabbed it a few times with a spoon. "You willing to kill, *vato*? 'Cause you go after Stirman yourself, that's what you'll have to do."

I didn't answer. The baby was trying to pick up an Apple Jack with tiny, clumsy fingers.

"Don't tell me," Ralph decided. "I see it in your eyes, man. I don't want to know. I'd have to tell Ana, *entiendes*?"

"Can you help me or not?"

He spooned some goop into the baby's mouth. Most of it dribbled down her chin. "I got a name."

I nodded, relieved but not surprised.

Ralph had spent years on the streets. He'd built a million-dollar pawn shop empire, occasionally branching out into less legally correct businesses. Until he'd stunned the town by marrying a police officer, Ralph had known the disreputable side of San Antonio as well as he knew the resale value of gold or used guitars.

"Guy's name is Beto Falcone," he said. "Pimps whores out of the Brazos Inn over on Crockett. He and Stirman used to do business, running fresh meat up from the border."

"Ralph . . ."

"Falcone would know Stirman's hiding places. Little persuasion, he might be willing to tell you. I got the number."

"Ralph, Beto Falcone got whacked six months ago."

Ralph stared at me.

"Couple of gang-bangers," I said. "Killed him for thirty bucks in cash. Beto's dead."

Something shifted between us, like the fulcrum of a seesaw.

Ralph turned to his computer. He stared at his items on eBay—the new heart of his pawn shop business. "Nobody told me."

It was a statement I'd never thought to hear Ralph Arguello say, right up there with *I'm sorry* and *Let's let him live*.

"You've been on paternity leave," I offered halfheartedly. "You've been out of it."

The lenses of his glasses flashed.

He turned to his daughter. He held out his little finger for her to grab.

Other than the fact she had no teeth, she looked a lot like her dad when she smiled. Her glee was so complete it could've been innocent or diabolic.

"I'll make some calls," Ralph said. "Give me a couple of hours."

"Be faster if we hit the streets."

Phones were unreliable for the kind of information we needed. We both knew that. Hell, Ralph hated phones.

But I sensed his hesitation—his completely un-Ralph-like reluctance to move.

The baby was pulling at his hand, trying to get the spoon.

"Haven't set foot in the shops for months," Ralph said. "Nowadays, I run my business from right here, you know? Some of the stuff I was into . . . I let it slide, *vato*."

I didn't respond.

"Ana and me—if we were going to stay together, something had to give. You understand?"

"And that something was you."

He acted like he hadn't heard.

He crushed an Apple Jack on the baby's tray, made a line of brown dust. "From what you're telling me, Barrow and Barrera stepped way over the line. They stole Stirman's money. Now you're telling me they killed his wife and kid, too."

"What's your point?"

"Stirman's got a legitimate gripe."

"Stirman's a sociopath. Doesn't mean Erainya and Jem should suffer."

Ralph stared out the windows toward Rosedale Park, the way he had always stared at the landscape of San Antonio—as if it was his private domain, as if he could feel everything happening out there. In a way, it *was* his domain. When he and Ana had moved into this house, their combined reputations had been enough to permanently halt all gang activity within a five-block radius. Nobody wanted to mess with Arguello and DeLeon's domestic bliss.

Ralph said, "You think Erainya kept the money?"

"No . . . I don't know. It just feels wrong."

"And if Barrow hid it from her—what would he have done with it?"

I shook my head. "Something self-destructive—something pathetic. Gambled it away. Maybe a whore stole it. Maybe it mildewed in a bus station locker until some lucky attendant busted the lock. Who the hell knows? I've gone through Barrow's case files. I've run every angle in my mind."

"Maybe he had better plans. Maybe if he'd lived, he would've tried to use it for a fresh start."

"Like hell."

"That's what I'd do."

The baby had gotten hold of her spoon now. She was trying to pull it away from her father, but Ralph kept his finger hooked around the handle.

"Good people do bad things," he said. "No surprise. Funny thing, though—you never think about it going the other way. Even fucking sociopaths can do something good once in a while. You know that? Nobody wants to live in hell, *vato*. Nobody."

"You've been reading too many picture books."

"Maybe you need to look at Barrow from a different angle, man. All I'm saying. And maybe Stirman can be dealt with short of killing."

"A minute ago—"

"I said if you went after him yourself, you'd have to kill him. But you could listen to Ana instead. You could let her help."

Ralph Arguello, lecturing me on trusting the police.

"I'll let you eat your lunch," I said. "Good seeing you, Ralph."

"Streets ain't mine no more, *vato*. You ain't gonna hold that against me, right?"

I listened for regret in his voice, heard none—just protectiveness of his new family, his new self. I tried to be happy for him. I tried not to feel unwelcome in his den.

"Sure," I said. "Hey, I understand."

"Call me in a while. I'll let you know what I find out."

I promised, though I knew I wasn't going to call.

Ralph walked me out. We shook hands at the door.

"What's the baby's name, anyway?" I asked.

"Lucia."

"Lucia."

"It was Ana's mom's name," he said.

"I remember."

"I'll be here, man, if you need me."

He meant it. But he was offering support, not backup, and there was a big difference.

I walked down his front steps. I felt like I'd just been fitted with someone else's Kevlar vest, and it was way too big for me.

When I turned at the curb, Ralph's expression was a mix of concern and relief, as if he was glad to watch me walk away, his violent past entrusted to the keeping of another man.

He turned inside and closed the door, leaving a thumbprint of tapioca on the doorjamb.

17

The note on Sam's refrigerator read:

I've got your car.
I'll come by this morning to check on you.
Stay put until then—Tres. 821-6643.

Hell of a thing. Somebody steals your car and leaves a signed note with his phone number. Tres was apparently the guy's name.

And this morning? It was already ten-thirty. No sign of the guy.

Sam thought about calling the field office, having this joker picked up and sweated in a locked room.

He paced around the kitchen in his three-piece suit. He ate a bowl of dry Frosted Flakes, took his medicine with a glass of orange juice and had to visit the restroom. When he came back, the WOAI radio news was talking about two fugitives shot dead in Omaha. Police were still looking for the leader of the group.

The leader's name made Sam anxious.

Will Stirman.

Sam went to his bedroom closet. He moved the shoeboxes

aside. The rifle case. The suitcases. He pulled out a large black duffel bag and looked inside.

The bag used to be fuller. And a lot heavier. He was pretty sure of that. He was also pretty sure he'd been waiting to do this for years.

He took his old service revolver and buried it in the bottom of the bag. Then he zipped it up.

He toted the bag to the kitchen and read the refrigerator note again.

He ripped it off and stuffed it in his vest pocket. The hell with staying put. He checked his regular sidearm, a Glock 9. He locked up his house, strolled across the street and hotwired his neighbor's Chevy Impala.

By the time the owner stumbled into his front yard, yelling obscenities, incredulous that the friendly neighborhood private eye was heisting his wheels, Sam was halfway down the block.

Should've left him a note, Sam thought.

It felt good to smile.

He didn't know where he was going.

He patted the empty seat next to him, looking for something—notes maybe? A case file?

The more he thought about it, the more anxious he felt, so he decided not to think. Just drive. If he kept the *why* and *where* below his radar screen, his instincts would take him where he needed to go.

Stirman, he reminded himself. *Will Stirman.*

He exited I-10 just before downtown, wove his way through the light industrial district by the Art Museum. The streets were a patchwork of railroad tracks, greasy rainwater and cement-frosted manhole covers.

He almost stopped at the museum. He managed security there. Maybe that's where he was heading. Something about the location, with the name Will Stirman—something seemed familiar.

But he didn't stop. He was looking for something he'd seen on television. Something on a videotape.

At Avenue B and Jones, the river had flooded its banks. A steady sheet of green shredded through the cement teeth of the bridge railing. In the swampy woods behind the museum, two young Latinos in black T-shirts and cutoffs were sitting on oil drums, fishing for God-knew-what.

Sam eased his stolen Impala across the bridge.

On the opposite bank was an old plumbing supply business. The storage yard was ringed in razor wire laced with Christmas lights and honeysuckle. PVC pipe was stacked on rotting flats. The two-story building had been imperfectly whitewashed, its boarded-up windows and garage-sized doors painted an odd assortment of olive and turquoise, like a little girl's face after playing with makeup.

This place didn't feel right either. It wasn't what Sam was looking for.

But something about it was familiar.

He parked by the gate.

Sam trusted his nose for locations. His tracking skills hadn't left him, any more than his ability to hotwire a car or shoot a gun.

He'd been here before.

He couldn't remember the names of the people he'd come with, but he remembered their faces with absolute clarity.

A husband and wife, and not very damn happy with each other.

The woman had sat in the back of the car. She had frizzy black hair, sharp features, eyes like chips of volcanic rock. She was scared of her husband—you could see that in the tenseness of her shoulders, the guarded way she spoke. But she was determined, too. She clutched the top of her handbag like it was a grenade pin.

Her husband rode shotgun next to Sam.

Sam didn't trust the guy. He was a big man, maybe a former boxer. Definitely a drinker. He had puffy eyes and a butterfly rash on his cheeks and nose. Cheap brown suit, a sidearm holstered sloppily at his belt. He had a casual way of telling his wife to shut up whenever she tried to speak.

The boxer turned to Sam. "You loaded?"

"What do you think?"

The boxer grinned in an unfriendly way. He was crude, but Sam remembered thinking: *a crude tool for a crude job.*

The woman said, "I'm going with you."

The boxer lifted an eyebrow. "You'll stay in the fucking car."

"*I* tipped you off," she insisted. "I got the information."

"Yeah, you give my informants hand jobs real well. So fucking what? Come on, Sam."

"Fred, I'm coming with you," the woman said.

Fred, Sam thought. *That was his name.*

Fred tried to stay cool, but Sam could see he was ready to blow up. Sam wanted to warn the wife, for her own safety. He wanted to tell her to hang back. You didn't make a guy like Fred lose face in front of another man.

The best Sam could do was look away, pretend he wasn't seeing it.

"Fine," Fred growled. "You want to come, Irene? Fine. You get shot, don't cry to me."

Back in the present, Sam opened his car door. He left the duffel bag in the trunk, and walked toward the warehouse.

The turquoise door wasn't locked.

Inside were pyramids of cardboard boxes, some still wrapped in plastic, some gutted by hopeful looters. The open boxes spilled bathroom tiles and brass sink fixtures across the floor. Scattered around an impromptu fire pit were dirty clothes, drug paraphernalia, broken lawn furniture.

Metal stairs led up to the second floor. A loft apartment, Sam remembered. He could hear movement above, footsteps trying not to creak.

The boxer had stopped at the top of the stairs. He drew his weapon, gesturing for his wife to stay behind them. Sam's FBI background gnawed at his gut, reminding him this was not the way to proceed, barreling into a high-risk situation with no backup, no reconnaissance, no plan of attack. Nevertheless, he followed the boxer's lead.

Reggae music pulsed from inside the apartment. There was another sound, too—one Sam couldn't quite place.

Just as the boxer kicked open the door, Sam realized the sound was a baby crying.

In the present, a scrawny young Anglo said, "Shit!"

He had been creeping toward the apartment door when Barrera busted it open. Now the Anglo kid stood blinking, bleary-eyed in the morning light that peppered down from the holes in the ceiling.

Sam pegged him for a two-bit junkie. He had piss-colored skin, deep bruises under his eyes. He wore smelly thirdhand fatigues. Behind him was a rats' nest of clothes, empty beer bottles and crack pipes. All the comforts of home.

Piss-face's expression was pure cornered-animal. Still, there was understanding, and fear, as he sized up Sam—a big well-dressed Latino, clearly some kind of cop. That aura never went away.

Sam felt a twinge of recognition. All users looked alike. Sam had dealt with hundreds. But something told him he knew this guy in particular.

Piss-face apparently had the same feeling. He went slack-jawed. "Barrera?"

Fred had fired the first shot.

Reggae music. A baby screaming. Sam dropped to a crouch in the doorway and Fred cut to the right.

A young Latina ran toward them, her arms raised as if to stop them. On the far side of the room, interrupted mid–phone call, a dark-haired Anglo with pale skin, dead eyes, a gun in his belt. Will Stirman.

Stirman was unprepared for the men busting down his door. He hesitated because of the woman who now stood between him and his enemies.

"Down!" Sam shouted to her. "Get the fuck down!"

The Latina was almost to the door, though what she hoped to accomplish, Sam couldn't imagine. She had the same grim look as an illegal, halfway across the Rio Grande, when the Border Patrol shows up. They keep running, knowing they are caught, but they have no choice but to try. It was as if she wanted to push the intruders out of her life.

For a moment, Will Stirman looked at Sam. Then Will drew his gun.

Fred Barrow aimed as the woman—who Sam wasn't sure Fred even registered—stepped in front of the gun, her arms raised like a long-lost relative.

*   *   *

Sam ignored Piss-face and scanned the room. Desolation where there had once been plush furniture, maroon wallpaper, reggae music on an expensive stereo. The only thing left was the crepe carpet, now coming apart in patches, water-stained, discolored in places from very old blood.

Piss-face's hand slid cautiously toward the pocket of his army surplus jacket.

"What are you doing here, Barrera?" he asked. "Scared the shit out of me."

Sam tried to refocus on the derelict.

Just his luck to find an old collar—or informant, stool pigeon, whatever the hell this guy was—sleeping in this warehouse, of all places. Then again, Sam had been on the streets so long it was hard to turn over any rock in San Antonio and not find some slimy thing he'd dealt with before.

"Get out," Sam told him.

He tried to put authority in his voice, but he didn't feel so good. He was remembering the pattern of the young Latina's dress, the look on Stirman's face as his lover fell.

Piss-face licked his lips. Hunger was slowly displacing his fear.

In his better days, Sam would've anticipated that shift.

"You remember me, right?" Piss-face asked. "Right, Mr. Barrera?"

His voice was dangerously polite, testing.

Sam counted bloodstains on the old carpet—two large ones, a constellation of lesser splatters.

Piss-face took a step closer. "Mr. Barrera?"

"Get lost," Sam murmured.

It didn't sound like his voice. It sounded like an old man, asking a question.

Piss-face was close enough now that Sam could smell the rotgut on his breath. "You don't remember me, do you?"

Sam had a gun. He knew he should draw it.

"What's my name, old man?" Piss-face asked. "Tell me."

The woman had fallen to the carpet. Will Stirman had fired, his shot taking out a chunk of plaster next to Fred Barrow's head. The second shot likely would've found Barrow's skull, but Sam opened up—aiming for Stirman's chest, getting his arm instead, then Stirman's shoulder as he went down. The couch probably saved Stirman's life, because as soon as Fred Barrow got over being stunned, he emptied his clip in that direction.

Sam had only shot twice. No more. He had not fired on the woman. He had not continued to fire, in shock, as Fred Barrow had done.

Sam's ears rang, and the music still throbbed, but there was a small hole of silence in the room that Sam registered only when Irene Barrow pushed past him, toward the crib. The baby was no longer crying.

In the present, Piss-face drew his gun. It was a small .22, but close enough to kill. He said, "Long as you're here, old man—how about a loan?"

His breath was downright flammable. His finger was tight on the trigger.

Sam felt something black and hard filling his chest. He stepped toward Piss-face, pushed his sternum against the barrel of the derelict's gun, forced Piss-face to take a step back.

"Do it," Sam said.

"I swear to God," Piss-face said.

"*Do* it!"

Sam slapped the gun out of Piss-face's hand. He took a handful of the kid's shirt. With his other hand, he hit the kid in the face, getting blood on his cuff, his coat sleeve, his college ring.

He forced himself to stop before he would kill the kid. He released Piss-face, let him fall in a trembling, whining heap.

"Get out."

Piss-face scrambled to the door and down the metal steps, his hands over his face.

Sam touched his own chest, where the gun had pressed against his heart. It would have been so much quicker than the darkness ahead, the slow painless disease that had begun wrapping around his brain.

He pulled out his own gun, just to steady his hand. He aimed it at the spot where Will Stirman had gone down.

After the shooting, reggae music had still blared: "Tomorrow People," a song Sam would find ironic in retrospect.

Fred Barrow had stared at the black duffel bag he'd inadvertently shot—one of two, filled with blocks of cash. A stray bullet had plowed a groove through the top layer of hundreds.

Standing over the crib, Barrow's wife was panicked, her voice desperate: "Christ, Fred. It's not breathing."

Sam had tried to forget the rest. He had tried for years.

Now God, with His sense of humor, was answering Sam's prayer for forgetfulness with a vengeance.

The Barrows had argued. Fred insisted that his wife leave before the police arrive, get the hell away. The two men would clean up.

And they had.

The division of the duffel bags—one each, no discussion. Such a simple matter to haul them downstairs, throw them in the trunk of the car, while Will Stirman was upstairs bleeding, dying, and the sirens were still a long way away.

Sam stared at his gun. He was getting farsighted. The match- grade handle pattern was only clear at a full arm's length.

His memory was like his vision. He had to hold something at several years' distance to see it clearly. Soon, he would be living in an eternal present. He would be unable to remember the beginning of a sentence long enough to reach the end.

He thought about the visit he'd taken, at his doctor's request. They needed a decision by Friday. When was that—tomorrow?

Sam could live in that brightly lit room, singing "This Land Is Your Land" with a group of old ladies, his name on a kindergarten tag to remind him who he was.

But he suspected the memory of the reggae music would only get clearer, the face of Irene Barrow as she looked into that crib.

He put his gun away.

There was still time to decide.

He walked downstairs, out of the abandoned warehouse, remembering the weight of the duffel bag so clearly it made his shoulders ache.

The car parked outside wasn't his BMW. It was a Chevy Impala, but it had already been hotwired, so Sam took it.

He drove toward downtown, then east, under Highway 281, until a scent caught him—a current, steering him toward the place he needed.

Will Stirman wouldn't have gone far from his old home. He would've chosen another warehouse, a place very much like the first. Sam had seen something on a video.

Every East Side street held memories for Sam, sunken like

land mines. The margarita-green house with the unpainted gables. The chop shop with the tiny American flags stuck on the fence posts. The abandoned lot, its cedar trees tangled with birdhouses and plastic grocery bags, the sidewalk bearded with wild cilantro. Sam had been to all these places. He had saved people, arrested people, discovered bodies. He was tempted to stop at every point, and stare, and try to remember why each was familiar.

But he kept driving.

He was looking for a red-brick building. It would be northeast of the Alamodome, in sight of the spires. He'd seen it on television.

The Impala rumbled down a desolate stretch of crumbling asphalt called Rosa Parks Way. The name struck Sam as pathetic. He remembered Rosa Parks. All that civil rights work, and the City Fathers made sure Rosa's memorial street was the geographic equivalent to the back of the bus.

A few blocks east of St. Paul Square, he pulled into a gravel lot.

Across the street, next to the Southern Pacific tracks, was a dismal four-story wedge of red brick. The faded black and white paint along the top proclaimed: CARRIZO ICE CO. 1907.

A loading dock wrapped around the building, an aluminum awning frayed and hanging down in pieces. The square freezer doors were thick wood, spray-painted with orange and blue gang monikers. Some of the windows had been bricked up. Others were boarded, or turned into doors for a fire escape that was no longer there. On the top floor, the windows were still intact—shiny glass, steel frames.

Sam thought he had the right place. He would have to watch it. He would wait for someone to arrive or leave.

He couldn't afford to move from this spot. If he did, he might lose his sense of purpose. He'd be swept off into the East Side, hunting memories.

He needed to stay here, and stay focused.

He patted his coat pocket, found a cell phone.

In his vest, he found a crumpled note—the name *Tres,* and a number.

After a moment's hesitation, watching a shadow move behind the fourth-floor windows, Sam decided it would be proper procedure to call for backup.

He looked at his watch: 1:34 P.M.

He dialed the number and got an answering machine. Sam left a message. He gave his position, reading the street sign N. CHERRY from half a block away. No problem with his vision, as long as he was at a distance.

Sam took out his gun and placed it next to him on the seat.

He had been on stakeouts before. He knew how to be patient.

He would wait for an opportunity.

He ignored his thirst, his irritated bowels, his dress shirt collar cutting into his throat. He ignored all discomfort, though he looked down from time to time, and wondered about the blood drying against his knuckles.

18

Maia leaned in the doorway of her condo, casually holding the Smith & Wesson eight-shot miniaturized cannon that passed for her sidearm.

She said, "You brought batteries, I hope."

Her ensemble du jour was topped off by a white linen jacket—the summer-weight fashion statement she'd had tailor-made to accommodate the Magnum's shoulder holster. Breezy, yet lethal.

"Batteries . . ." I looked in my bag of Whole Foods Market picnic supplies, which had seemed perfectly adequate a moment before. "What happened, the laser scope on your grenade launcher go out again?"

"Ha, ha. You have no idea how many double-As a Game Boy can go through in twenty-four hours. Come in."

A meteor had impacted on the smooth surface of Planet Maia. In the middle of the living room's milk-white carpet, Jem sat cross-legged, playing his Game Boy. He was surrounded by a debris ring of Nintendo cartridges and comic books and LEGO robots.

"Hey, champ," I said.

He didn't respond.

I exchanged looks with Maia. She pursed her lips.

"I brought lunch." I sat next to Jem and unloaded my goodies with a series of *ta-da* flourishes. Checkered cloth. French bread, cheese, wine for the adults. A juice box, pizza Lunchables, and a cup of Dippin' Dots futuristic ice cream for Jem.

He glanced at each item I produced, then went back to his game.

"Zapping good monsters?" I asked.

He lifted one shoulder. "My Gyarados is level thirty-five."

I would've understood the statement just as well in Japanese, but I tried to exude enthusiasm.

Maia sat with us. We munched on bread and cheese. I opened the wine. Jem let his bowl of ice cream dots melt.

"This isn't like you, Tres," Maia said. "A picnic? Almost romantic."

"Yuck," Jem muttered.

"Really," Maia agreed.

I thought that might coax a smile from him, but his expression stayed serious, his attention funneled toward the Game Boy like he wanted to pour himself into the tiny screen.

"Well . . ." Maia said. "I guess I'll put these ice cream pellet things in the freezer, Jem, if you don't want them right now."

"I don't."

Maia arched her eyebrow at me, giving me a silent command. She took the melting snack-of-the-future into the kitchen.

Jem kept playing his game.

I waited for the best moment to say something. The best moment proved elusive.

"Jem," I said at last. "You remember the man we saw at the soccer field?"

He pushed a few more buttons.

"That man's angry at your mother," I said. "She didn't do anything wrong, but he thinks she stole some of his money. Your mother is worried. When people are mad, they can do stupid things. Sometimes they might hurt people without think-ing. She didn't want you to get hurt."

"I know," Jem said. "She told me."

"Your mother is with that man right now."

Black bangs fell in his eyes. "She's at his house?"

"I'm not sure, champ. He's keeping her somewhere, like a hostage. He wants me to bring him money, to make up for what he lost. Once I do that, he'll let your mom go."

"We don't have any money."

"I'm working on that." My throat felt dry. "I'm going to see the man tonight. I'll make sure your mother is okay. I'll con-vince him she didn't do anything bad. I just wanted you to know—your mother loves you. That's why you're staying with Maia. More than anything, your mother wants to know you're safe."

Jem pulled his legs in tighter. He cradled the Game Boy.

"Light's red," he murmured. "I wish I had more batteries."

I tried to finish my wine, but it tasted like vinegar. "I'll clean up this stuff," I said. "Be right back, champ."

I found Maia at her kitchen window, staring out at the wooded canyon of Barton Creek. On her breakfast table was a spread of paperwork—her court cases, I assumed. Then I looked closer and saw they were news printouts about Will Stirman and the Floresville Five.

She turned toward me, held out her arms.

The wine tasted a whole lot better on her lips.

I said, "Missed you."

"Stay the night."

"I can't."

I told her why.

Maia's face got that battle-hardened look that always made me glad I was not the object of her anger. "Stirman asked for *Jem*?"

"Yeah."

My tone of voice must've unsettled her. She said, "You're not seriously considering—"

"No. Jem's safer here." I tried to sound definite about it, but something nagged at the back of my mind, something that had been there since lunchtime, when I'd visited with Ralph Arguello and his baby daughter. "I don't think Stirman would really try coming to Austin. If he did, he sure as hell wouldn't bargain for you."

Maia stared out the window. "Jem keeps talking about soccer. He wants life to be normal by the weekend. I can't blame him."

She didn't mention our last night together in San Marcos, or my promise to give her an answer about moving to Austin by this weekend.

I wondered how it had been for Maia, putting Jem to bed last night, taking care of a child. I found it hard to imagine her telling bedtime stories.

"You okay?" I asked.

"Just nerves." She waved toward the news clippings on the table. "This morning, I almost shot my neighbor when he came to borrow coffee. This is the first time I've opened my blinds since yesterday. I keep thinking, if Stirman had any skill with a sniper rifle . . ."

She gazed at the ridge across the valley.

The view was strikingly similar to the one from her old Potrero Hill apartment. The land fell away into a basin of green, hills on the opposite rim dotted with newly built mansions and condominiums. At night, the aquifer recharge zone below would be completely dark, but rimmed with lights, the Heart of Texas Highway strung red and gold across the void. A San Franciscan could easily imagine she was looking across an expanse of water at the Bay Bridge and the East Bay beyond.

The interior of Maia's new apartment was also a duplicate of the old—high ceilings, white walls, pristine tile work, milk carpet, a slight scent of jasmine in the air.

She'd re-created her living environment in Texas with such eerie precision it belied the risk she'd taken coming here—the career and reputation she'd left behind, the savings she'd burned, the chance she was taking on a guy who'd let her down before.

If asked, she would say the move was a life decision. The time had been right for her to reinvent herself. She hadn't moved just to be closer to me.

She would also swear her new home looked nothing like her old.

Maia shed her white jacket, folded it over the kitchen stool.

The gun in her holster looked enormous compared to the size of her hands, but I knew it fit her grip perfectly. The .357 was her preferred weapon. Anything smaller, and she felt poorly anchored.

"You can't negotiate with Will Stirman," she told me. "You know that."

I picked up one of the articles she had printed from the *Express-News* archives.

Human Trafficker Brought Down by Local Investigators 4/29/95.

Last night, working in conjunction with San Antonio police on the recent slayings at a Castroville ranch, two prominent local private investigators took part in a dramatic firefight leading to the arrest of Will Stirman, the alleged mastermind of a human trafficking operation which may have supplied the Castroville murderer with his victims.

None of the information was new to me. Late April, just as Ana DeLeon had said. Barrera and Barrow were portrayed as heroes. The statement from the SAPD's media relations officer was carefully restrained. *While we never condone private citizens taking the law into their own hands . . .*

No reference to missing money or a dead child. Soledad's death wasn't mentioned until the last paragraph—a completely subordinate fact, like a broken window.

"Tres." Maia sounded more insistent now. "If Stirman lost his family . . . he'll never let Erainya go. You'll have to find him before he calls the meeting. You'll have to kill him."

It was jarring, hearing her say that, but I wasn't surprised. Maia was the ultimate pragmatist when it came to sociopaths. She knew them. At her old San Francisco firm of Terrence & Goldman, she had been responsible for defending some of the richest sociopaths in the country. Under the right circumstances, Maia would have no problem putting a bullet through Will Stirman's forehead. She would not lose a moment's sleep.

"I'll find him," I promised.

But I was still looking at the article. Late April 1995.

Nobody wants to live in hell, vato. *Nobody.*

I imagined Fred Barrow—a big, brutish man with blood on his hands, his breath stinking of guilt and hate and violence, and a suitcase full of cash in the trunk of his car. I thought about what he might do with seven million dollars. I thought about Erainya's note from H., the package from Fred.

"You wasted time, coming up here," Maia said, sadly. "Three hours you should've spent looking for Stirman."

Domino moments are rare. One seemingly incongruous piece of information slips into place, and suddenly you've got a chain reaction of unanswered questions that all go down, one after the other. Investigators live for domino moments. On the other hand, the pattern you discover can sometimes scare the hell out of you.

"It wasn't a waste of time," I said. "I have to—"

I stopped.

Jem was standing in the kitchen doorway, holding his Game Boy.

"The batteries are dead," he announced.

Maia held out her arms. "Come here, sweetheart."

Jem came over and let her hug him, but his eyes were on me.

The kitchen floor was turning to liquid under my feet.

I said, "How long were you listening, champ?"

"Awhile," he admitted. "I want to go with you."

Maia tried to stroke the bangs out of his eyes to no avail. "You can't, sweetheart."

He pulled away from her. "That man wants me to come. I want to help my mother."

Maia looked to me for support.

I remembered Will Stirman's voice on the telephone, his tone that I hadn't quite been able to decipher: *We'll all be better behaved with the kid around.*

"I'll tell the man to let her go," Jem continued. "He won't hurt me. I'll talk to him first. Then if you have to, you can shoot him. That will be fairer."

His chin jutted out stubbornly, like his mother's. He sounded like he was describing a game plan rather than asking permission.

Not for the first time, I marveled at how much he'd changed since his preschool days.

He's still only eight, I reminded myself.

So what had I been doing at eight years old? I'd already found the keys to my dad's gun safe. I'd shot and gutted my first deer at the ranch. I'd spent hours hanging around the guards' desk at the Bexar County Jail, where my dad had his office. I already knew the difference between a con and a civilian. I'd had plenty of conversations with guys like Will Stirman, and I'd known instinctively—or at least I thought I knew—which ones would hurt a kid, and which ones wouldn't. If somebody had told me, at eight years old, that Will Stirman had taken my mom and I couldn't try to help her . . .

I could see Maia's disbelief growing as she realized what I was thinking.

"Tres . . ." she warned.

"Go pack your bag, champ," I said. "No mess on Maia's floor."

"Tres!" Maia said again.

"Okay," Jem said. "The uniform, too?"

I looked at him.

"It was in the bottom of the bag," he said. "You brought the goalie vest. That means everything will be better by Saturday. I'll get to play."

Maia glared at me as if I'd just sold the kid some real estate at the North Pole.

"I hope so," I told him. "We'll hope, okay? Now go get packed."

He hustled off, showing more energy than he had in days.

"How *can* you?" Maia asked.

When Maia got angry, she got cold. At the moment, her eyes could've frozen mercury.

"I need to use your phone," I said. "Local call."

"If you think, for one minute, I'm going to let you—"

"Thanks." I picked up her phone, dialed a friend of mine at the Texas Department of Human Resources. It took all of four minutes to ask an easy question, and get an easy answer. The organization I was inquiring about didn't exist. Nor, according to the state's records, had it existed eight years ago. I hung up, no doubt now, but feeling worse than ever.

"Well?" Maia demanded.

It would've been best to tell her.

I knew Maia would help me, if I explained. She would come to San Antonio, watch my back, fight my battles, do whatever she could to help save Erainya.

But it would be a mistake. I was already treading too far over the invisible line that separated our relationship from my work in San Antonio—the job Maia quietly resented. If I relied on her for more help, I'd be pushing us in the wrong direction. On some level she might never admit, Maia would take it as a sign of disrespect.

"Jem has to come with me," I said. "He's right. It may be the only way to resolve this without blood."

"You're absolutely insane."

"Stirman won't hurt him."

"You're sure of that." Her words were like mist off a glacier. "You're willing to risk his life."

Out her window, a hawk circled through the slow persistent drizzle over Barton Creek.

For the first time, I understood Erainya's dilemma as a parent—her sometimes crazy choices about what was best for Jem. The safest thing, the right thing, was rarely obvious.

I knew now why I had come to Austin. I knew exactly why Jem had to come back with me.

And I knew something else, too.

Standing in Maia's kitchen, so much like her old kitchen on Potrero Hill, looking out at the vista she swore was not the ghost image of her lost home, I knew where to find Fred Barrow's seven million dollars.

19

Will didn't mean for it to happen.

All he wanted was food and cash.

He passed up two convenience stores, convincing himself he needed to get farther away from the hideout.

He got on I-35, cruised down to Hot Wells Boulevard, turned into the South Side neighborhood he knew so well.

At the corner of South New Braunfels, the blue jeans factory he'd once used as a holding facility had been burned to crossbeams. The adobe house that belonged to his friend the Guide had been repainted lime green.

Farther down, on a ridge overlooking a swollen creek, the Estrella Barbecue Pit stood abandoned, its back deck sagging over the water.

Will had done business on that deck. He'd smoked cigars and drank Bacardi with clients while the air filled with brisket smoke, sulfur from the hot springs bubbling up in the creek bed, making soft milky rings in the mud.

Will and his clients would sit around the picnic table, negotiating the price of women.

Panamanian girls fought harder than Guatemalans. Girls from Coahuila turned the best short-term profit. The ones from the central mountains lasted longer. Twelve was too young to be reliably trained. Eighteen, too old. Glossy hair was a sign of health. Good teeth were a premium. Stirman wrote special orders on a yellow legal pad.

The following weekend, when Will got across the Rio Grande, he would find every girl on his shopping list, as if writing their descriptions made them appear—hopeful and eager and willing to believe his lies.

He made a right on South Presa, passed several more ice houses. He rejected one because he used to know the owners; another, because too many kids were Rollerblading outside.

His own hesitation irritated him. He should just pick a place and hit it.

He wasn't worried about being recognized. Since kidnapping Erainya Manos, he'd bleached his hair and shaved his five-day stubble. He'd gotten himself a pair of black rubber sunglasses, a blue Hawaiian shirt and jeans, boots that made him an inch taller. He doubted anyone would identify him right away, even in his old home turf.

Still he kept driving.

He turned on Dimmit Street because the name sounded familiar, and realized why only when he found himself in a dead end, facing a pink clapboard house. The hand-painted sign in the front yard read: TEXAS PRISON MINISTRY.

Will stopped his car in the middle of the cul-de-sac. He stared at the sign.

Pastor Riggs had always called his ministry headquarters Dimmit Street. Like it was some great central command, like the Pentagon or the White House.

But Will had never pictured it. He'd never realized where it was.

The front window had two bullet holes for eyes. Empty beer

bottles littered the flower bed. Parked in the driveway was the Reverend's black Ford Explorer, a dent in the fender where Elroy had backed into the Floresville Wal-Mart dumpster the first day of their escape.

Will's jaw tightened. He remembered Pastor Riggs fighting them in the chapel, forcing them to get violent. All of Will's plans had started to unravel from that moment.

After the head-bashing they'd given Riggs, the old man couldn't be alive. None of the news reports Will heard ever mentioned Riggs' fate. But if Riggs was alive, if he saw Will here . . .

Back up, Will's instincts told him.

He didn't.

He sat there stupidly as the door of the ministry house opened.

The tip of a bamboo cane appeared first, then Pastor Riggs, tapping at the stoop. Behind him, a scowling black dude, an ex-con judging from his posture, held the door as the preacher climbed down onto the porch.

Riggs had aged a decade in a week. The pastor's head was shaved and bandaged where Zeke's soldering iron had split the scalp. The left side of his face drooped like a Halloween mask.

The black dude carried a stack of books under one arm. Will wondered if they were donations for a prison library. Surely Riggs couldn't be doing outreach work anymore. His program was ruined. He'd been disgraced, discredited. No warden would let him within a mile of an inmate.

Suddenly, Riggs looked up. The preacher's eyes were unchanged—pale and startling blue. They stared straight at Will.

Will's hand went to the transmission.

His stolen Camaro had a tinted windshield. The setting sun shone straight against it. Riggs shouldn't be able to see through it any easier than through aluminum foil.

Still, their eyes seemed to meet. Will remembered prison Bible studies, moments when the heat and the preaching would wear through his pretense and Will would feel God. Or late at night, sketching Bible scenes on a yellow pad, when it almost seemed as if the rage could finally leave his mind, travel straight down to the tip of his pencil and onto the paper.

Will was sure, absolutely sure, that the Reverend could see him in this car.

He gunned the engine.

The Reverend raised his hand. Will slammed the Camaro into reverse. He fishtailed out of Dimmit Street, the pit of his stomach sloshing like a vat of sour milk.

He drove up South Presa, reassuring himself he hadn't made a mistake. It didn't matter. Stumbling across the old preacher didn't matter.

In a few hours, Will would have his money. He'd be on a chartered jet to Mexico, and from there, anywhere he pleased.

Navarre and Barrera would make the exchange, one way or another. They would bring the money, and the boy . . .

Will's hands felt sweaty on the wheel.

He wondered what Pastor Riggs would say if he knew his intentions.

You came to me on purpose, Brother Stirman. You want to be cleansed of that hatred.

Will wished it were so. But he knew what he had to do. He knew he couldn't be satisfied, couldn't put Soledad's spirit to rest unless Erainya Manos never saw her son again.

He pulled his Camaro over the railroad tracks and onto Roosevelt, passing storefront signs without reading them, fighting a desire to drive straight to the highway and head south— leave now, follow the road he knew so well to the Mexican border.

*　　*　　*

Eight years ago, his last night with Soledad, she had tried
to get him not to run. She sat next to him on the sofa while he
loaded his gun. She took his hands, and placed them on her
chest.

"If you run, *mi amor*," she said, "you'll be doing what they
want. Why please them?"

He could feel her heartbeat through the cotton dress.
Childbirth had swollen her breasts to a pleasant size, filled out
her face so she looked younger and healthier than when he first
brought her north from the burning sugar fields.

She smelled of honeysuckle she'd clipped that morning—a
fragrant clump of white and yellow flowers now blooming in a
water jar by the window. She'd taken such care with it, as if
she'd be here long enough to watch it grow roots.

Will had their bags almost packed. One for clothes; two filled
with enough cash to last a lifetime. He had three guns, two
phones, and an assortment of passports and fake IDs still to
pack. He'd already told Dimebox Ortiz he was leaving. He had
one last call to make—to Gerry Far, warning him to keep his
head down for a few days. Will and Soledad's plane would be in
the air in half an hour.

"I have to finish packing," he told her.

She carefully shifted her weight on top of him, her arms circling his neck. The warmth of her thighs pressed against his
legs. She kissed the bridge of his nose, the space between his
eyebrows. Her Saint Anthony medal dangled against his chin.

"Stay," she told him.

A Ziggy Marley song played—one of Soledad's favorites. She
always said the music reminded her of heat and salt water, of a
trip she'd made as a child to the beach near Matamoros. Soon,

Will promised her, she would live on the beach. She would have heat and the ocean every day.

He touched her necklace. "You never finished telling me about Saint Anthony."

She kissed him. "San Antonio, *loco* boy. My protector. He's the patron saint of lost things."

"What have you lost?"

She smiled, a little sadly. "Maybe *I'm* what was lost."

He realized his question had been stupid. She'd left her homeland, her aging father, her childhood. All for the sake of a better life in the north. And now Will was taking her away from that.

She unclasped the necklace, pressed it into his hand. "Stay with me here, *mi amor*. Cancel the flight."

She kissed him again.

He felt the blood stop pounding in his temples, start collecting lower in his body, stirring a different kind of pressure.

They hadn't made love since the baby arrived. It was probably still too soon.

She had not delivered in the hospital, of course. Stirman wanted no paper trails, no legal questions. Soledad was his creation. Their marriage had been secret for the same reason. He would not share her, or her child, with anyone.

But the delivery had been difficult. The old *curandera* midwife had commented on the amount of blood. For the first time, Will had seen fear and pain in Soledad's eyes, and he resented the child for that.

She slipped her hand underneath his belt, bit his ear.

Then the baby started crying, setting Will's nerves on edge.

He didn't want to take the child with them. He wished she had agreed to his idea of giving the baby away. He felt no guilt about this, only the need to not offend Soledad.

"Go on," he said, seeing her attention divided. "Tend to him."

Her lips brushed his forehead. "Let your enemies break against you, *mi amor*. They cannot hurt you."

"Don't forget to make an extra bottle."

She looked in his eyes for what would be the last time—the same undaunted look she always gave him, mutely reminding him that she had faced every horror a woman could face, some of those because of Will, yet she was not afraid. She had stayed with him this far. She didn't want to leave, but she would go into exile with him, or walk into gunfire. She would do whatever was needed to protect him, because as much as he claimed to own her, she had purchased him.

She rose to tend the child.

Will stared down at the silver necklace in his hand. In a flash of resentment, he dropped the medallion into the space beneath the floorboard where he normally hid his cash.

Let Saint Anthony stay in San Antonio. Soledad would have no more need of him. Will would protect her. He would make sure she never suffered loss again.

He closed up the secret place in the floor, and made his phone call to Gerry Far. A moment later, the apartment door exploded.

A police siren brought Will back to the present.

The patrol car was several blocks up Roosevelt, red lights flashing, the cop tapping his bullhorn as he pulled through traffic.

Will was prepared to turn on a side street, to run if he had to, but a block away from him the police car veered into a residential neighborhood.

Probably nothing to do with him.

He turned on the radio. Immediately, the newscaster said, "—alleged leader of the Floresville Five."

Will turned it off. He didn't want to know. His nerves were

frayed enough. It was seven in the evening, sun going down. He needed to find a store to rob.

Finally a corner sign caught his interest—ZUNIGA'S PRODUCE. The name sounded familiar, though Will was sure he'd never seen the place before.

Its walls were an odd color of stucco, like Chinese skin, so veined with cracks they seemed ready to fall apart. The doors were propped open with Black Diamond watermelons. Heaped outside were wooden crates of other produce—tomatoes, avocados, chili peppers, plantains.

No cars were parked out front. No customers at all, that Will could see. The store wouldn't have much cash in the till, but it wouldn't have surveillance cameras, either. Maybe the workers would be illegals. The owner would have no great desire to call the police.

Zuniga.

The name tugged at Will's memory, but he put it down to nerves.

He imagined Reverend Riggs' laser-blue eyes staring into him, trying to burn a hole in the small part of Will's conscience that still believed in God.

He parked the car. He'd hesitated long enough.

Inside were two aisles—one for groceries, the other for produce. There was no one behind the counter—just a curtain to a back office, a cigarette rack, a black-and-white television with a Spanish *telenovela* flickering on the screen.

In the produce section, an aging Latino in a tank top and sweat pants and rubber galoshes was spraying down the fruit. The line of mirrors over the vegetable bins all reflected his belly.

A cleaver, a heap of rubber bands, and a large mound of green onions sat next to him. The grocer's eyes were watering like crazy. Like he'd just taken a break from chopping and tying the *cebollas* into bundles. Or maybe he'd been following the *tele-novela*.

He looked over tearfully as Will picked up a shopping basket.

"Nice seein' the sun out there," Will told him.

The man shrugged. He went back to spraying his apples.

Will picked up three dusty soup cans, a loaf of Wonder Bread, Fig Newtons, chocolate bars—whatever didn't look too stale. He was conscious of the gun under his Hawaiian shirt, the grip digging into his abdomen.

He moved to the produce aisle, where things were much better tended. He picked up an orange, some apples, a pint of strawberries. The smell of the strawberries reminded him of the prison yard—hot summer afternoons, a thousand acres ripening in the fields all around Floresville.

Will brought his basket to the counter.

There were still no other customers. No one on the street. Just him and the old man.

The grocer looked over lazily. He called, "¡Lupe, ven acá!"

Will felt that uncomfortable memory tugging at the base of his skull. He had the sudden urge to leave.

Before he could, the back office curtain parted. A woman came out to help him.

She had been one of his.

He didn't recognize her, exactly, but he knew from the way she bore herself—the downcast eyes, careful gestures, as if she were walking through a hot oven. Her hair was prematurely gray, tied back in a bun. Her face, once beautiful enough to warrant a good price, was now drawn tight from years of hard work.

Will remembered something Gerry Far had told him for a laugh, years ago. Gerry had sold one of their acquisitions to a love-struck grocer, an old man who'd bought the girl for ten times her worth, cleaning out his savings and mortgaging his store to possess her. Will and Gerry had joked about how much the old man must like to squeeze ripe fruit. The man's name might've been Zuniga.

The woman didn't look at Will as she emptied his basket.

She ran her hands deftly over each item—estimating the weight of the produce, clacking prices from memory into an old-fashioned adding machine. She put everything into a brown paper bag for him, told him in Spanish it would be nineteen dollars and twenty-eight cents.

Will made up his mind. He would simply pay and leave.

He reached in his pocket, hoping to find some cash. Surely he'd overlooked at least one twenty-dollar bill.

But he didn't have time. Lupe looked up at him—straight through the sunglasses and the dyed hair and ten years of her own freedom—and she yelped with fear. *"¡Es él!"*

As if she'd expected him. Will realized the jailbreak must have dredged up her worst memories. The television would've kept his face constantly before her. Like thousands of others he'd brought north, Lupe must've been half expecting Will Stirman, her personal nightmare, to walk back into her life somehow. He had obliged her.

The rest happened fast.

The grocer Zuniga dropped his spray gun and grabbed the onion cleaver. He shouted at Stirman to get away from his wife. He told her to run, call the police.

The woman didn't move.

Will drew his gun. He told the old man to stop, to drop the knife.

Zuniga kept coming.

It's a fucking gun, Stirman thought. *Stop, you idiot.*

But there were years of the stored vengeance in the old man's eyes—resentment, poverty, desperate love for a woman Stirman had scarred. The old man wasn't going to stop.

Will fired a warning shot, but the grocer was already on top of him. The knife slashed into Will's shoulder.

Will's second shot was involuntary, a reflex from the pain. It caught the old man in the throat.

Zuniga went down on his knees, drowning as he tried to breathe. He crumpled onto the green mat. The spray gun he'd dropped hissed water, pushing a wave of red across the cement floor.

The woman didn't scream. She cupped her hands over her mouth and waited to die.

Will should have killed her. She could identify him. But his shoulder was on fire. Blood was soaking his shirt. The room turned the color of beer glass. He staggered outside, back toward his Camaro.

He was three blocks away before he realized he'd forgotten his groceries.

He pulled into a flea market parking lot. He stripped off his bloody shirt and wrapped it around his shoulder as tightly as he could. He wasn't sure how deep the cut was, or whether he'd stopped bleeding.

He made sure he still had bullets in his gun. Then he ditched the Camaro. He got lucky, found a decrepit Ford station wagon with keys in the ignition.

By the time he was on the road again, sirens were all around him, police cars racing toward the grocery store. The check-points would be going up soon. He had to get the hell away.

He tried to breathe deeply, lifting his bad shoulder so the pain would keep his senses sharp. Somehow, he made it back onto I-37.

He drove all the way south to Braunig Lake, then pulled over on a farm road, tried to control the rattle in his chest.

He pulled out his cell phone and called Pablo.

Five rings. Six. By the time Pablo picked up, Stirman was really pissed.

"You sleeping?"

Pablo hesitated. "No. Fuck you."

"Tell me you're holding the gun on her."

A longer silence. Pablo was probably looking for his goddamn gun. "Yeah."

"Point it at her head."

"What for? She's asleep."

"Pablo, tell me you're pointing the gun at her goddamn head."

"Okay. I am."

"It's going to go down faster than I thought. An hour, maximum, and I'll be back with the cash."

"It's only just getting dark."

"Don't turn on the radio. If I don't call back in one hour, shoot her. Listen for cops. You hear sirens, you think they might be coming for you, don't wait. Shoot her. You understand? Then get the hell out. You let her live, I swear to God, I'll find you."

"Slow down, man. I mean—shit."

"Pablo."

"Yeah, okay," he said. "I understand. But listen—"

Stirman didn't have time for more. He hung up.

Will knew what he had to do. He called the prearranged number. When Sam Barrera came on the line, waiting faithfully for instructions, Stirman told him how it would happen.

20

I almost didn't go home.

Looking back, I wonder which lives and deaths might've been exchanged had I driven straight toward the money.

But Jem and I both needed to use the little *caballeros* room. I figured we could make a pit stop at 90 Queen Anne and make our plans from there.

Besides, the radio news from Medina Lake was making me nervous. The Department of Public Safety had announced they could no longer guarantee the structural integrity of Medina Dam, which had been built in 1911 and never reinforced. Water was pouring 10.4 feet over the spillway.

My friend the Castroville deputy got a quote in, when asked how worried people should be. "That dam breaks, y'all can expect a sixty-foot-high wall of water. You tell me. "

Four towns downriver were being evacuated. Most of those half-million folk would be heading into San Antonio. It was no time to be on the highway.

Up next, the radio announcer promised, a breaking story about the Floresville Five. I glanced over at Jem and turned off the radio.

As he ran into my apartment, Jem yelled, "Cat!"

Robert Johnson opened one indignant eye.

Jem had long ago refused to believe cats could have surnames, so he'd taken to calling Robert Johnson by his species. It was one of the many humiliations Robert Johnson would endure from Jem without drawing blood, because he knew I would pay him off later with a king's ransom in kitty Tex-Mex.

"Do you have a paper bag?" Jem asked me, delighted.

As much as Robert Johnson loved playing sack-the-cat, I noticed the light on my answering machine was blinking.

I said, "Why don't you use the restroom first, champ?"

Jem was clearly more interested in tormenting my pet, but he'd started doing the cross-legged dance pretty bad. He dashed off to the john and rolled the door shut behind him.

Robert Johnson glared at me.

"It builds character," I said.

The answering machine told me I had two messages.

The first had come in at 1:35 P.M.

"Fred." Sam Barrera's voice sent a pang of guilt through my chest. I'd neglected checking on him much too long today. "I've found Stirman's hideout—North Cherry at Rosa Parks. Big brick building, Carrizo Ice Co. There's been nobody in or out, but I'm pretty sure he's keeping the woman there. I'll sit on the building as long as I can, but I need backup. Tell the field office to make it quiet this time."

I stared at the machine.

How Sam Barrera had gotten to a warehouse on the East Side when his BMW was sitting in my driveway, I didn't know. Perhaps he was imagining the whole thing from his armchair at home. But I had a sneaking suspicion the old bastard was truly mobile, and if Sam was knocking around the East Side looking for Stirman, he'd find trouble fast.

I grabbed my car keys.

The second message played.

This one had been left at 7:43 P.M., a few minutes before I'd walked in.

"Fred." Sam's voice again, tighter this time. "Where the hell are you? Stirman just called. I didn't . . . um, I tried to write it all down but I don't have my notebook. He's moved up the meeting time. He didn't sound good. Something's wrong. He wants us to bring the money to Jones and Avenue B right now. That's the museum, right? Shit, did we talk about money? Nothing's happening at this Carrizo Ice place, but I still think she's in there. I mean, the woman. You know. I'd better get over to the rendezvous point and stall him. If you don't get this— I'll think of something. I think I can take him down. He sounded like he might be hurt. I hate damn answering machines."

The line went dead.

"Jem," I called.

He came out of the bathroom. "You found a bag?"

"Champ, we don't have time—"

Red lights flashed against my windowpanes. A police car had pulled into the driveway, blocking my truck and Barrera's BMW. Ana DeLeon and her friend from the Fugitive Task Force, Major Cooper, got out of the back. Two uniforms got out of the front. They walked toward my porch looking like Death's Prize Patrol.

"On second thought," I told Jem, "how about you play with Robert Johnson in the backyard for a little while?"

My hand trembled as it hovered over the answering machine. I passed up *erase*, punched *rewind*.

A knock at the door. Ana DeLeon was two steps inside my living room before she asked, "May we come in?"

Behind her, the male cops stared at me. I could sense DeLeon was keeping them on a short tether. They would've liked nothing better than to tear me apart.

"Always glad to see friends," I said.

DeLeon formally introduced Major Cooper, the Task Force guy. Up close, I saw I was right about the linebacker thing. He had the cross-eyed squint of a former player, as if he'd spent too many years staring through a face plate. He wore a brown blazer with jeans and a yellow and blue tie that looked like Van Gogh had thrown up on it.

DeLeon said, "We have a problem."

I nodded. "You're right. He's a fashion disaster. But I don't think my clothes will fit him."

DeLeon managed to contain her mirth. "Twenty minutes ago, Will Stirman robbed a mom-and-pop on South Presa. The store owner stabbed him in the shoulder; Stirman shot the old guy dead. We blocked off the entire area, but Stirman still got away. Now we've got a wounded armed fugitive roaming the South Side."

"Straight down Broadway," I advised. "When you hit downtown, keep going."

"This is bullshit," Cooper said. "Cuff him."

DeLeon held up her hand. The uniforms stayed where they were.

"Tres, no games," she said. "The media is running with the story. Every cop in Bexar County who's not already on flood duty has been called up. We need to know what you know."

In the backyard, Jem was kicking his soccer ball at the patio table. He was trying to dislodge Robert Johnson, who was playing goalie. The score was zero–zero.

"You said it yourself," DeLeon reminded me. "If Stirman is forced to run, he won't bother keeping a hostage alive. We may have minutes rather than hours."

I glanced at Cooper. His face betrayed no surprise. He'd been fully briefed on Erainya.

I tried not to be angry. I tried not to feel like DeLeon had betrayed me by showing up unannounced with a bunch of bruis-ers. It wasn't her fault. She was doing her job, trying to help. Ralph had told me I should trust her, let her handle it. Maybe that's what decided me.

"Stirman called last night," I said. "He thinks Barrow and Barrera stole fourteen million dollars from him. He demanded we return it."

No one looked surprised about the amount of cash.

DeLeon said, "When and where?"

"Tonight. He's supposed to call after midnight and specify a drop."

"You found the money?"

"No."

DeLeon arched an eyebrow.

"Search the house," I offered.

DeLeon must've never heard of a bluff. She glanced at the uniforms. "Gentlemen?"

They tore up my apartment with gusto.

"While they're at it," she said, "mind if I search you for a weapon?"

Motherhood hadn't made her any gentler when it came to frisks.

Once she satisfied herself I wasn't carrying, and the cops found nothing more incriminating than my tai chi sword above the toilet and a cup full of HEB Buddy Buck coupons, DeLeon and Cooper exchanged looks.

"We'll tap the line," Cooper said. "Wait for the call."

"No," DeLeon and I chorused.

I'm not sure who was more embarrassed by our agreement.

"Stirman's wounded," DeLeon said. "If he's listening to the news, he knows we're on to him. He's not going to keep a sched-ule. He'll cut his losses and run."

"We've got every highway under surveillance," Cooper said. "We'll shut down the fucking city. He's not going anywhere."

"Right," I said. "You're just toying with him now."

Cooper took a step toward me.

DeLeon interposed. "Major."

"You vouched for this son-of-a-bitch," Cooper reminded her. "He knew Stirman was in town, maybe for days. If he'd given us a few goddamned details—"

"Major," DeLeon cut in, "as I explained at the hospital yesterday, Tres' boss may be in danger—"

"Hell with that. I should throw his ass in jail for aiding and abetting."

"You see that boy outside?" DeLeon asked. "His mother is the one Stirman took. Tres is trying to make sure she doesn't die."

"I don't . . ." Cooper stopped himself. His temples turned purple with the effort.

"You don't care," I supplied, "about anything except catching Stirman."

"Tres," DeLeon said, "if we knew where to look right now, it would be the San Antonio SWAT team who deployed. They're the only hostage force ready. I *know* them. They would do things right."

"If you knew where to look."

Her eyes held mine. "Stirman still wants his money. He might've called you after the robbery went bad, moved up the meeting time."

I thought about Sam Barrera, who would be arriving at Jones and Avenue B about now. *Minutes rather than hours.*

Cooper grumbled, "This asshole is holding back."

"I *know* that, goddamn it!" DeLeon snapped. She turned her attention back to me, tried to moderate her tone. "Well?"

I walked to the answering machine.

"I got home maybe two minutes before you walked in," I said. "This was waiting for me."

I pressed *play*.

As soon as Barrera's voice mentioned an address, Cooper whipped out his cell phone, but DeLeon said, "Wait."

She listened until I punched *stop*, then studied me uneasily. "Why did he call you Fred?"

"I'm the guy who works with Erainya. Sam's got Fred Barrow on the brain. You've never called somebody the wrong name when you were under stress?"

She thought about that. "He told you to call the field office. You've been talking with the FBI?"

"He means I-Tech, his agency. Look, I gave you what you want. Now get moving, or let me do it."

"Let's go," Cooper told the uniforms.

DeLeon hesitated. "You *will* stay here, Tres. You understand that?"

"I'm taking care of Jem. I have no weapon and no money to bargain with. Does it look like I'm charging into battle?"

DeLeon glanced toward the patio, where Jem was teaching Robert Johnson how to block corner shots.

"Sergeant," Cooper growled. "Now, or I leave without you."

Her expression was still troubled. She sensed something amiss. She said, "I'll get her back alive, Tres. I swear."

Their patrol car disappeared down Queen Anne Street.

I opened the patio door and told Jem to bring the cat inside.

"Time to go?" he asked, setting a relieved Robert Johnson down by his food dish.

"Time," I agreed. "You've got to be brave, champ. Can you do that for me?"

He nodded. "We'll get my mom back. He can't take us *both* on."

I tried to smile, despite the fact that I was betting everything—including our lives—on a guess.

I pressed *play* on the answering machine, let the tape continue from where I'd stopped it. I listened again to Sam Barrera's second message—the one Ana DeLeon hadn't heard.

21

Erainya dreamed of J.P.

He stood over her, telling her not to worry—he'd have the ropes off in a moment. She could smell his cologne. She was grateful for the familiar silver stubble on his cheeks, the strong line of his jaw against the broadcloth collar. His hands worked deftly at the knots.

But J.P. had been murdered. She had seen him fall in the alley behind Paesano's.

The man over her became Fred Barrow. He tugged at the ropes, clumsy and insistent, a gun in one hand, which made it impossible for him to get anywhere.

"Goddamn it, Irene." He smelled of cigars and bourbon. His belly pressed against her ribs, crushing her as it had the night she'd killed him. "Wake up. Come on."

Son-of-a-bitch.

She brought up her legs and kneecapped him in the face, sending him sprawling.

Erainya blinked, and came fully awake.

She was lying on a dirty pile of blankets, her arms bound behind her, her dress soaked with sweat. The man she'd just kneed in the head was the young fugitive—Pablo.

He got up, cursing, went to the table and exchanged his gun for a knife.

"Hold still," he growled, "or I'll cut your hands off."

Erainya felt the cold metal blade slip between her wrists. Pablo tugged, and the ropes snapped. She sat up, tried to move her arms. She felt like someone had poured boiling water into her veins.

Pablo stepped back, retrieved his gun. "Do the rest yourself."

Her fingers were numb. She managed to peel back the duct tape from her mouth.

"Get up." Pablo stood by the plywood-barricaded window, peeking out a sliver of sunset at something below. "We don't have much time."

She fumbled with the knots that bound her ankles. She wanted to feel hopeful about being untied, but she didn't like the urgency in Pablo's voice. He had that wild, angry look in his eyes he got every time Will Stirman yelled at him.

She must have missed something. Had Stirman called? Erainya cursed herself for falling asleep.

"Stand up," Pablo ordered.

"My legs are numb."

He turned toward her, the light from the window making a luminous pink scar on his left cheek. "Get over here if you want to live. You need to see this."

Erainya got unsteadily to her feet.

At the window, Pablo put the gun against her spine. "Quietly."

The evening air felt good on her face—better than the stifling heat inside anyway.

At first, Erainya saw nothing special—train tracks, a half-flooded gravel parking lot freckled with rain, empty loading docks and gutted warehouses. The sun was going down through a break in the clouds.

Then she noticed the blue van with tinted windows, parked under a chinaberry tree at the end of the block. She caught a flicker of movement on a rooftop across the street. A glint of metal in an upper window that should've been empty.

"Cops," Pablo told her. "Your friends broke faith."

The muzzle of his gun dug between her vertebrae.

Erainya tried to steady her breathing. "I don't see anything."

"You won't see them until they break down the door, huh? They're setting up a perimeter. We've been screwed."

His breath was sour from lack of sleep and canned food, his eyes red with shame, like a kid who'd just been beat up in the locker room.

Give him options, Erainya told herself.

Pablo had used the word *we.* He was desperate and alone. He was looking for help.

"Get away from the window," she told him. "You're giving the snipers a target."

He pulled her back, shoving her toward the mattress. "Your friend thought I wouldn't shoot you? Is that what he thought?"

"You're not cold-blooded, honey. You just cut me loose."

"I can't shoot a woman sleeping and tied up." His voice quivered. "I wanted you to see them out there. This ain't my fault."

A big rig rumbled by outside, drawing Pablo's attention to the window.

Erainya could try to disarm him, but her limbs were sandbags. She'd grab for the gun only as a last resort. She was afraid that decision might be just a few seconds away.

"Shooting me won't help," she said. "Don't listen to Stirman."

Pablo's face was beaded with sweat.

"I can still run," he said. "The loading dock in back—"

"They'll kill you as soon as you step outside."

"I'm not going to mess with a hostage, miss. I'm sorry."

"Let me go out there," she said. "I'll tell them Stirman forced you. That's true, isn't it? They'll treat you fair. I'll stay with you, honey."

Pablo blinked.

It had probably been a long time since anyone had offered to stay with him in a crisis.

He raised the gun. "I'm not going back to jail."

"You don't have to kill me."

"If I don't, Stirman will find me—doesn't matter if I'm in jail or out. I have to get home. My wife . . ."

Erainya imagined a SWAT team moving silently into position. A flash-bang grenade would roll in the door first. Maybe tear gas. It wouldn't be soon enough. Pablo and she were both going to die.

"There's another way," she told him. She tried her best not to make it sound like a lie. "I have an idea."

His finger was white on the trigger. "No time, miss."

"Listen to me."

Pablo shook his head, his eyes bright with anger as if he were still hearing Stirman's voice giving him orders.

Erainya started explaining anyway, describing her last-resort idea as Pablo took aim at her heart.

22

The Art Museum was supposed to be closed for flood repairs, but when Jem and I got there the entranceway blazed with light. The glass front doors were propped open with a trash can.

Two cars sat at the curb—an old Ford station wagon and an '83 Chevy Impala with naked-lady-silhouette mud flaps. Neither struck me as a typical art patron vehicle.

"I've been here on a field trip," Jem informed me.

"That's good," I said. "So you know where the bathrooms are?"

He nodded. With his active bladder, Jem had men's room radar.

"If I tell you to run," I said, "go to the bathroom. Lock the door if you can, and call 911. Okay?"

"Okay." He slipped his mother's cell phone into the pocket of his shorts. "Next time we do a heist, can we go to Malibu Castle?"

"*Rendezvous*, champ. Heists are what the bad guys do."

I pulled my truck up to the Grand Avenue Bridge and parked behind a dark stand of cottonwoods next to the swollen river. I wasn't sure why. I just didn't feel right leaving the truck in plain sight.

We walked back to the museum entrance.

I used my Swiss army knife to puncture the tires on the Chevy and the Ford. I was tempted to cut off the Chevy's naked-lady mud flaps, but we were in a hurry.

Jem took my hand. It was the first time he'd done so in almost a year. We looked up at the two towers rising into the night, the glass skywalk between them, crisscrossed with neon. I wished they still made beer here. I needed one.

Together we walked up the front steps.

The night watchman was slumped over the security desk. His gun holster was empty. He had a nasty lump on the side of his head. Spots of blood dribbled from his earlobe onto the security monitor.

"Is he okay?" Jem asked.

"Oh, sure." I squeezed Jem's hand and pulled him away. "Probably just tired."

Dripping water echoed in the vastness of the Great Hall. Three stories above, damaged skylights sent a steady stream of runoff onto the café tables and the chocolate Saltillo tiles, completely missing the buckets. At the top of the staircase, two windows had been blasted out by the storms, replaced with plastic sheeting. The hanging catamaran sculpture that always reminded me of a da Vinci contraption was wrapped in a tarp.

I glanced into the gift shop. No crazed killers.

The other direction, plastic-wrapped statues of Marcus Aurelius and Vishnu flanked the entrance to the Ancient Cultures wing.

A man's voice crackled with static: "Upstairs."

It came from the unconscious guard—or rather, from the two-way radio clipped to his belt.

"Hope you're not as empty-handed as it looks," Stirman's voice said. "Mr. Barrera hopes so, too. West elevator. All the way up."

I looked around for a security camera. I didn't see one.

"Let's go," I told Jem.

"You sure this isn't a heist?" he asked.

The West Tower elevator was one of those see-through glass and steel jobs, set in the center of the room amidst Anubis statues and Middle Kingdom hieroglyphics. Getting inside made me feel like I was becoming one of the displays.

We ascended past Chinese porcelain and samurai armor. The pulley system went by, its brass wheels and silver weights clicking. We stopped on the fourth floor. Tahitian masks and Aboriginal fertility statues stared at us from the shadows.

The gallery space was tiny at the top of the tower. There was no place to go but the skywalk.

Will Stirman stood at the far end, holding a two-way radio and a gun. Sam Barrera sat cross-legged in front of him, a black duffel bag at his side.

"Come across halfway," Stirman told us.

We stepped out over the void between the towers.

To the north, past the rooftops of the smaller galleries, Highway 281 cut a glittering arc around the woods and the river. To the south glowed all of downtown—the Tower of the Americas, the enchilada-red library, the old Tower Life Building.

Stirman hadn't needed a security camera to see us approaching. From this vantage point, you could see straight down to the front of the building, and inside the Great Hall through the skylights.

It was difficult to say whether he or Barrera looked worse.

Sam was dressed in his suit and tie, but looked like he'd been broiling in a hot car all afternoon. His face glistened. His expression was blank with pain. His hand appeared to be broken. He cradled it in his lap, the fingers purple and swollen.

At least he wasn't covered in blood.

Stirman's shoulder wound made him look like something out

of a Jacobean tragedy. I tried to convince myself the amount of blood soaking through his makeshift bandages wasn't as much as it appeared, but it looked pretty damn bad.

His feverish eyes studied me for a moment, then rested on Jem. "I see the child, but not the money. Why is that, Navarre?"

"You need a doctor, Stirman."

He swayed back about five degrees. The guy had to be going into shock. If I could just wait for the right moment . . .

"Don't get ideas," Stirman warned. "Barrera got ideas. You can see they didn't help him."

"You okay, Sam?" I asked.

Barrera tried to move his swollen hand, winced. "Where's Fred?"

"Dead, Sam. Dead eight years."

Stirman threw his walkie-talkie against the window so hard the glass shuddered. Next to me, Jem flinched.

"The old man keeps yammering about Barrow like he's still alive," Stirman complained. "He looks at me like he doesn't know who I am."

"Barrera's ill." I tried to keep my voice even. "He's losing his memory."

I could tell from Stirman's face that he didn't want to believe me. He wanted to buy into Sam's dementia—to think Fred Barrow really was coming back from the dead, that he would show up any minute to get his just deserts.

"He brought me this." Stirman picked up the black duffel bag, tossed it toward me. "What the hell is *this*?"

The zipper split open when it hit the carpet. Paper spilled all over the skywalk.

Not money.

Photographs. Old yellowed photos. In some of them, I recognized Sam Barrera's face—a much younger Sam, grinning with his arms around people I didn't know. There hadn't been a single photo in Sam Barrera's house—but here they all were, a lifetime's worth, stuffed in an old loot bag.

"More memory problems?" Stirman asked.

"It's the right bag," Barrera insisted. "Tell him, Fred."

Stirman raised an eyebrow at me.

"Barrera spent his share of the loot years ago," I said. "Used it to build up his company. He's got nothing left."

Stirman jabbed his gun to the back of Barrera's head. "Too bad for him. Where's Fred Barrow's share?"

"You didn't give me time to retrieve it."

"But you know where it is."

"Yeah."

"Then you'll take me there."

"Look at yourself, Stirman. You're in no shape to go anywhere."

"You'll take me there," he repeated. "And if you're lying, you will wish to God you weren't." He looked at Jem. "Come here, boy."

"Jem, no," I said.

Stirman blinked at me. He was swaying a little more now, his face blue in the walkway's neon lights. "They took everything from me, Navarre. I mean to collect."

"You'd take Jem from Erainya."

"Yes."

"You'd take revenge on a little boy—"

"It isn't revenge."

"—a single mother, and an old man who doesn't even remember why you're mad at him. Is that satisfying? Is that what Soledad would've wanted?"

For a moment, I thought I'd pushed him too far, misread him completely.

But then he looked at Jem, and Stirman's face took on that same hunger I'd seen at the soccer field. Again, he forced himself to contain his anger. Stirman had been telling me the truth on the phone—he *did* need Jem here. The boy's presence was the only thing keeping him sane.

Stirman told me, "I know what I'm doing."

"Don't lie to yourself," I said. "This isn't about what Barrow and Barrera took from you eight years ago. This is about what you ran away from. *You* failed Soledad. You stayed silent about her baby. All this time, you let the past stay buried. You can't make that right now."

Stirman's jaw tightened. "Be careful telling me what I can and can't do."

"Listen to Jem," I said. "Listen to what he wants."

"I want my mother back," Jem managed.

"Your mother . . ." Stirman's eyes drifted, as if looking at Jem had suddenly become painful. "Boy, if you knew about your mother . . ."

At that moment, Stirman looked very much like Sam Barrera—like a man whose lifelong focus had started to unravel.

"Put down the gun," I told him. "Surrender to the police."

Stirman exhaled, a humorless laugh. "That's your advice, huh? Death Row?"

"You won't survive another day on the outside. If you want any time to make amends, if it's really not about revenge, then prison's your only choice. It's the only place you belong now."

Stirman's face had gone clammy. His bandaged shoulder glistened with new blood. The simple act of holding the gun to Barrera's head must've been torture for him.

"Tell me where the money is," he said. "Maybe I'll let you and Barrera go. But the boy comes with me."

Sam Barrera said, "Like hell."

He started to get up.

"Sit down, old man," Stirman ordered, pushing Barrera's collarbone with the gun.

Barrera ignored him. He got unsteadily to his feet. "I didn't come this far to let him run, Fred."

I said, "Sam—"

"Go ahead and shoot me," Barrera told Stirman. "You think I don't remember? *I* shot your wife. Don't take it out on Fred and this little kid. You gonna shoot somebody, shoot me."

Stirman stared at Barrera in disbelief. "But . . . it was Barrow . . . I saw him. Why are you—"

"Shoot me," Barrera ordered. "Last chance. I got the whole goddamn FBI surrounding this place."

Stirman took a step back—a deeply ingrained human instinct: Get away from the crazy person.

Barrera grabbed the gun.

It discharged, cracking the glass wall behind Barrera's head. I yelled, "Jem, run!"

He followed my orders too well. With perfect eight-year-old single-mindedness, he ran toward the nearest restroom, which happened to be the wrong way—directly past Stirman, in the East Tower.

"No!"

Another shot drowned out my voice. A tube of red neon exploded. Stirman shoved Sam Barrera against the glass, which buckled, shattered, and Sam Barrera went backward into the void.

Stirman turned as Jem brushed past him. He tried to catch the boy's shirt. I tackled Stirman. The butt of his gun slammed into my ear.

The next thing I knew I was on the carpet. A photograph was stuck to my cheek.

I got up, my vision doubled. I leaned against the railing, now open to the wet night air, and I saw a pale human shape fifteen feet below, sprawled on the lower gallery roof. Sam Barrera's body.

I didn't have time to think about that. Stirman hadn't stayed to finish me off.

He had gone after Jem.

23

Just as she heard the shot inside the warehouse, Ana DeLeon's phone vibrated against her Kevlar vest.

The SWAT team was too well trained to react to gunfire, but they all looked at her to see what was rattling.

She ripped the phone out of her pocket and stared at the display.

Ralph Arguello.

He never called her at work. She imagined the baby in the emergency room, the house burning down—what would it take for him to call like this?

There was nothing she could do. She stuck the phone back in her pocket and took out her sidearm.

The lieutenant in charge waved the team forward. Four guys in body armor moved into the warehouse, DeLeon in the rear, the unwelcome guest.

She wasn't worried about her own safety, or about capturing Stirman.

SAPD had the whole area ringed with snipers, cordoned off with a double perimeter, two helicopters on standby. If Stirman was inside, he was screwed. The problem was getting Erainya out in one piece.

They secured the first floor in twenty seconds. Stairs led up, exactly where the schematics said they should. The shot had come from above—third or fourth floor, about where long-range mikes had zeroed in on voices.

Sixty-three seconds later, the team was in the fourth-floor corridor. DeLeon was melting from the heat and the Kevlar. She forgot about that when she heard Erainya's voice—yelling for help.

There was an open doorway at the end of the hall.

Smaller voices—two men in conversation.

"In here!" Erainya yelled. "Anybody?"

It wasn't the voice of a woman being held at gunpoint. But something felt wrong to DeLeon.

The SWAT lieutenant looked back at the entry team—not a question, but a silent warning. He, too, sensed the wrongness of the situation, the team's uneasiness. But his look made it clear they would be following the plan.

Their point man moved to the doorway, threw in the flash grenade.

The subsonic boom shook the plaster. Anyone within twenty feet would be knocked senseless.

The team moved in.

Their laser sites made a cluster of red dots on the source of the men's voices—a portable radio.

Under the window, next to an overturned table, Erainya Manos lay stunned, her legs bound and a duct tape gag half peeled off her mouth. Her hands had been tied behind her, but one of them was partially free. That hand gripped a pistol.

DeLeon scanned the scene with disbelief. Erainya had crawled from the pile of filthy blankets in the corner, managed to kick over the table, where her captor had foolishly left a gun. She'd gotten her fingers free enough to grasp the pistol and fire a shot for help.

That was what had happened. No doubt. But where the hell was Stirman?

The team checked the rest of the floor. The rooms were empty. The lieutenant radioed the situation. Within thirty seconds Major Cooper was inside with a second team. He ordered a sweep of the roof.

By the time Erainya was coherent enough to speak, DeLeon knew there was no one else in the building.

"Left," Erainya said. "About . . . I don't remember."

She was clearly confused, dehydrated, scared out of her wits. She said there had been two men, Will Stirman and a young Latino Stirman had called Pablo. Stirman had left to get ransom money. As soon as he was gone, Pablo disobeyed Stirman's orders to guard her and fled. She didn't know where either of them went. Her son was in danger. Stirman wanted to kill him. That's all she cared about.

"Damn it," the SWAT lieutenant said.

Major Cooper looked equally miffed. It was all fine and good to rescue a hostage, but with no capture, no blood, DeLeon knew it was a wasted evening for him. They had a whole city to search now. Their energy had been directed the wrong way. Sam Barrera and Tres Navarre . . . she would be having a serious conversation with both of them. She hated private eyes.

Her phone rattled again. She had completely forgotten about Ralph.

She stepped to the window and answered the call.

"I found him," her husband said.

"What? Is Lucia okay?"

The baby was fine. Ralph told her about Tres' visit earlier in the day.

She felt the old resentment building—the near-panic that

fluttered in her chest whenever Ralph got close to his old life, his old habits.

She controlled her voice. "You went out looking for Stirman?"

"No, just some calls, *mi amor*. But that's not the thing. I know where they're supposed to deliver Stirman's money."

"We're already at the warehouse. Stirman isn't here."

"You're a couple of miles off. I called Tres—"

"You gave Navarre information first?"

"Just listen, will you? I called to tell him I'd had no luck tracking Stirman. I got Tres' machine. I was worried, so I figured what the hell, I'd retrieve his messages, see if he'd gotten anything—"

"You can retrieve Navarre's messages?"

"How long have I known him, Ana? Shit, yes. I could use his ATM card, if I wanted to."

She fought back the bite of jealousy. "That doesn't matter. He played us the message."

"The second message?"

Time slowed. Ana said, "What second message?"

Ralph laughed appreciatively. "Shit—Tres don't change. The meet's at the Art Museum. It's closed for repairs but Barrera runs security. He's got the keys. And Ana?"

She was already moving, waving frantically at the SWAT lieutenant. "Yeah?"

"Try not to shoot Tres, okay? He can't help himself."

24

Somehow, the gun found its way into my hand.

It may have been the one smashed out of Barrera's grip, or the one taken from the security guard's holster. Maybe Barrera had hidden it at the bottom of the black duffel bag.

I figured there was some inverse property to the old statistic—carry a gun, and you are the most likely one to be shot with it. Perhaps if you didn't carry a gun, you were likely to find one you could use to shoot someone else.

At any rate, the old-fashioned .45 service revolver was lying there on the carpet. I scooped it up and ran into the gloom of the East Tower.

My ears were ringing. I was pretty sure the left side of my face was bleeding. Two blurry sets of steps kaleidoscoped in front of me, then two bathroom doors, then I was inside the men's room, staring at a bloody handprint on the stall door, but no Jem.

I ran back into the gallery. An alarm went off—bells in the distance; the floor lights dimming red.

I wondered what kind of stupid alarm system sounds only when you try to escape the bathroom. Then I noticed the open glass doors leading to the rooftop, the stenciled warning: EMER-GENCY EXIT ONLY. ALARM WILL SOUND.

I stepped outside, sinking to a crouch. The rooftop space was L-shaped—a railed patio with a walkway that ran along the back side of the tower. Rain made the tar shingles soft under my feet.

I crept around the corner and could just make out Jem's shape toward the end of the walkway.

His back was to me. He stood frozen, looking at something—perhaps Sam Barrera's body below.

As quietly as I could, I called, "Jem."

No reply.

Stirman must have missed him. Stirman had given up when he heard the alarms. The police cars would be heading this way. It couldn't take them long.

"Jem," I said. "Come on—I'll get you out of here."

I stepped closer and froze.

Jem wasn't staring over the edge. He was staring at Will Stirman, who was crouching in front of him at the edge of the walkway.

He was telling Jem something, pointing his gun at the boy's feet. I could've sworn he was giving Jem a lecture.

Stirman saw me. He rose, calmly. We leveled our guns at each other.

I could hear police cars now. Tires slashing through water, turning onto Jones. They were running without sirens, but I knew they were cops. There is something unmistakable about the sound of police engines.

"It's over," I told Stirman. "Let Jem go back to his mother."

Stirman blinked slowly. He seemed to be losing his grip on consciousness.

A single police light flashed—circling once across the neon skywalk and the face of the West Tower. An officer must have hit the switch accidentally while getting out of his car.

The light snapped Stirman back to his senses. He looked around. He was backed into a corner, forty feet in the air.

"Tell me where the money is," he said.

"It's too late for that," I said. "You'll never get out of the building."

"I owe Soledad. I can't give up."

"It isn't giving up. It's deciding to live. If you run, you'll die."

Down in front of the museum, car doors were opening.

I had to get Jem away from Stirman. I had to get him out of the line of fire.

Stirman held my eyes. He seemed to understand what I was thinking.

He put his hand on Jem's shoulder, gently pushed him toward me. "Go on, boy."

Jem dug in his heels. His hand was closed, as if he were holding something small. "But . . ."

"Go on," Stirman ordered.

Jem shook his head stubbornly. "But you told me—"

"It's all right." Stirman's voice cracked. "Just go on, now."

When Jem was finally safe behind me, Stirman said, "Now tell me about the cash. Quick."

I didn't see what difference it would make. I told him where the money was.

Understanding dawned on Stirman's face—the sense that what I said had to be true. "Goddamn Fred Barrow."

I imagined the police inside the building, the slow pulse of the glass elevator as it rose through the galleries, filled with heavily armed men.

Stirman took one last look at Jem—hesitating long enough to erase any chance of escape.

"Bear witness, Jem," he said. "Be good to your mother, hear?"

Then he jumped. The drop should have been enough to break

his legs, but he hit the roof of the lower gallery on solid footing and cleared the other side, dropping into the darkness behind the museum. There was at least a square mile of woods and flooded riverbanks back there. The police would have to search it on foot. But they would find him. I was sure of that.

Jem stared at the spot where Stirman had disappeared—wet treetops hissing in the rain.

I wanted to put my hand on his shoulder, but I sensed the barrier he was putting up. He wanted no more hand-holding, no comforting.

"He won't come back," I said.

"I know."

His tone wasn't what I expected from an eight-year-old who'd just had a conversation with evil. He sounded wistful. He wore the same expression he'd worn the night we watched his mother's van go floating away down Rosillio Creek.

He slipped his hand into his pocket, depositing whatever he was holding.

Before I could ask what it was, I heard a groan from the roof below us. A man's voice said, "Hell."

"Stay here," I told Jem.

I lowered myself over the railing. Stirman had done it. How hard could it be?

I dropped.

Stupid, Navarre.

I lost my footing immediately and slid down the slick roof. I would have gone over the edge and into the skylights below had I not caught the wet bottom rung of a service ladder. Slowly, I managed to crawl back up to where Sam Barrera was lying on his back, his arm bent underneath him at an ugly angle.

"Damn bastard," he muttered. "You get him, Fred?"

I sat next to him, too exhausted to correct his ragged memory. "Yeah. I got him."

That seemed to comfort the old man. He put his head back and let the rain fall on his face. Police were popping up in all the windows of the museum now—SWAT team members on the skywalk, aiming assault rifles at me.

"Thanks," I told Sam, "for trying to save us up there."

"Did I do that?"

"Yeah, you did."

"I always was pretty damn brave," Barrera said. "I don't know about taking the money, though. It feels wrong."

"Maybe it is," I admitted.

"And the baby?"

I looked at him, and asked carefully, "What about him?"

"Did your wife get him out okay?"

I was silent for a long time as the police moved in, DeLeon now visible above us, not looking happy, or in any hurry to call off her firing squad.

"Yeah, Erainya got him out," I told Barrera. "The baby is fine."

I looked up at Ana DeLeon in the broken glass and neon. I raised my hands in surrender.

25

The plane was a twin-engine Cessna, so old no self-respecting drug-runner would use it anymore, but it could still make the flight to Mexico below radar in under an hour.

The pilot waited in the drizzle on the tarmac at Stinson Field. He checked his watch. His client was late.

It was a crummy night to fly, but anticipating his payment made him feel better. He imagined the money in his bank account. He would make separate cash deposits, space them out carefully, keep them under the mandatory reporting limit.

He was deep in thought about a comfortable retirement when somebody put a gun to his back.

Long after the police took Erainya Manos away, Pablo had waited in the ventilation shaft.

He expected the woman to sell him out. Any second, the muzzle of an assault rifle would poke its way into his hiding place.

But Pablo kept waiting.

When he couldn't stand it anymore, he crawled out. No one was waiting in the storage room to ambush him. His gun was still lying on the floor by the window. They hadn't even bothered bagging it for evidence.

Why would the police leave the scene so fast?

He checked the magazine. Still loaded, minus the bullet Erainya Manos had fired to rattle the police.

Dangerous, he had told her.

It'll throw them off balance, she said. *When they find out I fired the gun, they'll relax their guard about everything. They'll believe I'm alone.*

He hadn't trusted her, but he'd gone along. He couldn't run. He couldn't surrender. He couldn't bring himself to kill her.

He crept down the stairs, spotted two uniformed cops at the front entrance. They looked bored, like they'd been put there to keep people out. They weren't paying any attention to the inside of the building.

Pablo slipped out the back, onto the loading docks.

The rain felt good on his face, but he told himself he would never make it across open ground. There were probably still snipers on the surrounding rooftops. His shoulder blades tensed for the bullet he expected in his back.

He jogged down a dark alley. Nothing happened. He made it three blocks away, came out next to St. Paul Square. A bunch of tourist rental cars were parked on the street. He strolled down the line, glancing casually through windows. A Dodge Neon had the driver's keys just sitting there on the front seat.

Too easy. Had to be a trap.

The police would surround him as soon as he turned the ignition. The engine would explode. Something.

But he got in, started the Neon, and pulled away from the curb.

By the time he got to the highway, he was crying like a child.

He had come *that* close to killing Erainya Manos, and she'd been telling him the truth.

*   *   *

The pilot found himself facing a young Latino with cob-webs in his hair, ragged clothes, dirt and scratches on his arms like he'd crawled out of a collapsed building.

The pilot tried for calm. He raised his hands. "I got nothing you can rob, partner. Unless you want an airplane."

"Actually," the Latino said, "that is exactly what I want."

The pilot blinked. *"You're* Will Stirman?"

"You know the Calabras airstrip, south of Juárez?"

"Sure." The pilot didn't feel the need to mention he'd flown heroin from that airstrip a dozen times. "You have my hundred grand?"

The Latino smiled. He nudged the pilot's nose affectionately with his gun. "Actually, *señor,* there's been a slight change of plans."

Will Stirman found his money, right where Navarre said it would be.

The black duffel bag was lighter than when Will had packed it, eight years ago, but that was to be expected. Fred Barrow must've used a good half million.

Will stuffed a couple of hundred-dollar bills in his pocket, rezipped the bag.

He had one last score to settle.

He climbed the wooden stairs out of the basement, the knife wound in his shoulder throbbing so badly he could hardly think. He found an intact section of roof to stand under. Rain was blowing through the skeletal remains of the house. The dark hills around him smelled of wet juniper.

Will called the SAPD. He was pleasantly surprised to get a connection so far from the city. He told the dispatcher he was the outside accomplice who'd helped Will Stirman escape, and now he had a guilty conscience. He gave her enough details about the jailbreak to be sure she was taking him seriously. Then he told her where they could find one of the missing Floresville Five. A hunting cabin in the woods of Wisconsin. He gave her directions.

Will hung up, feeling satisfied.

With any luck, his guess would be right. The Guide might be stupid enough to lay low there. He might have thought Will had forgotten about the Wisconsin property, which the Guide had shown him once, years ago—his little retirement dream house. But Will never forgot a good hiding place.

He walked back to the main road in the dark—a good half mile, through mosquitoes and mud and brambles. Down toward the river, the only visible light was a kerosene lamp glowing in a curtained window. A caretaker's cabin, maybe. Will avoided it.

He hadn't seen another human being for thirty miles, since he exited the main highway. Every farmhouse had been dark, every road abandoned. Anybody crazy enough to ignore the evacuation orders, Will wanted to stay clear of.

He climbed into the truck and stared at the empty seat next to him.

You *failed Soledad,* Navarre had said. *You let the past stay buried.*

The words weighed on Will's heart.

Eight years ago, he had taken the coward's way out. He'd never tried to find out what really happened to Soledad's baby—*his* baby.

He'd assumed the worst, nursed his anger, promised himself that he would get revenge in the long run. But he'd stayed silent. In his most secret thoughts, he'd been relieved not to be a father anymore. Relieved the child was gone. And his guilt had fueled his anger.

Now . . . what had he accomplished?

He'd left hardly a ripple on the lives of his old enemies. He'd had a chance to settle his debts, salvage something from the past. But here he was again, doing the only thing he was good at—running away. He never had Soledad's courage for staying put.

Would she forgive him?

Maybe if she'd seen Jem Manos' face . . .

Will started the truck's engine. He set the duffel bag next to him. All his pleasure at finding the money had drained away.

He realized bitterly that Navarre was wrong on one count. He would *not* die on the outside. Will Stirman was too good at hiding and running. Nothing could catch the Ghost.

He would make it across the border, then eventually down into Central America. He would get the shoulder wound treated and live to a ripe old age on some tropical beach, alone, dreaming every night about the people he had killed, waking up every morning with no one, remembering the face of Jem Manos, and wishing he was not a coward.

A distant rumble rattled the truck's windows. Will thought at first it was thunder, but the rumble didn't die. It grew louder, building toward a crescendo. Thunder didn't do that.

Will put the truck in drive and eased forward, toward the bridge.

In his headlights, the Medina River was doing strange things. It was churning with foam, waves sloshing over the road. The ground was shaking.

Will looked upriver. He could see nothing but that single yellow light on the hillside.

He turned on the radio. Static.

It occurred to him then what might be happening—what they'd said on the news.

But that was impossible.

The roar filled his ears.

He looked north again, and this time his heart nearly stopped. The horizon was curling toward him, the earth lifting up like the edge of a carpet.

For a moment, his hand drifted toward the stick shift. He could punch the gas. He could run for higher ground.

Then a sense of calm came over him. He realized Navarre had been right on every count. So much for the uncatchable Will Stirman.

He killed the truck's engine and got out. He wanted to be standing on his own two feet for this.

The yellow light on the hill comforted him, letting him know he wasn't alone.

He heard Soledad's voice: *Maybe* I'm *what was lost.*

He remembered her last kiss, and waited to be scoured away with all the other ghosts of the land.

The Cessna flew above the South Side, angling into the rain.

Pablo did not relax his guard, but he couldn't help watching the lights below—the great expanse of San Antonio, and south: the smaller towns of Poteet, Kenedy, and there, Floresville. He was almost sure he could see the prison.

He had no money. No resources. Nothing but a gun and a pilot who would betray him at the first opportunity.

But the airstrip was secluded in the mountains, in territory he knew well.

He had already used the pilot's phone to make a call to El Paso—to an old friend who would relay a message to Angelina. It was risky, revealing his location like that. What Angelina would do with the information, he didn't know. Perhaps she would be waiting for him. Perhaps the Mexican police would.

He had sent her instructions many times in his letters—always indirect references that she alone would understand. If she'd read the letters, if she wanted him back, she would know what to do.

She was to tell her friends and family to look for a yellow cloth tied around the front porch post—the kind people left out for soldiers overseas. That would be her signal to them—the only goodbye she could give—to let them know she had disappeared on purpose, gone to join him.

Pablo wondered if she would do that.

The Cessna climbed higher, above the flooded farms and the dark ranch land of South Texas.

Pablo thought of El Paso, and his wife's face.

For the first time since Floresville, since the last morning circle when he'd joined hands with his five brethren and Pastor Riggs, Pablo prayed.

26

That bastard Will Stirman stole my truck.

While I was busy getting chewed out by DeLeon, and the paramedics were tending to Sam Barrera, and the police were fanning out across every square foot of riverfront behind the museum, Stirman crept around the side of the building—exactly where it was most suicidal to go. He found my F-150 by the river, found the extra key I kept in the wheel well, pulled away over the Grand Avenue Bridge and disappeared.

It was twenty minutes before I noticed the truck was missing and we figured out what had happened.

By then, Stirman was long gone.

That same night, two hours later and twenty-five miles north-west of town, in the lightest rainfall of the month, Medina Dam broke.

The old McCurdy Ranch was right in the path of forty billion cubic feet of water. Century trees were uprooted. Boulders disappeared. New gorges and ravines were carved into the rock, and the cabin of Gloria Paz was reduced to a concrete slab and a few dark gold cinder blocks.

I don't know what happened to Gloria. I'd like to think she got out, but somehow I imagine her standing on her front porch with her shotgun and her tin cup of goat's milk and coffee, her milky eyes staring north as the wall of water came toward her. I imagine her smiling, thinking of her long journey on the Green Highway.

Perched on its high hill, the McCurdy ranch house itself was spared.

I didn't need to go into the basement to see that Will Stirman had been there. The tarp had been stripped off the abandoned building supplies. Dug out from the middle of the lumber and paint cans was a lockbox—now busted open and empty, a box the perfect size to fit a duffel bag full of cash.

Fred Barrow was the San Antonio businessman who had purchased the McCurdy property. The mildewed fishing painting over the mantel was one of his, just like the ones hanging in Erainya's study.

After shooting Will Stirman, Barrow had only lived a few weeks, but in that time he had managed to buy the land, set up a trust, and allow Gloria Paz a safe place to live for the rest of her life. Barrow had planned to use his stolen millions to cleanse and remake the murderer's ranch. A feeble, guilty gesture, but I knew Fred had been trying to put the victims' spirits to rest, to make amends.

This did not make Fred Barrow a good man. It did not excuse the way he treated Erainya, or make me sorry that the asshole was dead. But he had redeemed one life, one small cinder block cabin. He'd been remembered as honest by an aging blind woman. It made me wonder if I could've done any better with dirty money.

*   *   *

Much to the Fugitive Task Force's relief, Will Stirman's body
was found forty miles downriver. The Green Highway had, for
once, reversed course, its cleared lanes providing the path of
least resistance for thousands of tons of flotsam swept south by
the flood. Many of the dead were never recovered, their bodies
buried deep under a new geological layer of silt and debris. But
Stirman's body was easily identified—tangled in downed power
lines, his arms wrapped around the cables as if he had inten-
tionally held on—as if he wanted to be sure there was no public
doubt about his death.

My truck, being heavier, had not been carried quite so far. It
had melded into a sandbank half a mile downstream from the
McCurdy Ranch entrance. Only the back fender showed.

Will Stirman had found his money. He died reclaiming something from Fred Barrow. But the duffel bag was not in the
truck, nor on his person. Whatever was left of Stirman's seven
million dollars floated away in the flood, and is still buried
somewhere in the South Texas landscape.

The final incidents in the Floresville Five case were pretty
unsatisfactory for law enforcement. The first was a shoot-out at
a Wisconsin hunting cabin where an unidentified man resisted
arrest, opened fire on police and was killed by an FBI sniper.
The slain man was not, as originally thought, one of the escaped convicts, but he fit the description of an Anglo who had
been seen in the company of Elroy Lacoste and Luis Juarez in
Omaha. Perhaps he was one of Stirman's old associates. Embarrassed police were still working to establish his identity.

The fourth convict, C. C. Andrews, was discovered when rain
eroded his shallow grave in an Oklahoma riverbank. A farmer
went out to dig some new fence posts one morning and was

startled to find a dead African-American in an expensive Italian suit floating in the middle of his creek.

This left only one escapee unaccounted for—Pablo Zagosa. Publicly, police remained confident of his eventual capture, but when pressed, they admitted they had no solid leads. Pablo's estranged wife in El Paso had disappeared, and family members said it was because she feared her husband's vengeance. But this did not explain the yellow cloth police found tied to Angelina Zagosa's front porch rail. Privately, Ana DeLeon told me the Task Force was baffled. They were starting to reconcile themselves to the idea that Pablo Zagosa might be the little fish that got away.

As for Dimebox Ortiz, he was spending a few nights in the county jail, but he was confident that his brother-in-law would eventually soften and bail him out. And I was confident I would be bounty-hunting him again soon after that.

Saturday, two days after the Medina Dam broke, the sun blazed down at the Lady Bird Johnson YMCA field.

After six billion dollars in damage, thirty-seven lives lost, the attention of the network news, the president, the governor and the National Guard, the floods decided they'd had enough fun. Like spoiled children, they went off to throw a tantrum somewhere else.

Jem manned the goalie box in his yellow vest.

The rest of my team clumped midfield around the ball as the Saint Mark's coach yelled orders to his kids about crossovers and wings and a bunch of other maneuvers I'd never heard of.

"Get 'em!" Erainya yelled next to me.

Which pretty much summed up our strategy.

Technically, parents weren't allowed on the players' side of the field, but Erainya had decided she was now my assistant coach.

The Garcia twins slammed into each other, but got up before the ref could halt play. Jack fell down in one of his slide-into-home kicks, shooting the ball straight toward the Saint Mark's guards, who just shot it right back.

"I love this," I said. "So much more relaxing than a firefight."

Erainya said, "Huh."

Her dark eyes glittered as she scanned the field. "All right, honey. What's that kid's name—Peter?"

"Paul."

"*That's* it, Paul!" she shouted. "To the goal!"

By that time Paul had run past the ball, let Saint Mark's intercept, and was busy checking out a really cool rock he'd found on the field.

"J.P. got off the ventilator today," Erainya told me. "We talked a whole ten minutes."

I heard the relief in her voice—the return of that love-struck optimism that had infuriated me for months whenever she talked about her boyfriend.

J. P. Sanchez had beaten the odds. His friends at the Medical Center had called in a few favors. They'd imported the best specialists from Houston and Los Angeles to oversee the reconstructive surgery. Sanchez would be in the hospital for weeks, physical therapy for months, but his long-term prognosis was good.

"I'm glad," I said. And then, when she gave me a skeptical look, I added: "Seriously."

"He'll be asking you to serve as best man," Erainya said. "Just so you're warned."

The sun suddenly felt a lot warmer. "Me?"

"I'd ask you to be a bridesmaid, honey, but the dress would

look terrible on you." Then she shouted, "Come on, Laura! Good!"

The ball made another futile loop around the field. It sailed toward Jem. It bounced off Maria.

Erainya turned to me. "Honey, look, J.P.'s only got his daughter. No male friends he's really close to. He knows how Jem and I feel about you. He wants you there. Think about it."

I felt a weight on my chest, the unresolved need to say something I couldn't quite say.

Jem crouched at the goalie net, his hands down, knees bent—the exact position I'd told him to keep. He wore the same crazy grin he always got whenever he was on the soccer field. Saint Mark's had only scored one goal off him so far. Then again, we'd scored zip.

"Guess you're closing the agency?" I asked Erainya.

She shrugged. "I can't run it anymore."

"Oh. Right."

She looked completely unconcerned. "You'll get along."

I had expected this. I should not feel bitter. Maia Lee would be delighted.

"Besides," Erainya said, "I'll be around if you need advice. I ain't going to turn it over to you just to let you run it into the ground."

"Excuse me?"

"Don't look at me like that, you big idiot. I'm giving you the Erainya Manos Agency. My clients. My files. My fabulous resources. My unpaid bills. With both me and Sam retiring, we've got to have one decent PI in town. And if you're smart, you'll keep the name. It's lucky."

Paul was taking the ball in the right direction. Somehow, he managed to kick it to Jack.

"Well?" Erainya asked me. "You're not gonna disappoint me, are you?"

Will Stirman was gone. Erainya was happy.

I could say nothing.

But the weight was there still, smooth and hard as a river rock.

"Laura!" I yelled. "To the middle! Help him out!"

Only because it was her love interest Jack, Laura followed directions.

Jack passed. Laura kicked. The ball sailed into the net.

Our team erupted into cheers, dog barks, taunts about Saint Mark's being poop-butts.

The ref blew the whistle.

The kids swarmed us—sixteen hot sweaty little bodies, dying for water and a chance to play forward.

The last quarter: 1–1. Jem wanted to keep the vest.

I hated the idea. Saint Mark's only needed one goal. I didn't want Jem responsible for losing the game.

Still, nobody else wanted the job. We ended with seven forwards and Jem as keeper.

"You doing okay, champ?" I asked him.

"Yeah." He looked up a moment longer, squinting into the sun, like he understood he needed to prove to me that he really was okay. Something silver glinted around his neck—a Saint Anthony medallion I'd never seen before. He said, "I'm good. Watch."

They went out on the field again.

Erainya stood next to me, cupping the sun out of her eyes. I thought about how many times she'd whacked me with that hand, or cut the air at some stupid comment I'd made.

"Stirman talked to Jem," I said, "the night at the museum."

She kept her eyes on the field. "Yeah?"

"They had maybe a minute alone together, out on the roof."

"Miracle Jem wasn't hurt."

"No miracle. Stirman never wanted to hurt him. I wouldn't

have brought Jem along otherwise. Stirman wanted to take him."

The ref's whistle blew. Saint Mark's kicked off. The ball was lost in a forest of little cleats and shin guards.

Erainya looked at me the way she normally looked at Sam Barrera—as if I was about to snatch away her last bread-and-butter contract.

"So," she said, her tone carefully neutral. "What do you figure he told Jem, in that one minute?"

"I don't know," I said. "Maybe he told Jem the truth."

Saint Mark's drove the ball toward our goal. Their coach yelled for their best kicker to stand ready at the penalty line.

Erainya was silent, watching me.

"Jem's birth date was the same day Stirman was arrested," I said. "Other than that, the adoption papers were a pretty good forgery. You never went to Greece that year, did you?"

She hesitated a couple of heartbeats. Then the shield she'd been trying to put up melted. "Fred didn't want me to keep the baby."

"That's what your last argument was about—why you shot him," I guessed. "He wasn't just threatening you. He was threatening the baby, too."

She flexed her hand, as if remembering the trigger of the gun. "That night in Stirman's apartment, the baby had stopped breathing. I guess the shock of the gunfire . . . I don't know. I did CPR. I brought him back to life. Fred . . . well, I wasn't going to lose the child after all that. After I shot Fred, I sent Jem to stay with a friend of mine, lady named Helen Malski, until the trial was over."

"I found a letter she wrote you. Jem was the package she was keeping safe."

Erainya nodded. "Once I was released, Jem and I disappeared

for a while. I'd done enough work on adoption cases. Faking Jem's paperwork wasn't hard. I made up his birthday. I kept thinking somebody would question . . . Stirman would raise hell. Barrera would squawk. But nothing like that ever happened. Eventually, I figured Stirman thought the child was dead, or he just didn't care enough to protest. I felt safe enough to come back home, take over the agency. I couldn't have left a baby like that, with his mother dead."

"You made Jem's birth date a clue."

"I know. Stupid."

"Classic guilt. Part of you wanted to get caught."

"Stop talking like a PI." There was a challenge in her eyes, but it was frail.

She was a few weeks away from a whole new future. She was about to re-create herself for the second time. I could bring it all crashing down if I wanted to.

"You caught me," she said. "Question is: What are you going to do about it?"

The game caught my attention. I shouted, "Jem, heads up!"

He crouched, ready for a challenge.

The Saint Mark's kicker drove the ball straight toward the goal.

Jem dove. The ball sailed right past him into the net.

The other team cheered like crazy.

Jem picked up the ball, ran it to the line, and threw it like it was still in play. He kept smiling like everything was good. The Saint Anthony medallion had come untucked from his collar. It gleamed silver against his goalie vest.

"Honey?" Erainya said to me, her voice growing tense. "What do you want to do?"

Maybe everything *was* good. I caught Jem's eye and gave him the thumbs-up sign.

He grinned, delighted.

I didn't know what Stirman had told him. It didn't matter.

The ref blew the whistle. Game over: a 2–1 loss.

"Not as bad as I'd feared." I looked at Erainya. "For one thing, I'm going to insist on a legal name change."

Erainya looked grim, but she managed to keep her composure. "If you seriously think . . ."

"The Tres Navarre Agency," I said. "Much better ring to it."

Then I did something I had never done. I kissed Erainya on the cheek, left her startled and blinking, and went out to give her son a big high five.

27

A week later, I got a call from Alicia, Sam's personal secre-
tary.

She couldn't reach Sam at home again. He hadn't reported to
the office. She was worried, and I had become the person to call.

Maia and I were at my apartment, having an argument with
Robert Johnson about who made better cheese enchiladas. The
cat was playing silent and diplomatic. He wanted a cook-off.

I hung up the phone and looked at Maia, who was dressed
for work. She had a court date in Austin that afternoon.

"Problem with Sam," I told her.

I hadn't gotten a replacement for my truck yet, so I asked if
she could spare an hour to drive me.

"That depends," she said. "Are we going to talk on the way?"

So far, I had successfully avoided the subject of my hypothetical move to Austin. It hadn't been easy keeping Maia's mind off
the topic. She'd made me work pretty hard at it all night long.

She knew I'd agreed to take over Erainya's agency. She'd re-
ceived that news so graciously I was pretty sure she was contemplating murdering me later.

What she wanted to know now is where I'd be living.

She was sure I could run the business from Austin. I could

commute to San Antonio a few days a week, maybe hire one of my friends to cover for me part-time. I could slowly shift my clientele base to Austin, where business would be better.

The agency had no physical office space, anyway. Few assets. Even fewer steady clients. Maia wanted to know what was wrong with her plan.

I said, "Did I mention how outstandingly beautiful you look this morning?"

She picked her gun from the counter, pointed it at the front door, and said, "Walk."

I had a pretty good hunch where Sam would be.

We found him sitting on the front porch of his childhood home on Cedar and South Alamo, the photographs from his black duffel bag spread around his feet. It looked like he was trying to group them by subject matter and year.

"Morning," he told us.

He was dressed in a three-piece suit, clean-shaven, marinated with Old Spice. His left arm was in a cast, but it didn't seem to bother him much.

I thought I'd taken all his guns away, but he'd found an old Smith & Wesson somewhere and stuck it in his shoulder holster. He had a Frosted Flake stuck to his chin.

"Hi, Sam," I said. "It's me, Tres."

"I know that, damn it."

"This is Maia Lee."

I didn't ask if he remembered her.

Sam picked up a photograph. "Lot of faces. Some of these are twenty, thirty years old. Nothing more recent than ten, I'd guess."

"Your family."

Barrera looked up at me. "What would you think—a guy who has a bagful of pictures like this? What's your read?"

"Estranged," I said. "But maybe he doesn't really want it that way."

Sam considered. "Maybe."

Foot traffic went by on South Alamo. A *paleta* seller chimed the bell on his bike. A couple of tattooed, orange-haired Latino kids walked by with artist sketch pads. An Anglo mom chased her toddler, who was waving a half-eaten flour tortilla. The mom paused at the FOR SALE sign in Sam's yard and took the last flier from his tube.

Sam pointed his thumb toward the front door. "I used to live here."

"I know," I said.

"Second bedroom upstairs. Downstairs, when I was first retired, I thought about putting my PI office in here, you know? But the neighborhood was going downhill then. Bad place for a business."

He looked at Maia, who smiled in a daughterly way. If she was anxious about being late for her court date, she didn't show it. Patience was one of her great investigative assets, which explained why she was still dating me.

"Now they call the neighborhood Southtown," Sam told her. "Look at this traffic. When did the center of town move south again?"

I needed to get Sam home. I just wasn't sure how to do it yet. The gun wasn't the hardest part. It was moving the photographs. He would get upset about that.

"What would you charge," he asked me, "for a job like this?"

"What job, Sam?"

He waved at the photos. "Finding them. Putting names back to the faces. It's bothering me."

"Look, Sam," I said, "the folks at the office are worried about you."

"My office?"

"Yeah. I-Tech. You were supposed to go in today and sign some papers."

"I'm retiring," he said.

"That's right."

"Before they kick me out."

His eyes showed no hint of confusion—just the sadness of a man who knew exactly what was happening to him.

"Alicia and my doctor have it all planned," he said. "I'm supposed to sell my properties. The money will pay for this assisted living program. They do studies with new drugs, like on rats. They say it's my best shot. I don't want to live with a bunch of people like me."

"Sam—let's get you home."

"This is my home."

Down on South Alamo, *conjunto* music played from a car stereo. The morning air was heating up, filled with the smell of wet magnolia leaves from Sam's front yard.

Sam picked up a tintype of an old Latino in a starched shirt, suspenders and a bowler. It could've been Sam's grandfather.

Right then, I knew what I would do. I realized I'd been thinking about it for days.

I wasn't excited. I figured I might as well make myself a T-shirt that said COACH FOR LIFE on one side and KICK ME on the other side. But I knew I had to do it. I'd never forgive myself otherwise.

I looked at Maia.

I kept looking until I thought I'd conveyed my question right.

She hesitated, then leaned over and kissed my cheek. "I think I'll stroll down the block for a while, gentlemen. Nice meeting you, Mr. Barrera."

When it was just Sam and me, I said, "You want all of those people found?"

"Yeah." Sam studied the old picture. "Names to faces, you know? Bothering the hell out of me."

"Big job. Lot of hours, plus expenses."

"I've got money."

"I was thinking more like a trade."

He scratched his ear. "Like what?"

"This house. We split it. I take the downstairs for my office, rent-free. You keep upstairs to live in."

He stared at me.

"But no deal if you don't live here," I said. "I want the landlord close, in case I have a problem. Plus, you know, this'll be a private eye agency. I'll be just starting out. I'll expect free consultations with you."

Sam looked away. A group of college girls chatted their way down the sidewalk, heading toward the coffeehouse.

"We got a deal, Sam?"

"Yeah." His voice was hoarse. "We got a deal, Fred."

"My name is Tres."

"I know that, damn it."

"I've got to go talk to Maia Lee. You want to come with me, Sam?"

"No. I'll wait here. I like the porch."

"You've got some cereal on your chin."

He brushed it off.

When I got to the bottom of the steps, he called, "Tres."

I turned, surprised that he'd remembered my name.

"Call the FBI for me, will you? Tell them I'm going to work at home today. I just got an idea."

"I'll tell them, Sam. Be right back, okay?"

He didn't acknowledge me. He was too busy rearranging his

photos, as if he'd just figured out how to break the case wide
open.

Maia Lee stood across the street, looking in the window of
Tienda Guadalupe. She was admiring the folk art devils.

"The one with the furry butt looks like you," she said.

I told her about my deal with Sam. I got the feeling she wasn't
exactly surprised.

"I think I'll buy that devil to hang on my back porch," she decided. "By the neck, maybe."

"I love you."

She turned toward me, gave me a long kiss. A family of
tourists walked the long way around us. A couple of Chevy-
cruising *vatos* made some appreciative catcalls.

Maia gently pushed away from me. She said, "I won't ask if
you understand what you're getting yourself into. I know you
better than that. But if you need any help with the legal stuff . . ."

"I've still got a hotshot attorney in Austin?"

She looked down at the grimy sidewalk, the same brick path
San Antonians had been walking since the 1800s. "You can't get
free of this place, any more than Sam Barrera can. I might as
well admit that."

"Where does that leave us?"

"Long-distance," she said. "I've got to go now."

"I don't have a car."

She kissed me once more for the road. "You don't need one,
Tres. You're home."

ABOUT THE AUTHOR

Rick Riordan is the author of five previous award-winning novels. He lives in San Antonio, Texas, with his wife and two sons, where he is at work on the next novel in the Tres Navarre series.